Voyage to the Twisted Memory

JANMESH

BLUEROSE PUBLISHERS
India | U.K.

Copyright © Janmesh 2025

All rights reserved by author. No part of this publication may be reproduced, stored in a retrieval system or transmitted in any form or by any means, electronic, mechanical, photocopying, recording or otherwise, without the prior permission of the author. Although every precaution has been taken to verify the accuracy of the information contained herein, the publisher assumes no responsibility for any errors or omissions. No liability is assumed for damages that may result from the use of information contained within.

BlueRose Publishers takes no responsibility for any damages, losses, or liabilities that may arise from the use or misuse of the information, products, or services provided in this publication.

For permissions requests or inquiries regarding this publication, please contact:

BLUEROSE PUBLISHERS
www.BlueRoseONE.com
info@bluerosepublishers.com
+91 8882 898 898
+4407342408967

ISBN: 978-93-6452-922-8

Cover Design: Sadhna Kumari
Typesetting: Pooja Sharma

First Edition: January 2025

*To Bhagwan Shani, the faith personified,
I dedicate my work to you.*

Contents

The Call	1
Something Dodgy	11
Formation of Clique	28
Invited Trouble	40
Into The Ferry	50
The Sight of the Start	57
The Town	69
The Crow Talk	79
The Last Bliss	86
The Hoax	96
The Blue-Eyed Crow	106
Amber Eye	115
Back to the Fort	124
A Real Deal	158
Give in to Go in	165
The Place He Most Feared	174
The Quiet City	182
Action in the Moonlight	197
Tribe of Mumbai	209
Helping Hand	231
Creator-Nurturer-Destroyer	247

Chapter 1
The Call

Aryan was seated in his private office, leaning on a chair with his face turned to the left, gazing out of the glass window. His eyes were fixed as if he was daydreaming--- and indeed, he was. Perhaps about his work, Aryan is an auditor at a reputed company. Or maybe he was dreaming about what his wife would be doing now? Would she be preparing a tasty meal today?

He turned his face, exhaling. Outside the door, there were rows of murmurs, a constant sound of a telephone ringing, with shadows moving here and there.

I am bored.

There was a knock on the door, and Aryan sat up straight.

"Come in."

A person entered, neatly dressed, but seemed a little nervous. He walked and came right in front of Aryan's desk.

"Boss, the Chairman said…he needs those account books he gave to you…including the balance sheet," said the person, looking at Aryan.

Aryan nodded. He then opened a drawer above his right leg, taking some files from it. As he lifted his head, there was a low sound, as if something had fallen inside his drawer. That caught his attention, and he looked down inside his drawer for a moment, then shook his head and passed those files to the person.

"Joshi, before giving those files to Chairman, do have a look for errors or mistakes," said Aryan bossily.

"As you say, Boss," replied the person with a nod.

The person almost reached the metal handle of the door when he turned back. Aryan noticed this sudden action, the person's face clearly indicated hesitation. Aryan, on the other hand smiled, having a hunch of his employee's nervousness.

"The project details are almost done… I know the due date is getting closer every day. Do not worry, I will complete it on time," Said Aryan in good spirits.

Aryan's employee smiled and gave him a respectful nod before leaving the room.

Aryan sighed, looking down into the drawer. He picked up the rectangular photo frame and gazed at it with an expression that conveyed a sense of longing for those days.

****

Aryan opened the door and entered his house. Right in front of the door, at a distance, laid a couch, and on that couch was seated his gracious wife, Ekta.

"You're late again," said Ekta, getting up and walking towards him.

She took the bag off his shoulder, and Aryan kissed her on the head. After removing his shoes, he went straight to her and wrapped her in his arms.

"I am sorry, Ekta, but what can I do? I have this big project on my head, and there might be more days ahead of me coming a little late."

Ekta broke off and eyed him for a second. She looked down and sighed.

"It's okay, I understand."

Aryan smiled and started to take steps towards the kitchen when Ekta caught his hand. Aryan turned with a look of bewilderment.

"What's troubling you?" asked Ekta.

"I just told you, Honey, the look is because of that damned project."

"Nope, something else is troubling you. Don't lie to me, or I will surely get mad and throw things at you."

Aryan laughed softly, taking her arms. He walked up to his bag, which Ekta had placed on the table beside the couch. He let go of her hand and, opening the middle chain of his bag, took out the photo frame he was looking at earlier in his office.

"Your friends!"

"This picture is the proof of our last trip as a group," said Aryan, with happiness in his eyes but sadness in his voice.

"I remember this; back then, we were just dating. It was like…"

"Six years and eight months ago. I also remember that I could not take you on this trip because we had that rule *not to bring any outsiders* on our group trip," said Aryan with much excitement.

Ekta always adored her husband's bubbling-with-excitement voice.

They had dinner together. Then Aryan went to the bathroom, while Ekta set the bed, which was already settled. Aryan came back, kissed

Ekta on her cheek, and sat on the bed, taking out a book. Ekta did the same. She also took out a book from her side of the drawer beside her bed.

Ekta shut the book and turned herself, facing Aryan.

"Aryan, I don't think I will be able to go to my office anymore," said Ekta seriously.

Aryan closed his book, and just like Ekta, he also turned himself on the bed towards her.

"I knew it you were sick. You hurled like a dinosaur this morning—okay, sorry, do not give me that look—why cannot you go to the office?"

"I am not telling you."

"What?"

"I will tell you only if you promise me one thing."

"Ekta, whatever you want, I will give it to you," said Aryan, placing his palm on her cheek.

Ekta smiled and immediately leaned back, getting off the bed. The drawer from which she took her book, she opened that again and took out a small leather purse. She came back to bed and passed the purse to Aryan.

Aryan, puzzled, opened the purse. There was only one thing in it. Aryan immediately looked at Ekta. Ekta's eyes were filled with tears, happy tears. She nodded.

"I AM GOING TO BE A FATHER!" screamed Aryan, jumping on the bed.

Ekta too got up on the bed, and Aryan wrapped her in his arms. He wiped those sparkling tears from her face. He had not let go of the pregnancy test tool yet.

"Don't forget—I want something from you."

"Whatever you want—just demand it and it will be at your feet, Ekta."

"I want you to go on a trip with your friends, just like old days," said Ekta solemnly.

Aryan, eyes wide opened, took a minute to reply.

"What?—I cannot, you know that I cannot do that. Besides, my friends are busy people now. It is not like six years back, that time we did not even know what a proper job feels like." said Aryan.

"But you promised," cried Ekta.

"Look, I have a project to deal with. And you are pregnant now? Do not think for a second that I will leave you in this condition," said Aryan, coming forward and tucking her hair behind her ear.

"Then—then do not plan a long trip, just a week. In that time, I will go live with my sister," insisted Ekta.

Aryan did not say anything; they just stood there on the bed, looking deep into each other's eyes.

"Please?"

Then Ekta leaned forward and rested her head on Aryan's chest. Aryan ran his hand through the back of her head, smelling her hair and kissing her.

"Fine, if you want that, then I will fulfil it," said Aryan, calmly.

Ekta leaned back with a charming smile on her face. She happily jumped on the bed. Aryan, too, smiled and then laughed out loud seeing her.

"But...," said Aryan. Ekta stopped jumping. "If anyone disagrees, then the plan is off. That means I will stay here with you, got it?"

Ekta nodded; she knew that Aryan would say that.

"Call the most persuasive guy or girl in your group." said Ekta. "Does your group have any person who can convince the whole group in an instant?"

"Oh, yeah!" said Aryan with a beaming smile.

****

There was a constant sound of clarinet in the wedding hall, people in their finest costumes, smiling, greeting each other, embracing the environment. The aroma of fine dining spread all over the hall. A beautiful scenario of a wedding.

Daksh was far, way far, from the mandap where the groom and bride were to be wedded. Daksh was an average-height male, his physique suggested that he sweats it out daily in workouts, but without any additional weights. With his amusing charm, he approached everyone. He owns a photo studio, and now he is here at the wedding ceremony.

"Oh, c'mon, ladies, I know you can do much better than that," said Daksh charmingly.

The group of teenage girls in front of him giggled and changed their poses. Click—Click.

A man approached Daksh from behind, he was a couple of inches taller compared to Daksh, and he looked like he exercises with heavyweights. He grabbed Daksh from behind and pulled him towards his side. Daksh got imbalanced but saved himself from falling. He turned and saw that his subordinate, Ganesh, was the one who pulled him.

"What are you doing, Ganesh? Can't you see I am working here?" snapped Daksh.

"Daksh, we are getting paid for taking pictures of the groom and the bride, not some—what is this—group of teenage girls, how ridiculous," said Ganesh, sourly.

Daksh looked at Ganesh with a blank expression.

"You know very well that my dream is to be a high-paid professional photographer who takes pictures of beautiful models—"

"And you think clicking photos of these girls will fulfill that?"

Daksh turned his face down and shook his head. Ganesh tapped him on the back.

"Reality disappoints me."

"It always does, my friend. Now let us go and do some real work."

Together they clicked many photos of the groom and the bride, with their family, and without their family. Daksh, momentarily, got distracted as some of those girls came back and asked for his acquaintance, but Ganesh volunteered to leave Daksh with the groom and the bride. After what felt like eons, a man approached them, probably the father of the groom or bride, Daksh did not know.

"Gentlemen, the food counter is now open. Do not forget to enjoy it," said the man politely.

Daksh smiled and nodded. He looked at Ganesh and saw a beaming smile appear on his face upon hearing the most enjoyable part of any wedding.

Now Daksh and Ganesh were seated on chairs, their plates on a table in front of them, which was covered with yellow cloth. Ganesh was enjoying every bite of the food on his plate, as was Daksh.

Just then, the phone rang, and Daksh realized it was his. He took out his phone from his pocket. Seeing the number of the caller, his expression changed immediately. He picked up the call.

Ganesh turned and saw several emotions on Daksh's face. At first, it was surprise, his eyes were wide open, then a happy, charming smile, and finally, a suspenseful grimace.

As Daksh hung up the phone, he got up from his seat and started walking towards the exit.

"Where the heck you going?" asked Ganesh, standing up from his chair and holding his plate in one hand.

Daksh turned, "I am sorry, Ganesh, but I have to leave—something really important came up…" said Daksh in haste.

"What about the food?"

But by then, Daksh was already turning behind the exit. Ganesh sat back down, shrugged, and continued eating.

****

Aryan was standing on his eleventh-floor balcony, gazing at the sky. Seeing those twinkling stars always calmed him down. Then he turned to look down at the streets.

He was excited with all his heart to go on a trip, but now Ekta is pregnant, so his mind is diverting a bit.

He turned and saw Ekta leaned on the side window, her eyes fixed on him. By the looks of her, Aryan got the fact that she knew what he was thinking. They both went inside their bedroom and sat on the bed.

Ting-ting.

Aryan checked his phone and stood up on his feet to read the message Daksh had sent him. It read:

Hey, Freak, I missed you a lot. Everyone agreed to FaceTime tomorrow, around ten at dark. So, be ready—and how is Ekta?

Ekta smiled as she read the message, observing the rejuvenating smile on Aryan.

"Sure, I knew it from the start that you would call Daksh."

The next day arrived, and so did the big bubble of excitement in Aryan's body. He went to the office in full spirits of goodness, apart from the project pressure, he had a great day over there.

Aryan arrived earlier than usual, which surprised Ekta.

"So, you have time for your friends but not for me, huh?"

"Hey, you were the one who insisted on me doing it."

"Yeah, like you didn't want to."

Aryan noticed the playful moodiness in his wife. He came forward, he embraced her, he asked,

Suddenly, why so moody?

"Hey, I am a woman; I have the right to be moody," said Ekta quickly.

Aryan laughed and hugged her; she gripped him tight.

"I love you so much, my Ekta," said Aryan over her shoulder.

"I love you too, my Aryan."

They had a delicious dinner together, then they spent some time talking about what happened in the office and how his project is going. Then Ekta went to bed while Aryan sat in front of his desk beside his living room window with his laptop.

Aryan's heartbeat rose, seeing the clock hitting the target of half-past ten.

"Did they ditch me? No, this cannot be."

Just then, there was a Bing Sound, and Daksh appeared on the screen.

"Hey—where are the others? I swear to God, if they ditch us, I will – "

A Bing Sound and it added one more person: Yash. Another Bing and Oviya came on the screen. Two more Bings, adding two people, Mahir and Ruhi. And at last came Aadhaya.

They all started conversing with a blow of elation. Every one of the seven showed their gratitude for being able to reunite again. Seeing them, talking with them was a great joy Aryan had not felt in years, of course, finding out he is going to be a father was a wonder too.

They were united by the universe since their school years, hence the topic about the past was a harbinger. Then around half-past eleven, they started to debate whether they should go on a trip or not. At this moment, Aryan closed his eyes, even though he knew that no matter what, his vote is on both sides.

YES.

Came the answer from every seven of them. Daksh showed his playfulness in that too. Oviya planned to meet in person so that they can all plan the whole trip properly. Every soul agreed to this joyous plan of Oviya. But now the question arrived: where to meet?

Aryan answered that he told them they would meet at the place where they used to hang around back in their school time, the place where they used to go to escape (or bunk) classes.

Everyone adored Aryan's idea and set up a day to finally meet, laughing at each other's faces. The decided day was Saturday, in the evening.

Chapter 2

Something Dodgy

Saturday came in a blink of an eye, and Aryan got out of bed hopefully. All he had to do now was wait for a couple of hours, and then he would meet his group—the one that lasted until their last trip. Even the thought of meeting them brought elated feelings in him.

Aryan spent most of his day talking to Ekta, then he took her to the doctor and the morning went like this. Ekta noticed the constant elevation of her husband's mood and got a little jealous.

The afternoon arrived, and Aryan got dressed. He wore a navy blue full-sleeve t-shirt with light blue washed jeans and sneakers. This costume suited him, as he was tall and lean. He also set his long hair back.

Ekta whistled when he came out of the bathroom.

"Have fun with them!" said Ekta, approaching him and running her hand over his sleeve.

"Fun? We have not met in six years—there is going to be a lot more than fun."

Aryan got surprised seeing Ekta's expression turn to a concerned look. He came close and rested his hand on her cheek.

"Anything bothering you?"

"Nothing, just don't overdo it—I know how friends get, but…"

"What are you trying to say, sweetie?"

"All I am saying is—don't come home—drunk."

Aryan laughed out loud, he controlled his laughter, with some difficulty, seeing Ekta's face.

"Answer me this: when have I ever came home drunk?"

"I know, but—"

"If it makes you feel any better, I will only have one beer and not a drop more, ok?" said Aryan pacifyingly.

Ekta smiled and hugged him, Aryan kissed her. Then he bent down and kissed Ekta's belly.

"Cannot forget to kiss her—or him."

And Aryan walked towards the door, picked up his car keys from the table beside the door, and turned. Ekta waved him by, and he shut the door behind him.

Aryan was driving his car, taking turns here and there, and then straight.

How lucky I am to have Ekta as my wife. She saw right through me. Thank you, Ekta. Thank you so much.

He happily matched the tone of the music playing on the speaker with his soft series of whistles. When the area started to appear more and more familiar, he turned off the music and paid attention to every turn he took. He turned left and looked to the left; there it was where it all started—their school. Aryan smiled, he knew that somewhere nearby, there was a narrow road. He reached there and parked his car. Aryan exited from the car and walked back where he came from. He was almost in front of his school's gate when he saw someone familiar on the other side of the road, looking at him.

As it was afternoon, there were very few people on the road, and the milieu was humid. Aryan ran towards his friend Yash. Yash was a tall man, taller than Aryan. His body was lean like Aryan's, even though Aryan had an excellent jawline; Yash's jawline was like some of those models you see in magazines. Yash wore his hair long, just like Aryan.

Yash opened his arms and welcomed Aryan. They hugged and jumped together, making monkey noises.

"I missed you, freak," said Aryan, coming back, his head was going to explode with happiness.

"Oh, you don't know how much I missed you…" said Yash, "this last six years, all I did was go to college, come back home—and that's it."

"Same here Yash, same here!"

They turned their glance towards the five-story building, widely spread on the other side of the road. No vehicle bothered them as they were standing on the footpath.

"Remember lunch breaks?" asked Yash with a soft laugh, without turning.

"How can I ever forget those—we did all sorts of weird stuff instead of eating our lunch."

They looked at each other with thankful expressions.

"Bringing back memories, I suppose?"

The deep voice came from the back. Aryan and Yash turned and saw a figure who was an inch or two shorter than Aryan, and he wore his hair flat on the right.

"DAKSH!" roared Aryan and Yash together.

They embraced each other and got back to staring at the school building, with Daksh on the left, Aryan in the middle, and Yash to the right.

Out of nowhere, Aryan started laughing so hard that he had to clench his stomach with his hands.

"Quick, Yash," said Daksh in an emergency tone, "there is a chemist right on that left turn."

"What—why?" said Yash, puzzled.

By then, Aryan stopped his sudden laughter and was looking at Daksh.

"To get his lunatic pills, of course," said Daksh, amusingly.

Yash and Aryan gave him bemused looks.

"Why that sudden burst, Aryan?" asked Yash.

"Remember that break time; we were playing 'IT' "? And Daksh came to strangle you in that corner at the edge of the building, suddenly a—hi—"

"Those senior girls came in between me and Daksh, and he strangled one of them," said Yash, laughing.

"How pitifully he cried when one of them slapped him so hard."

They both laughed while Daksh looked bemused, eyeing them.

"It was a mistake," said Daksh.

"Oh-oh," laughed Yash while speaking, "I can still hear your girlish cry."

And they laughed even louder.

"Hey, guys—GUYS!" screamed Daksh, "Did we plan to meet here, on the footpath?"

Aryan and Yash controlled their laughter and looked at Daksh.

"Not actually, we decided to meet in that house," answered Aryan.

"Yeah, I know that too. Shall we go then?"

Aryan and Yash looked at each other. It is not every time that Daksh gets annoyed, because he was always the annoyer. But he was right, they did not decide to meet here. They both nodded and started walking together.

They walked straight. Aryan looked at the school building, which was now walking backward. They continued going straight, then turned right and walked straight. They were now walking on a narrow road with buildings on each side. Trees on the sides covered the road in a beautiful shade of grey, it was peacefully quiet as it was siesta time.

"Ah, look at it—still looks dodgy," sighed Yash.

All three of them were now in front of a rusted gate, which wasn't even locked. Behind the gate was a shady— two-floored building colored in a somewhat off-yellow hue. The paint of the building was peeling from every wall and corner, with numerous cracks visible. They called this place the dodgy house because it looked dodgy.

Back when they were in school, this building was started but left unfinished, the construction abandoned for some reason. Since then, they used it as their base to skip classes when some mean teacher's lecture was on. All seven of them, Yash somewhat, loved this place because it provided them with the most demanded thing: personal space. Despite the fun and emptiness, they avoided coming here at night. Daksh was the one who told them about some adults coming here for suspicious activities.

"Wow, it still looks the same," said Daksh, "terrible."

"Yeah, it does," said Aryan, "I think it got abandoned again."

"Hey, I remember an event that occurred here," said Daksh, looking at Yash.

"What event?"

"I remember how you cried like a baby in one of those second-floor rooms," said Daksh mischievously.

"HEY, YOU GUYS LEFT ME ALONE IN THAT GODFORSAKEN ROO—"

A roaring sound of some vehicle disturbed Yash. Everyone tilted their heads to the left and saw a bike approaching. The bike's noise was heavy and ear-pulling. The master of the bike parked it across the road. As the road was narrow, they were able to see the person. Judging by the figure, the person was a woman wearing a green bomber jacket over a black t-shirt, dark jeans, and boots. She took off her helmet and looked towards them with a beaming smile.

"My God, that's Ruhi," said Aryan.

Ruhi started walking towards them, her helmet in her right hand. She was slim and good-looking, her dark hair matched with her dark brown eyes. Her height almost matched Daksh's.

"Wow, she turned into a good ooh!"

Aryan and Yash punched Daksh before he could finish his vulgar comment. Ruhi came close.

"If any of you said that you didn't miss me, I will kill you right here."

Aryan and Yash laughed, and Daksh was rubbing his stomach.

"Of course, we missed you, Ruhi," said Aryan.

They embraced each other and started conversing.

"Long hair looks good on you, Aryan. And Yash, are you planning to start modeling? Cause your face is giving me that vibe for sure." (Yash blushed). "Daksh, finally, after all that nagging, you started exercising, see, you don't have a belly anymore."

"Well, thanks for noticing, Ruhi," said Daksh, looking at Aryan and Yash.

"What, you look the same to me," said Yash teasingly.

Daksh avoided that comment and turned back to Ruhi.

"You have changed a lot too, I mean, you don't look like the shy girl I remembered."

"The fashion world changes you a lot once you enter," said Ruhi. "But I liked the comment."

"Daksh is right, you look like a girl who's got style."

"Thank you, Aryan," said Ruhi, going red. "Shall we wait for others or go inside directly?"

"I think we should wait—"

"Let's go!" said Daksh, cutting in Yash. He gave him a teasing smile, and Yash returned it with a sound of gritting teeth.

They moved towards the gate of the building; Yash walked unwillingly.

The gate gave a high-pitched ehhh sound when pushed by Daksh. Yash shuddered at that sound. They walked in and saw the entrance, which was in front of them and opened, as it had no doors. On the land was a jungle of weeds and some other wild plants. Together they walked inside, as it was afternoon, there was no need for flashlights, as the room had many windows. Besides the light, the building was shadier from inside, with some more cracked walls. The paint was completely off the walls, leaving the concrete fully naked.

"Great, this place smells like flowers—which has been rotting since time began…" said Daksh, covering his nose.

"Oof, you're right," said Yash, covering his nose too.

The ground floor was widely spread, but the smell was killing them. So, they decided to go a floor up. They turned left from the entrance and saw those deadly stairs. They were normal stairs, although there was one thing missing: side supporters. If a person loses his/her balance, it will be a journey straight down.

"I think I found the cause of this smell," said Aryan disgustingly.

All of them came forward and saw where Aryan was pointing, under the stairs. They made a noise of disgust, and Ruhi immediately turned her face when she had a good look at it.

"Look at it, even the dead rat is rotten," said Daksh with a laugh. "I mean, seriously, look at his insides, instead of red, they are turned to black."

"Eww!" snarled Ruhi and slapped Daksh on the back.

They started climbing the stairs, Ruhi at the front, the rest of them following her.

"OH MY GOD!" screamed Ruhi.

"WHAT?" asked Aryan, Daksh, and Yash together.

"I think—I think I stepped onto something," said Ruhi, breathily.

They all looked down at her feet, except Ruhi, she had no courage to do so.

"Oh, it's nothing—just a big fat rat," said Daksh, looking at Ruhi.

"WHAT…"

"No, it's not, he is lying," said Aryan. "Just some old rug, that's it."

Ruhi looked down and calmed herself, she then turned her red face towards Daksh.

"You are still that shy little girl, aren't you?"

"I will grab you by the neck and squeeze the life out of you."

"No time to fight—let's go," said Aryan straightforwardly.

They reached the first floor, and in front of them was a long, narrow hall. On the left, there was only one room, and on the right, two rooms. They always chose the left room as it was big and bright, unlike the others, which were the opposite. They entered and remembered those fun moments that occurred here. The sunlight was coming fully from the only window which was in front of the entrance. Right below the window, a little bit to the right, were two wooden benches. Suddenly—

"BOO!"

Everyone screamed and jumped to the other side of the room, heart-pounding heavily. Together they turned.

They saw a girl like their age, she had a square jaw just like Daksh, but firm. Her lush brown hair flowing backward with sparkling brown eyes. Her height was like Ruhi. Oviya was laughing mercilessly.

"OVIYA! That. Was not funny," snapped Ruhi.

"Outrageous," said Yash.

"I—am—sorry," said Oviya trying to take back control of her voice. "I just saw you and thought of having some fun—now come along give me a hug."

They all hugged and parted. Daksh and Yash picked up those two benches and brought them close. They placed those benches against each other.

"Oh—crap," said Daksh suddenly.

"What happened, Daksh?" asked Ruhi.

But Daksh did not answer and stormed outside the room and left the building. They all stood there looking at each other.

"Maybe he forgot something," said Oviya.

"Yeah, his brain," said Yash.

Everyone laughed and sat on those benches after cleaning them.

Aryan and Yash sat on one bench, and Oviya and Ruhi on the other facing them.

"So how are things going in the hospital?" asked Aryan to Oviya.

"Hospital?" echoed Yash and Ruhi together.

"Uh, hello, I am a doctor now," said Oviya, looking at Yash and then at Ruhi.

"When did that happen?" asked Ruhi and Yash together.

"How self-occupied are you guys," said Oviya, coldly, "I texted each one of you, two years ago that I passed my medical exams."

"Oh, yeah, I remember now," said Yash, but it was obvious that he was lying.

Oviya turned her face to Ruhi, who looked like she was now done for it. Just then, Daksh came back, so her attention went to him, and Ruhi sighed. Everyone beamed and clapped, not for Daksh, but for those two beer cartons he was carrying.

"Guess who I just ran into?" asked Daksh, smiling.

"Hello, fools."

The feminine voice came from Daksh's back. Daksh came inside, and Aadhaya followed. She was taller than Ruhi and Oviya. She was lean, her diamond-cut face glowed graciously. Aadhaya's hair was the most striking feature of her.

Everyone ran towards her and embraced her, except Aryan, who stayed back with Daksh.

"I want you guys to meet somebody," said Aadhaya, turning, "This is Sam."

A man came from behind her, looking like those people who spend at least five hours in the gym. His face was firm but had a calm look. Chest spread wide with built shoulders and back. His height was like Aryan's.

"Hi, I am Sam, Aadhaya's—boyfriend," said Sam, waving his hand.

"Hey, I didn't know we were allowed to bring a date," said Yash. "If I'd known, I could've—ouch."

Oviya pinched Yash, and they welcomed Sam, giving a look to Aryan.

"And now the fun begins," said Daksh, raising those cartons of beer.

Sam came and shook hands with Aryan, and there was an awkward vibe when that happened.

"Speaking of fun," said Ruhi, "I have also brought something."

Ruhi buried her hand inside her jacket's pocket and took out a small plastic bag. In it, there were two boxes of cigarettes.

"Is that what I think it is?" said Daksh, his voice jumping with excitement.

"Yep"

"YOU SMOKE?!" said Oviya in her top voice.

"Oh, c'mon, Oviya," said Ruhi.

"Oviya, it has been six years, and I know you are now a doctor, but—" Aadhaya stopped as Oviya turned her face to Aryan.

"What are you looking at me for?" said Aryan, "I am not going to stop them."

There was no point in arguing with Yash or Daksh as they were hopeless from all perspectives. Oviya turned her face and sighed.

"Alright, fine, but I am allowing only this time."

Everyone jumped and beamed, cheering for Oviya. As Daksh was looking at the packet dearly, Ruhi passed it to him.

"How neat is the smell!" said Daksh, taking one of those out and examining it.

"I have my fair share of experience," said Ruhi elatedly.

Daksh gave back the packet, Ruhi passed it to Yash, then Yash gave it back. She offered it to Aryan, but Aryan refused.

"What happened to you?" said Ruhi, puzzled.

"And don't say that you don't smoke," said Daksh, backing up Ruhi. "We smoked a number of things together."

"It's not that," said Aryan shaking his head. He took a glance at Aadhaya. "Ekta—I promised Ekta that I will only have one beer, and that is it. I am sorry."

All of them nodded. Ruhi took back the packet and hid it behind her back. They all took a quick glance at Aadhaya, who was speaking with Sam.

"I almost forgot that you are married," said Oviya, remembering.

"Well, your loss," said Daksh looking at Aryan, "but I am smoking."

Daksh borrowed the lighter from Ruhi and lit it. It almost touched his cigarette when a strong voice came.

"I cannot believe you guys started without me."

They turned and saw Mahir standing at the entrance. He was tall, dark, and his body was comparable to Sam's.

Mahir ran in and picked everyone up in his arms. He was always the most excited one.

"Man, it's good to see you all."

They all got seated on the long bench, Ruhi passed a joint to Mahir. He and Aryan started talking. Everyone was facing each other, telling what has been happening in their lives, except for one callow person.

Daksh had his back to them and was facing the entrance.

"What are you doing?" asked Oviya, bewildered.

Daksh turned, "Oh, nothing, just facing the entrance in case somebody else pops up."

HA-HA-HA! echoed the group, bemused.

"Everyone is here now, you idiot," said Yash. He slid on the bench to make room for Daksh. Daksh sat beside him, and they both started smoking.

"Wait a minute," said Mahir with a confused look, then he pointed at everyone with his fingers, "Aryan, Ruhi, Oviya, Yash, Daksh, Aadhaya—who the hell is this strong man?" said Mahir looking at Sam.

Sam got up, "I am sorry I didn't introduce myself, I am Sam."

"I am Mahir," said Mahir. "By the judge of your arms, you had your arms day this morning, I guess."

"Yes, and by the judge of your flexed legs, you had your leg day today." Said Sam, still shaking hands.

"He is my boyfriend," came Aadhaya, hugging Sam from his side.

"OO..." said Mahir in a squeaky voice, he looked at Aryan and immediately turned, "Nice to meet you."

"I'll open those beers," said Aryan as silence fell.

"And I will help you," said Aadhaya looking at him.

They both went towards the window where those cartons were placed foolishly on the edge of the window.

Except for Sam, everyone shared a look, they all sat back on the bench and started their conversation.

"So, how are things going on in the hospital, Oviya?" Said Mahir to divert everyone.

"It is going great," said Oviya, before giving a cold look to Yash.

Yash exhaled smoke out of his mouth, "People forget things, Oviya. I AM SORRY, plus it was the time when I got the job at the university, I was busy."

Oviya turned her face away. Sam smiled awkwardly, looking at Ruhi, and Mahir turned his gaze from Yash to Oviya. Ruhi tapped him on the shoulders.

"He didn't know that Oviya is now a doctor," said Ruhi playfully.

"Okay, for future reasons, let me narrate everyone's vocation here — so let's see…" Yash started to point out their profession, "Ruhi is a Fashion Designer" (Ruhi nodded), "Daksh, here is a photographer" (Daksh didn't pay attention), "Oviya is a doctor" (Oviya looked at him with pursed lips), "Aryan is working in a company as an accountant — "

"I am not an accountant — I am an AUDITOR," said Aryan, loudly.

"Well, that's that. I don't know what Aadhaya does for a living, neither do I know about Sam — and not about you too, Mahir."

"And you never will," said Mahir, grinning.

"I am a gym trainer," said Sam, facing Yash. "And Aadhaya is about to start her own salon."

"Impressive!" beamed Oviya and Ruhi together.

"Thank you, ladies," said Aadhaya, taking out a beer bottle from the carton.

"Hey, you!" said Ruhi, looking at Mahir. "Are you going to tell us or not?"

"Yeah, what's with the secrecy?" asked Oviya.

"Hey, guys, come back, and let's discuss the trip," said Mahir, avoiding Ruhi and Oviya's question.

Ruhi and Oviya narrowed their eyes at Mahir and nodded. Mahir looked at them and turned his face again.

"I have already planned everything," said Aadhaya, walking close towards them.

"We know," said everyone. They knew since their first trip Aadhaya was the one who planned everything, she loves doing that.

"You are still our planner, you know…" said Oviya, as Aadhaya sat beside her. They awed and hugged.

"Well, we have gone on trips everywhere from Goa beach to… well, everywhere," said Aadhaya. "But now I have decided to go somewhere unique, like we have never experienced before…"

"…I have found a place, in that place, there are a number of forts, beaches, and it is a hill station, too," said Aadhaya enthusiastically.

"All under one roof, now that's my type," said Daksh.

"Sounds good to me," said Aryan.

"But there is one problem, though," said Aadhaya, biting her lips.

"What?"

"The only way to reach there is through a ferry—which leaves at sharp six in the morning," said Aadhaya gravely.

"It means we have to leave our house by—four," said Oviya.

"That's not a problem," said Sam.

"Yes, we can get ready by then," said Aryan.

"I agree," said Yash.

"Me too," said Ruhi, giving a high-five to Yash.

"But I have a problem," said Daksh.

Everyone turned to Daksh and gave him a threatening look.

"Enough with the jokes already," said Mahir, annoyed.

"I am serious, you freak," said Daksh. "The thing is, at that time, the dogs in my area go crazy. And if I come out riding my bike, they will chase me to my death."

The walls of the room shook with the rumble of laughter.

"See, this is what happens when you speak seriously," said Daksh.

"Don't worry, Daksh, I will pick you up," said Aryan.

"I will bring the camera then," said Daksh simply.

"I'll go get a beer," said Aadhaya.

"Let me help you with that," said Aryan.

They both walked away towards those cartons. Instead of bringing them here, they stood there talking.

"This is weird," Sam coughed out the smoke.

"No, that is weird," said Mahir, pointing at the place where Aryan and Aadhaya were talking.

"Why?" asked Sam.

"Because they were in a pretty long relationship," said Mahir waving his hand. "They were together since school."

Then Mahir's eyes met Daksh; he looked like frustrated. He got the same expression from Ruhi, Yash, and Oviya.

"Wait, you didn't know?"

"No…I didn't," said Sam, looking at Aadhaya.

"There is no need to worry, Sam," said Daksh, airily, nudged Sam. "Aryan is a taken man—he is married."

Daksh looked at others with wide-open eyes, angrily.

"Yeah, he is married," said Ruhi.

"Happily married," said Yash, nodding.

Sam eased his body and smiled. Aadhaya came back shortly and sat beside Sam. He kissed her on her cheek. Aryan came shortly and passed the beer bottles.

The discussion about the trip went on. They decided to start their trip on the upcoming Tuesday and not to come back home until they had visited every famous tourist spot over there. All agreed to this, and with cheers, they gulped down the beer.

When the sky turned orange, they left the building and came out into the open. Daksh kept annoying Aryan by reminding him to pick him up. Aryan said "Yes" for the hundredth time, satisfying Daksh.

Everyone went their ways, only to come together on Tuesday. Aryan sat in his car, unable to wait to tell Ekta all about this God-gifted day.

Chapter 3

Formation of Clique

Aryan was seated comfortably in his private office, leaning on the chair with his laptop in front of him, but his attention was somewhere else. His mind could not stop wandering about how the trip would start. Initially, when he woke up this morning, he thought it would all go away, maybe just a dream. He heaved a sigh of relief when Ekta came in and told him to drop her at her sister's place.

Looking at the screen, he scrolled thoughtlessly. Aryan dropped Ekta at her sister's house, and she was more excited about the trip than Aryan, even though she was not going with him. That is when Aryan got cold feet; he told her that he could stay with her and enjoy that time too. Ekta told him that he can do that, just as she playfully hit on Aryan's head and said, "A promise is a promise." Then he safely dropped her at her sister's place, and she was also happy to help. Ekta gave him an affectionate kiss, they told each how much they would miss the other and Aryan left.

"Come in," said Aryan, as there was a knock on his door.

His employee came in, looking more confident compared to his past appearances.

"You called me Boss?" said his employee.

"Yes, Neel, I want you to give this to the Company Secretary as quickly as you can—no, go now," said Aryan bossily.

Neel took the envelope from Aryan's hand and gave it a scanning look.

"I know that I mustn't ask—what's in it, Boss?"

"In it, there is a letter saying that for a couple of days, I will be going on a trip, and she will be the one taking care of the Audit department during those days."

Neel gave him a perplexed look; Aryan knew what that look was about but chose to toy with him.

"But—but what about the project?"

"Oh, dear, Neel... take that chair and sit beside me, I want to show you something."

Neel took the chair from the front of the desk and placed it beside Aryan. Aryan smiled and turned his laptop towards Neel. Neel looked at it with deep thought and then scrolled up and down, while Aryan grinned, observing the change of emotions on Neel's face.

"How did you it...?"

"Spent all of Saturday night, then after dropping my wife, yesterday I continued, until today's sunrise," said Aryan cheerfully.

"You're amazing," said Neel, admiringly.

"That I am. Can you give the letter to the Company Secretary now?"

Neel smiled and rushed out of the office, Aryan leaned back on his chair and relaxed.

****

"For God's sake, Daksh!" said Ganesh.

"What?"

Daksh and Ganesh were in the photo-shoot room, which was square and had many background curtains in various colors. There were four lights, with a white umbrella in front of it. Ganesh was the model, seated on the chair, unwillingly. Daksh was annoying him with his topic of 'how to work while I am gone.' At first, Ganesh was listening to what Daksh had to say, but then Daksh started to act like Daksh, showing him how to click photos.

"...you see when the camera makes this sound," Daksh clicked a photo of Ganesh, he was now resting his hand on his hand, "It means the photo has been clicked and saved in memory."

"It is already evening, Daksh," Sighed Ganesh.

"So? What is up with you today?" asked Daksh, putting away the camera.

"What is up with me?" mimed Ganesh getting up from his chair, Daksh got started with this sudden moment. "The question is what is up with you?"

Daksh and Ganesh stood there looking at each other for a second. Then Ganesh grabbed Daksh's hand and started to move out. Daksh could not resist in front of Ganesh's tall, wide figure. Ganesh dragged him out of the room to the office. The office area was somewhat narrow but long, its walls yellow in color hidden behind countless photo frames. Most of them were nicely figured women.

"There is no need to worry, Daksh," said Ganesh. "Look at all these photos you and I took together, I know how to take pictures."

Daksh heaved a sigh and nodded.

"I am sorry, Ganesh. It is just...I never went out for more than a day since I started this business."

"I understand, Daksh," said Ganesh, placing his hand on Daksh's shoulder. "But I can handle the business for a couple of days."

"Fine, I will stop annoying you," said Daksh quietly.

Ganesh smiled and hugged him.

"Handle the business in my absence, brother" said Daksh, tapping on Ganesh's arm.

"I will, brother," said Ganesh, "Now go and get some sleep."

"Sleep? It is evening now, you idiot."

"Hmm, I thought you told me that you are leaving by four in the morning."

"Oh, Boy,"

****

BANG!

The door of the hospital swung open with a rumble. Pulling the stretcher were two male nurses and one female nurse. From the left came Oviya, adjusting her coat, she took a good look at the body on the stretcher.

"What do we have here?" asked Oviya hoarsely.

The Nurse beside Oviya gave her all the details about the patient.

Oviya picked up the pad and went through the pages. They pulled the stretcher to the right, and at the end of the passage was a big two-door-in-one-frame with I.C.U. written on it. They entered the room and it got shut behind them, turning on the red light above the heading.

After about two to three hours, Oviya came out, removing her gloves and mask, she threw them into a metal dustbin. She walked straight, and then the passage turned right. She leaned on the edge of the wall.

"They are his family," said the female nurse coming from behind.

Oviya peeked through the wall and saw the passage turning right. Just beside a door was a bench, and seated on it was a woman dressed in a green sari, sobbing. There was a boy beside her, barely an adult, consoling his mother.

Oviya approached them, and the woman inquired about her husband with teary eyes and a wobbling voice. Oviya reassured her that her husband was fine and out of danger. The woman jumped up from the bench and hugged Oviya. Oviya smiled and left the nurse with them.

Now Oviya was walking straight, passing by many other doctors who gave her a formal nod. She took a left and stood in front of a door with a label on it that said "Nina: Head of the Department," She exhaled and knocked, entering when a voice told her to do so.

The room was painted in two colors, with the upper wall in pink and the rest in blue. This room had the best view of the hospital. Right in front of the window, a woman was seated, probably a year or two older than Oviya. Seated behind her desk, her attention was on some papers she was scribbling on.

Oviya cleared her throat. "I just came here to tell you that tomorrow I will be leaving—and don't know when I will be coming back, probably by next week."

Nina stopped writing and looked up at Oviya, taking off her glasses. She was a firm-looking woman with a strong jaw.

"Yes, I know that," said Nina, curtly. "You told me yesterday."

Saying that, she continued her work by putting on her glasses.

Oviya gave her a stern look and turned towards the door, reaching for the knob.

"Wait," said Nina.

Oviya turned and saw that Nina was getting up, leaving her glasses on the desk. To Oviya's left was a couch, and Nina gestured for her to sit. They both took a seat, with Nina to Oviya's left.

"Look, I am sorry for my behavior," apologized Nina.

Oviya closed her eyes and nodded.

"I know you have a lot on your hands."

"A lot."

They both laughed.

"Take the leave for the whole week," said Nina, placing her hand on her shoulder. "I am so very jealous of you."

"Jealous of me?" said Oviya, unbelievingly. "You are the one who got promoted."

"That is true, though you have no idea what sort of people I must deal with now—investors of this hospital—ugh! They are always at my throat for reports...or even if I request new equipment for the research team...Why do you need that? What sort of result can we expect? How much time will it take to give us results?"

Oviya laughed softly. Nina gave her the approval she needed. After some informal talk, she left her office, closed the door behind her, with her back rested against the wall just beside the door, she heaved a sigh and walked away.

****

The shop's floor and walls were made of fine marble that shone brightly. It was a big, widely spread clothes shop for women. The starting price of clothes here was more than someone's house rent. Many mannequins were displaying their finest work behind the glass wall, tempting onlookers to discuss the design and lavishness of the material.

A woman entered the shop and approached the reception area.

"I want to buy a dress," she stated directly.

"Of course, Madam," replied the receptionist. "One of our best designers and curators will be with you in a second."

After a moment, Ruhi arrived, and the woman walked towards her. Ruhi was wearing a white turtleneck firmly tucked into her trousers. They both passed through the second door and entered a space filled with millions of clothes to choose from. The woman explained the occasion for which she needed a dress, and Ruhi began suggesting options accordingly. After a few rejections by the client, Ruhi finally found a dress that would complement the client's personality.

"I would suggest this yellow one, it will bring out your natural tone," Ruhi suggested, taking the beautiful dress from her subordinate, and showing it to the buyer.

The woman was surprised to see that Ruhi was right, the dress indeed enhanced her color when she tried it on.

A man approached Ruhi and said "Boss wants to see you."

Ruhi nodded and turned to the buyer, she tapped on her back as she was admiring herself in a huge mirror.

"Madam, from here, he will take care of the rest. If you want to make any changes, you can," Ruhi assured her.

"No, this dress is perfect. Thank you for suggesting this so quickly," said the woman, beamingly.

Ruhi smiled and nodded. She turned and started walking towards her boss's office, moving hastily. She knocked on the door before entering.

The office was clean, square-shaped, with walls painted in plain white. Behind the desk was seated a woman with short, blonde hair. She looked at Ruhi and gestured for her to sit. Ruhi took a seat in front of the desk and noticed the piece of paper her boss was reading—a second passed, and she realized her boss was reviewing her leave letter.

"Look, boss, I know what your answer is going to be, so I will just—"

"And how do you know that?" interrupted Ruhi's boss, looking at her.

She stood up behind her desk and came beside Ruhi, then seated herself in front of Ruhi, on the desk. Ruhi said nothing, just gazing at her boss absent-mindedly.

"Okay," said her boss after a minute.

"Okay?" asked Ruhi.

"I am giving you permission to go on your trip, all expenses paid," announced her boss.

"But this is our peak sales time, and if I went, then my career will be in…" said Ruhi compellingly but stopped as her boss got up.

Ruhi's boss patted her back, and she looked at her.

"Ruhi, darling, you think way too much," said the boss calmly. "But you are one of my favorites, you remind me of how I was at your age."

"Thank you!" said Ruhi with a note of admiration.

"It'll be fine, and I am giving you a paid leave—I haven't given that to myself yet."

"Thank you so much," said Ruhi graciously.

"Now go and enjoy."

****

A classroom filled with students, boys were all drowsy while girls were attentive to learn and to see their handsome professor, Yash. Yash was on the platform, and behind him was the massive board.

"You all know Economics will not leave you as long as you are in the commerce field, and just like that, the story of Demand and Supply will go on. So where were we—oh, yes, we were talking about how Demand and Supply are not equal but dependent on each other. That concludes the third point, and now the fourth poi—" Yash stopped abruptly, he remembered something. He went into deep thought, just recalling that he forgot to submit his leave letter.

Boys and girls looked at each other in confusion, caused by their professor's sudden silence. In the upcoming second, many unusual activities occurred as their professor ran out of the class as if a dog was chasing him. Many students got up from their seats. Their professor came back in sliding.

"The lecture is over, your math professor will be here soon," said Yash, hastily.

Yash was running so fast that he knew if someone came in the way, he would strangle them. He hated the fact that the campus was huge. Students and professors backed off immediately as they saw Yash running like a madman.

As Yash entered the staff room, he ran towards his desk and opened a drawer. He started throwing unnecessary things, which was most of it. He did not care about the fact that he was not the only one in the staff room, there were other professors too.

"Looking for something?" asked a woman's voice.

Yash turned and saw one of those professors, she was of his age, wearing a blue dress. The specs she wore did not give out a boring vibe but instead enhanced her beauty. She stood there for Yash to reply.

"Yes, Professor Rose, an envelope," said Yash without turning; he maintained his speed of throwing things.

"Oh, can I help you, Professor Yash?"

"Thank you, Professor—but I think...FOUND IT!"

Professor Rose chuckled, so did Yash as he got back up.

"Is Madam Principal in her office?" asked Yash, looking at her visage.

"I think so," answered Professor Rose, "Do you have a minute?"

Yash turned "I doubt that—but do speak your mind."

Professor Rose did not speak or was just not able to. She just stood there looking at him. She opened her mouth but then shut it again.

"Can you make it quickly, Professor? I am in a slight rush," said Yash, impatiently.

"I was—I was wondering that—that if you—if you would want to—go on a dinner with me tomorrow?"

"I can't."

After a minute, Yash realized what he bluntly spoke. He saw Rose adjusting her spectacles, looking down, and then she turned. As she did that, Yash walked towards her.

"What I meant is...," said Yash

Rose turned.

"Yes, Yash?" said Professor Rose, looking straight into his eyes.

"I am going on a trip tomorrow and not be back by next week. How about we go on a dinner—next Saturday, if you are free?" said Yash, charmingly with a touch of humbleness.

"Saturday sounds nice," said Professor Rose, her cheeks went red.

"Now, if you will excuse me, I have a very important thing to do."

Saying that, Yash took off to the principal's office. As it was summertime and most of the portion was already taught by Yash, he got his leave approved. He came out with a beaming smile and a dreamy look on his face. By this time tomorrow, he will be on a beach with his beloved gang of fools.

****

Mr. Shankar was seated on his chair, more like a throne, reading a newspaper. With one hand, he was stroking his handsome beard and mustache. He was a well-dressed man, and the room he was in had many rare items he bought in an auction. His reading got disturbed when his daughter stormed in.

"Father—Father—speak to mother, she has started again," said Aadhaya, outrageously.

A few minutes earlier, Aadhaya and her mother had a conversation in which Aadhaya mentioned her trip. Mrs. Shankar plainly denied, saying she cannot go without her mother with her on the trip.

Mrs. Shankar arrived shortly in the yellow-lit room. She always detested the fact that the beautiful walls of the room were hidden behind rows of the bookshelf. Aadhaya paced up towards her father.

"Father, what is my age?" asked Aadhaya looking at Mr. Shankar.

Mr. Shankar chuckled but frowned when he saw a dreadful look on his daughter's face.

"Twenty-Seven—soon going to be Twenty-Eight," Said Mr. Shankar putting away the newspaper.

Mrs. Shankar came close and halted beside Aadhaya. Mr. Shankar looked at his wife and then his daughter.

"Suddenly, why are you asking me about your age?"

"Tell her that, tell her what my age is," said Aadhaya looking at her mother. "I told her that I am going on a trip with my friends and she forbade me to go like I am still a school girl...every time its the same story."

Mrs. Shankar narrowed her eyes at Aadhaya. Mr. Shankar scratched his head, and then he looked at his daughter.

"I think you should go; you are a grown-up now—you know very well what one must do and what one must not."

Mrs. Shankar gave a disapproving look to her husband.

"Seriously?" said Mrs. Shankar.

"My dear darling, we must face the fact that our little Aadhaya is an adult now. Her salon is about to open, in all that work she barely dines with us anymore. This trip will relax her."

Mr. Shankar took hold of Mrs. Shankar's hand and gestured her to come close.

"And what if she finds that special person of her life on that trip, you understand right?" whispered Mr. Shankar.

Aadhaya opened her mouth, as she clearly heard what her father just said to her mother but chose not to rebel about it. All she wanted was to go on the trip.

Mrs. Shankar looked at Aadhaya, Mr. Shankar got up from his seat.

"Alright, fine you can go," said Mrs. Shankar in a dry voice.

"Woo-hoo!" screamed Aadhaya in joy.

She jumped and wrapped Mr. and Mrs. Shankar in her arms. They embraced her fully.

Chapter 4

Invited Trouble

Ah, the day arrived. Aryan had not slept at all. He took a shower, and by half-past three, he said goodbye to his house. Driving his car, he went straight to Daksh's place. A strange feeling passed through him as he was the only one driving on the road in which he was the driver along with the darkness. He prayed that this feeling may never touch him again.

"See, I told you!" said Daksh, entering the car.

Aryan had to agree with that; there were many stray dogs roaming around in the middle of the road. And not those humble ones you see on social media.

They drove straight to the Dodgy house, that is where they are meeting again. The lord of light still has not kissed his beloved, so there was nothing but darkness, with only artificial light showing them the way forward. To keep company, the Prince of Night was accompanying our Earth. Aryan did not know that the Moon shines this long. He was able to hear the unpleasant song of those dogs. Daksh was thankful that Aryan came to pick up otherwise, it would be a whole other situation for him.

Aryan and Daksh were the second to arrive the first were Oviya and Ruhi. Ruhi did not come on her sports bike instead, she came with Oviya, in her car. Then arrived Aadhaya and Sam, in her car. And lastly, Yash and Mahir arrived, Mahir accompanied Yash. While Aryan was enjoying a soft breeze coming from the north, he straightened up when he counted that everyone is here now.

"We are not going in there, right?" asked Yash, anxiously looking at the building.

"No, Yash," said Ruhi, with a soft laugh.

Yash sighed in relief, Mahir smacked on his back, playfully. They formed a circle, every eye on Aadhaya now, as she was the planner of this whole operation.

"OKAY, NOW LISTEN UP!" said Aadhaya, bossily.

"For God's sake, Aadhaya," said Daksh. "It's almost four in the morning, people will get suspicious about what we are doing in the corner of the road."

"Well, yeah, you are right, got a bit over-excited," said Aadhaya, avoiding eye contact with anyone.

Everyone laughed and shushed themselves, then told Aadhaya to continue.

"Now," said Aadhaya in an appealing tone, "we will ride and stop at the Gateway of India, and nowhere else. There will be a ferry waiting for us over there. By the time we reach there, it will probably be six, so the ticket counter will be open. I have already decided with Oviya and Ruhi regarding the hotel over there, so do not worry. Now, the most important note, and I will not say this again, that none of you—and I am pointing at you boys—do not go roaming around and reach straight to the destination, agreed?"

"Hey, why are you looking at me?" said Daksh.

Everyone agreed, Aryan tapped on Daksh's shoulder and went inside their car. The rest of them did the same, starting their engines, they began to move.

The sequence of cars looked like: Aadhaya's car was in the lead, to her back was Oviya's car, second to the last was Yash's, and finally, at last, was Aryan's. As there was little to no traffic, Aryan enjoyed riding on this empty road. His car moved smoothly, like abuse from an angry man.

Daksh opened his side of the window and was enjoying a gentle breeze. He turned to look at Aryan.

"Aryan, what time it is?"

Aryan, with his right hand on the wheel, checked the clock, which was cuddled up on his left wrist.

"Ten minutes remaining to hit the five-fifteen target," said Aryan.

Further came a four-way, and they took a left. Aryan gazed sideways and saw nothing but taxis zooming around. He turned to look at Daksh and was almost scared. Daksh's face looked like an ironic humble person. He took out his cellphone from the upper pocket of his denim jacket and dialed.

"Hello, Mahir."

"What are you doing?" snarled Aryan.

"Oh, shut your face," said Daksh. He put the phone on speaker, "Mahir, put the call on speaker so Yash can hear us too."

"Okay," said Mahir "Done, Daksh."

"Let's go and have something to eat," said Daksh.

Aryan screamed at him, even letting go of the steering wheel, which he grabbed again when Daksh pointed it out.

"Are you crazy?" came Mahir's irritated voice from the speaker.

"You heard Aadhaya," said Yash, "we are not allowed to go wandering around, she will kill us."

"I agree with the killing part," said Aryan, looking gravely at Daksh.

Daksh shook his head, knowing just the way to convince them.

"Come on guys, I can bet on this that none of you had anything to eat since dinner," said Daksh, seriously. And if I am wrong, I will let us say—yeah, I will stop joking around—for life."

Daksh knew by the silence that his prediction of a full-toss ball was right, and it hit the six.

"Yeah, you are right about that," said Yash, "I mean I cannot get something at this early in the morning."

"I am hungry too," said Mahir.

"I know just the place," said Daksh in excitement, "there is an Idli stall, which is not far from the Gateway."

Daksh then peeked out of the window by letting his head and half of his chest come out from the window. He analyzed where they are now and came back.

"Are you mad? If traffic police were nearby, he would have slapped you right there."

Daksh completely ignored Aryan's comment and continued to talk with Mahir and Yash on the call.

"Yep, not far from here said Daksh."

"My stomach is making noises now, let's go," said Yash uneasily.

"Yup, I would also like to have a nice plate full of Idli and Samb—"

"You guys are mad," roared Aryan. He snatched Daksh's phone out of his hand.

"Hey, not cool" said Daksh looking at Aryan.

"Let's go, Aryan" came Mahir's voice from the phone.

"Besides, we are going to reach way too early over there, I mean look at the time," Yash's voice came.

"I know, Aryan, that Ekta was certainly not home yesterday," said Daksh leaning forward. "So, you had a lousy dinner, and excited as you are, you left your house in a rush, hence did not have breakfast. What do you want to do, follow Aadhaya, and reach the Gateway way too early and listen to her talking, or come with us and have a plate full of Idli, with such a mouth-watering chutney and the lovely Sambar?"

Aryan gulped and looked away, then his stomach talked in its unpleasing voice.

"Ok—ok, fine," said Aryan.

"Hey, Daksh, what if they see us taking a wrong turn?" asked Yash.

"Don't worry, my friend because here comes the signal" said Daksh in high spirits. He, just like before, moved his head out of the window like a dog, he came back inside. "There are very few vehicles, so we have to do the activity quickly, they will take the right, and we have to take the left, understood Yash?"

"Got it," answered Yash.

Cars got stopped as the red signal was on. They waited patiently. As the light turned green, Yash and Aryan took a left turn, while Aadhaya and Oviya took the right. As there were a couple of taxis in between, they could not notice.

They arrived at a place that was crowded, not that much, even at this time of the day. The Idli stall was placed at the corner of the road, right outside the entrance of the train station. On the road, there was a queue of taxis, drivers were out screaming their routes. Just in front of the Idli stall, there was a man at a distance with his own petit stall, selling all kinds of cigarettes astonishingly, it was more crowded.

"See, I told you it is not far from the Gateway," said Daksh, cheerfully.

"Not far? We are at the train station," said Aryan, waspishly, he slammed the door shut.

"Cheer up, Aryan," said Mahir. "We are way too early—my God, the smell of Sambar!"

Aryan was about to speak acid, but Daksh grabbed his lips with his fingers.

"Before you say anything, hear me out," said Daksh, as Aryan slapped his hand to free his lips. "Now, at first, we will have a delicious breakfast, and after that, a puff of smoke, then we will be on our way to the Gateway."

Aryan, outnumbered, agreed to this plan.

"Listen, guys, don't eat too much," said Yash informatively. "You are aware that we are going on a ferry...things get projectile on the waters."

"Fine, Professor," said Daksh.

Idli was indeed mouth-watering, and what was the taste of coconut Chutney and Sambar! Even Aryan enjoyed it. They all were so ready for another round, but the cold look of Yash lagged them behind. Now the time was fifteen minutes left for the clock to show six. It was around this time they moved to the stall of bad-goodies.

Aryan went aside to attend a phone call while others bought a cigarette each for themselves and exhaled the blissful filth.

"Who do you think he is talking to?" asked Mahir, looking at Aryan while exhaling a cloud of smoke.

Aryan had his back to them and was about a meter away from them.

"I don't know, but not Aadhaya," said Yash with a short laugh, conjuring a cloud of smoke.

"He must be talking with Ekta, you idiots," said Daksh, lighting his cigarette.

"Ah, the wife," said Yash, nodding.

"Call me crazy, but I sometimes imagined that Aryan and Aadhaya will get married one day," said Mahir, dreamily.

"Yep, me too."

"Everyone did."

"I am not judging, but aren't you a professor?" said Daksh, looking at Yash.

"I know I shouldn't, but life gives you only one chance, only one day to do this kind of filthy stuff," said Yash, looking at his cigarette.

Daksh nodded by listening to those words of Yash.

"Pfff, but sadly," sighed Mahir, "Wait a minute, I don't recall how they broke up, or why they broke up, do any of you know?"

Daksh shook his head, saying—"It happened in college, I barely attended college."

"You must be knowing though, right, Yash?"

"Well, I don't know anything about the why part," said Yash, "but I do know about the how part."

Mahir and Daksh looked at Yash straightly, their looks were enough for Yash to continue.

"I don't know what happened exactly, but I do know some of it."

"Well, I should have asked you instead of Ruhi," said Daksh with disappointment.

"Ok, let me see—yes—it was very gloom—"

"Hey, watch out," Screamed Daksh, waving hands of Yash let out a spark on Daksh's jacket. "Do you know how much this jacket cost me?"

"Cut it out, Daksh!" Said Mahir, roughly. "Continue…"

"I was in the class, attending a lecture," Went on Yash, "You know that Aryan and I were in the same class. But that day he did not come, he ditched me that day. Anyway, suddenly voices started to come from the outside hallway, of someone having a rumble with someone. After a minute or two, the voices grew louder, even that grumpy Professor of ours took notice of it. So, he went out, and I did too. And there they were, in the middle of the hallway, fighting. Aadhaya was turned all red, and frustrating tears were coming out of her eyes. As always Aryan was calm, but I was the one who took notice of his tearless sobbing. She was screaming about some betrayal and cheating, I do not know. You know the rest, right?"

"So that is what happened, that's how it all ended?" said Daksh with a bewildered look, he looked at Mahir. "As we got separated in college, and my class was a floor up. But that day, I was out, on the second floor, hanging out with that beautiful chi—"

"Daksh!" said Mahir, "I went to a different college."

"Yeah, sorry. As I was saying, I was on the second floor that day. I heard noises and came out into the hallway. What I saw made me confused, like your face is right now, Mahir. Students were gathered in the middle, I thought maybe someone must have fallen. But then, breaking out of the crowd came Aryan, straight towards me. I felt his tears on my shirt. I knew that something uncertain had happened. He never told me what you just said to us, Yash. Whenever I asked him, he changes the topic or says he has no such power to speak about that."

"It was indeed a gloomy day," said Yash with an expression of *What-if-this-never-happened.* "It was Ruhi who took away Aadhaya out of the crowd."

"Wow, sure it was a nasty day," said Mahir, solicitously.

"Oviya was also studying in a different college, but I think Ruhi must have told her all about it," said Yash.

"Hang on, what was the real issue they were—"

"Sshh!"

Daksh shushed Mahir as Aryan was walking towards them. All three of them nodded awkwardly at him, and Aryan ignored it. He took a cigarette and lit it, sighing in relief and letting out a cloud of smoke.

"So, how's the wife?" asked Mahir, to break the silence.

"Fine, I guess."

At that very moment, Yash let out a giggle.

"What?"

"Nothing, just imagining what Aadhaya might be wondering about our slight delay," said Yash, airily.

"Stuck in traffic," said Mahir.

"Don't worry, you guys, I have got it all figured out," said Daksh, boldly. "The ferry departs at six-thirty, it will take us, what, like ten minutes to reach the Gateway from here, still, we will have twenty minutes as spare."

Mahir grinned, so did Aryan, but Yash's face turned blue as something very unpleasant was trying to come out of his body.

"What happened, Yash?" asked Aryan, seeing Yash sweating.

"She said it leaves at six..." said Yash, in a low hush voice.

"Sorry?"

"SHE SAID THE FERRY DEPARTS AT SIX!"

Everyone straightened up hearing Yash's loud voice.

"No-way," said Daksh in denial. She said "I want you boys to come straight to the Gateway because the ferry leaves at…oh, dear."

"Wh—what's the time?" asked Yash to Mahir.

Mahir's hands trembled, he looked at his watch, and his face went pale.

"It—it's five minutes past six."

"YOU IDIOT!" screamed Yash, looking at Daksh.

Mahir looked full of rage and was advancing on Daksh, he went a step back when—

"Oh-God."

Everyone turned towards Aryan, he was looking petrified. He went all stiff, he even stopped blinking. They approached.

"Now, wait a minute, who were you talking to on the phone?" asked Yash.

"I—I thought it would be a good idea to inform…"

"YES?" said three of them together.

"Sam."

Their eyes were wide opened when Aryan said that name. Pictures of Aadhaya going all merciless on them came in front of their eyes.

Together they let out a big cloud of smoke, they threw their cigarettes and ran towards their cars.

Chapter 5

Into The Ferry

How the rays of the sun adored the look of the Gateway, marvelous! The sun had bloomed on everyone, visitors had started to enter, including some locals. The ferry queue was about to start soon, the genial breeze would turn into a hot wind that would stick your shirt to your back.

It was half an hour ago that Aadhaya, Ruhi, Oviya, and Sam passed through the entrance.

"Argh! I am going to kill those dumb monkeys."

Aadhaya was very uneasy about the fact that our boys went on playing wandering. Her rage kept piling up, and the queue of the ferry was not doing any good. Ruhi and Oviya were seated on a bench, in front of them was Aadhaya pacing left and right. They were looking at her anxiously. They took notice of the boys being late when the queue came into view. Aadhaya was so mad, she decided to stand right in front of the entrance so that she could see when they would arrive and pound on them like an angry tigress. On their left was a lavish hotel introduced by a heart-rich family. Ruhi was looking at it and was deep in thought, but Aadhaya's one more of her angry grunt disturbed her.

"I knew something was fishy when I noticed from the side-mirror Daksh poking out of the window like a dog," said Ruhi, seated beside Oviya, both looking at Aadhaya.

"Oh, the boys are in deep trouble," said Oviya, aside to Ruhi.

Ruhi nodded without taking her eyes off Aadhaya. She pressed her pointy fingers hard on her phone.

"Huh, their phones are switched off—all of their phones are dead, like they will be if they don't show up in a few seconds."

Aadhaya was shaking in anger now, by the looks of her, someone might not make it up to the ferry, let alone the trip.

"Try calling Aryan," suggested Ruhi.

Aadhaya rang him once—second—and third, all of them unanswered.

"Why isn't he picking up my calls?" said Aadhaya, looking at Ruhi.

Ruhi shrugged, "Wow, he never does that."

That did not pacify Aadhaya at all. She only became more irritated.

"What the…"

"What happened, Oviya?" asked Aadhaya and Ruhi together.

"The queue—it's moving."

Aadhaya, Ruhi, and Oviya watched the scene with a horror-struck expression. The queue was moving forward, which informed them that the ferry had started to invite people in, and soon it would leave. Many tourists cheered and beamed as they got inside the ferry. Aadhaya closed her eyes, she could not handle this. Ruhi and Oviya were on their feet, watching the ferry. Then the ferry echoed its horn and started moving.

Aadhaya gritted her teeth so hard that Ruhi and Oviya moved a step away from her in case she blew up on them.

"Hey, look, it's Sam," said Ruhi, pointing towards where the queue was.

Sam was running towards them, his well-built body moving swiftly. In seconds, he was in front of them. Ruhi, noticing that the boys had gone wandering around, had asked Sam to inquire about the ferry and if there was another in case if they missed this one, which they did.

"I got some information," said Sam, looking at them. "They told me not to worry because there are five more ferries like this that will drop us at our destination."

Ruhi and Oviya heaved a sigh of relief, but Aadhaya was not pleased at all, maybe she did not listen to what Sam said.

"Why is Aryan not picking up my calls?" asked Aadhaya, turning towards Ruhi and Oviya.

"Honey, I don't know," said Oviya calmly.

"Hang on, Aryan just called me—like fifteen to twenty minutes ago."

"WHAT?" said all three girls together.

"Yeah, he told me not to worry, they are just having breakfast near the station," said Sam. "He said that they were having Idli and smoke—" Sam realized he spoke way too much.

"Did you say smoking?"

"They are having Idli?"

"I shouldn't have said that, should I?"

The face of numbers, in which two sticks show us their dance, willingly or unwillingly, who knows. Those both sticks came to a halt on the number six.

Four of them passed through the entrance hurriedly and saw the massive Gateway of India. Panting, even though they came by car, they started to search for a woman around five foot eight, her face probably red from boiling anger inside her, ready to burst on them.

"Thank the Gods, there was not that much traffic," said Aryan, pacing forwards.

"Aryan, do you think—they left us?" asked Yash, anxiously.

"Pff, there is no way they would do that."

In response, Daksh received a stern, cold look from the three of them. They paced forwards and now, moving their heads like an owl searching for rats, they started to search for their other halves.

Yash was looking at the center, the rays moved away as a cloud came in between, and then right in front of him, at some distance, was standing Aadhaya. She was already looking at him.

"Hey, guys..."

Aryan, Daksh, and Mahir came close to Yash and matched their gaze with Yash's. They saw Aadhaya, her hands rested on her waist, to her right was Sam waving at them awkwardly, and to her left were Oviya and Ruhi. They looked at them and got up from the bench. Even from this distance, they saw the devilish smirk on Oviya and Ruhi's visages.

"Oh-boy, this is bad," said Mahir, looking at Aadhaya.

"Very bad!" said Yash.

"It is not that bad...I am sure she will take this calmly and let us g—"

Daksh stopped his nonchalant tone when Mahir put his massive arm on his right shoulder. Daksh looked at Aryan and Yash they had their up-to-no-good smirk. Yash stayed at his right, but Aryan moved to his back.

"What the—hey, what you lunatics—what are you doing..."

Daksh cried out when the three of them started to push him forward straight towards Aadhaya. Daksh shook his body with all his power, but he failed as he was no match for the three of them together.

"We will tell her that it was you, the only one, who was smoking," said Aryan, pushing Daksh from behind.

"Yes, and we will tell her that--that you forced us to divert the routes," said Yash, pushing Daksh by his shoulder, while clenching his left hand firmly so he could make no moves.

"You guys are SICK—STOP PUSHING ME!"

"And we will tell her that you told us the wrong time," said Mahir with no mercy, pushing Daksh firmly.

Dragging Daksh towards Aadhaya, to meet his doom by her hands, they conversed about the plan. Daksh was insisting on talking things out, but none of them listened to him and continued pulling. They also did not mind people watching. Our girls, and Sam, were enjoying the show. Sam was not enjoying it as much by the looks of his guilty expression. They knew that Daksh would be the only one who did all this.

As they came close to the rest of them, they acted as if Daksh was dragged willingly towards her. One final push by Mahir, and Daksh was right in front of his impending doom.

"Hi, girls—and Sam, you are looking marvelous today," said Daksh in a fake cheerful tone, avoiding looking at Aadhaya.

"Look, it was all his plan!" said Yash, pointing at Daksh.

Daksh groaned, glancing back. His eyes met Aadhaya's, and he quickly turned his gaze towards Ruhi and Oviya.

"We were—I am I," said Daksh, as Aryan kicked him at the back of his leg, "was having breakfast. By the looks of your faces, you might have probably heard about this by now. We—I mean I had Idli. You people are hungry too, but unlike you, I like to act on things."

Ruhi and Oviya gave him a disbelieving look.

"Mumi…"

Daksh brought his hands forward as Ruhi raised her fist to punch him. He opened his eyes and got surprised—Aadhaya caught hold of Ruhi's fist, she saved him from getting punched.

Aryan, Yash, and Mahir shared the same look. Then Aadhaya looked at them, let go of her hand, and turned. She started to walk towards where the ferry queue started. They all grinned together.

"Told you guys, she has lost her touch since our last trip," said Daksh, turning back to face the three of them.

"I think so," said Aryan, puzzled.

"Phew, I thought something terrible was going happen to us," said Yash.

"You guys are a band of fools," said Ruhi, tartly. "We have to line up so that we can go on the ferry, and thanks to you guys, we missed our first."

"And who knows," said Oviya, coming forward and looking at them, "Once on the ferry, and there will be nowhere else to run. She will show you guys her true colors."

"Maybe throw you out of the ferry, into the deep ocean," said Ruhi, unpleasantly.

They both laughed devilishly and walked towards Aadhaya. The four of them stared at them with a horror-struck face.

"Sorry to interrupt your stare, but we have to catch that ferry," said Sam.

"Yeah," said Aryan.

"Absolutely," said Yash, starting to walk.

"Yay, the trip begins, don't know how it will end though," said Mahir, following them.

"If she decides to throw us out, the first one to go for a swim will be Yash, not me this time."

Chapter 6

The Sight of the Start

They all came to the upper deck, which was open for sky-watching and had shade at the further part of the ferry's upper deck. They were the only group up there; the rest were some locals and a couple of voyagers like them. There were seats at every edge of the ferry, except at the back, a space where most people take pictures of themselves. Shortly, Aryan, Daksh, Yash, and Mahir arrived, as they forgot their bags in their car. The rest of them were seated on the right edge of the ferry. Middle rows of benches were empty as people preferred edges, where the cold breeze was ethereal in the summertime.

They turned their gaze to observe the vast ocean, here and there, they were able to see expensive yachts and speed boats. And with that, the ferry started moving. Everyone went to the stern (back edge) of the ferry and saw the Gateway of India going far away. A small island came into view, but the ferry did not stop there. As per Aadhaya, it would take them a minimum of one hour and thirty minutes to reach their destination, and it is the last stop of the ferry. They came back and seated on those immovable seats. To their right was the bow (further edge) of the ferry.

"Hey, look at that," said Aryan, getting up from his seat and turning backward.

Countless seabirds were keeping pace with the ferry, some flying above it.

"How lovely!" sighed Oviya as she looked at them.

They all got up at once as the seabirds came close, seated at the right edge, the seabirds were flying behind them. These birds had a white-feathered body and a yellowish beak, looking no-way harmful.

It was astonishing when a guy from the opposite side walked towards the stern of the ferry where there was no shade. He lifted his arm, holding a corn stick in his fingers. One of the seabirds came in a whoosh and snatched the corn stick from his fingers with its beak, as if they were trained birds.

No sooner than later, everyone on the upper deck started doing the same. The birds flew towards them, taking the corn sticks out of people's grips. The birds flew passionately, and the girls looked at them with eyes that spoke for them.

Aryan, Daksh, Yash, and Mahir ran down to the lower deck and bought packets of those corn sticks, at an unevenly high price. Yash was outraged, as those packets showed the price of ten rupees, but the seller was selling them for fifteen. The rest of them reminded him about more pressing matters, like Aadhaya. He sighed and let go of that poor man.

Oviya and Ruhi giggled whenever the seabirds came and took the corn stick out of their hands. Everyone enjoyed it, plus it felt good to give those birds something to eat. Ah, what new entertainment! Daksh went towards the seats they were resting on, just beneath them where they had all their bags. He found his bag and took out the camera.

When he did that, his bag lost about half of its weight, as if there was nothing in there except the camera. He ran towards the tail edge of the ferry and took countless pictures of them and the seabirds, of course.

Ruhi was persistently asking Daksh to click the picture exactly when a seabird would take the corn stick out of her hand. She stood on the edge, raised her hand, and held the corn stick in her fingers. A seabird did come to snatch the corn stick, but it was a clumsy one, so the bird took the corn stick and messed up Ruhi's hair by almost stepping on them. The group burst into laughter, and Daksh even took a picture of that. Ruhi begged him to delete it, but Daksh was not going to do that, her nose turned red with anger. They took some group photos and some individual shots.

As the ferry continued floating towards the horizon, the seabirds went to a different part. They watched them fly away and came back to their seats. Ruhi's head was resting on Oviya's shoulder, Daksh and Mahir were seated facing them on the middle row, while Yash and Aryan were seated beside Oviya and Ruhi. In all these ethereal moments, no one took notice of what Aadhaya was doing, and even Sam was seated beside Daksh, talking about some game.

Aadhaya stood up from her seat, pulling her jeans up to her waist. Silence fell upon them, and Aryan knew exactly what was about to happen. He looked at Mahir and Daksh, and saw the mirror of his own expression of *and-here-comes-the-hell*. Turning to Yash, he saw his eyes fixed on Aadhaya, his lips moving, possibly in silent prayer.

"UP!" shouted Aadhaya, gesturing with her pointy index finger.

They immediately stood up on their feet, and Ruhi lifted her head from Oviya's shoulder. They looked at the four of them grinning, while Sam turned his face, avoiding any eye contact.

"Move over there," commanded Aadhaya, pointing in the direction where they had been having their pleasant time with the seabirds.

Daksh was at the last edge, to his right was Mahir, to Mahir's right was Yash, and at last, Aryan. Behind them, there was nothing but the metal border of the ferry, so there was no chance to retreat. Right in front, facing them, stood Aadhaya.

"Because of you foolish boys, we missed our first ferry," said Aadhaya in such a calm tone that it could successfully scare even Ravana.

She took steps forward, and they all started to walk back until their hips touched the edge bars of the ferry.

"Look, Aadhaya," said Daksh in an even tone, as if he did nothing wrong, "We were just having breakfast, that's all."

"Oh-really?"

They all nodded, looking at Aadhaya, lips pursed in a feeble attempt at innocence.

"Then answer my one question, Daksh," said Aadhaya in a honeyed tone.

"What question, Aadhaya?" Daksh replied.

Aadhaya came close, very close to Daksh. Their noses were just inches apart. She sniffed and looked straight into his dark eyes.

"Why do you smell like you just came out of a tobacco factory?" asked Aadhaya, simply.

Everyone knew that in mere seconds, this would turn into a very awful scenario, except, of course, for our callow friend.

"Oh, that—you know—women adore the smell of tobacco, it's manly," said Daksh with an attitude.

Aadhaya knew that it was a plain lie, she gave him a honeyed smile and moved even closer.

"See, it's working," said Daksh.

Sam slapped himself on the head, he knew Daksh was going to regret this so much. He did not mind at all that Aadhaya was now uncomfortably close.

Aadhaya sighed, looking at him, and then she ran her fingers over his jacket. When her fingers moved upwards towards his chest, he closed his eyes. That is when she grabbed him by his collars, swung her right foot back, and—

"OOoooo…"

Daksh screamed in agony and fell hard. Aadhaya kicked him straight between his legs, and the poor man rolled with his hands between his legs. Other people on the upper deck got up hearing the victim's scream. Just then, Ruhi and Oviya got up and applauded, they sat back down as they knew they were in the same group.

Aryan, Yash, and Mahir trembled to see their friend rolling on the deck in pain. They shared a look of horror, and just then, Aadhaya looked at them, her face hidden behind her lush hair.

"Now—the hunk," said Aadhaya, spitting hair from her mouth as she walked in front of Mahir. "DON'T YOU DARE MOVE, or I will throw you out of this ferry," she yelled as Mahir tried to move away.

"Lo—look Aadhaya…it was his fault, it was all HIS PLAN, I swear to God," said Mahir, his voice vibrating.

"Kick him, Aadhaya!" said Ruhi at the top of her voice.

"Yeah, kick him straight in the—"

Oviya stopped, and their cheers died away as Aryan and Yash gave them their cold look. Sam was looking at all this with his half-closed eyes.

"Why were you not picking up my calls?" asked Aadhaya.

"I—I—"

"I—I?" mimicked Aadhaya.

"I was busy eating Idli."

"And what about smoking?"

"Fine, I was smoking that time so couldn't pick up your calls."

"I am sorry, Mahir," said Aadhaya, she didn't mean it, "but because of your smoking, we missed our first—"

"But we are on the move, right?" said Mahir audaciously, "I mean, what happens if we are a little late? It is not like the world is going to fall."

Aryan and Yash looked away; they knew Mahir would die soon. Aadhaya's mouth was shut, but one could see her cheekbones moving. In the blink of an eye, like a cat, she came close to Mahir. To outsmart her, he immediately covered his crotch behind his hands. Aadhaya smiled, as if she knew he would do that. She screamed, and with all her force, she punched him right in the core of his stomach.

Mahir screamed and went to the edge of the ferry, there stood a pole, and he got the support he needed.

"Now, the pretty boy," said Aadhaya, nastily.

Yash's eyes widened as he saw Aadhaya moving towards him. He looked at Aryan, even though he knew it was of no help.

"Hey—hey" said Yash as Aadhaya was advancing on him, he put his long arms forward, "my phone—my phone was switched off the moment I left home, how would I pick up your call then? I always pick up your calls."

Aadhaya looked at him, slightly puzzled.

"He is lying" said Daksh, getting back on his feet with those corner poles, "He switched off his phone purposely the moment we started smoking. He said, "I am switching off my phone so I do not have to listen to Aadhaya's bickering." I heard him."

"YOU BRAT!" screamed Yash at Daksh, "I did not say that—I swear I didn't say that."

"My bickering, huh?" said Aadhaya, smiling like an evil witch, walking towards him, "Plus, you lied to me, you know very well I hate liars."

Yash was breathing heavily, a crazy idea struck his head, and he chose to act on it. He ran towards Aadhaya, pushed her aside with his shoulder, and ran towards the middle rows of the bench. There stood another pole, and he grabbed it like a Koala to a warm tree. The pole was in front of Ruhi and Oviya and beside Sam.

"Cheating," roared Ruhi.

"That's not fair, Yash," said Oviya.

Sam got up, Ruhi and Oviya came close. They both tried to take Yash off the pole but failed, as he had grabbed it with all his might. Others on the upper deck laughed at this struggle between Ruhi and Oviya.

"Huh-ha! You cannot do anything now," said Yash, happily side-faced as others were at his back, "Now you cannot throw me out of the ferry, Aadhaya."

Aadhaya breathed fire, hearing her grunt, Yash firmed his grip. She came marching towards him, her fist was already warmed up. Aadhaya groaned and punched Yash right at the back of his head. It got two outputs as his front hit the pole.

Yash let go of his pole and started to rub his head, with his right hand rubbing the front and left back of his head. He looked and saw Aadhaya was still angry, she gritted her teeth and punched him right in the stomach.

"Ooofff!"

Yash fell on the bench where Sam was seated a minute ago. Ruhi and Oviya high-fived Aadhaya beamingly. Sam came and sat beside Yash.

"You okay, man?" said Sam with sympathy.

Everyone again went quiet as Aadhaya turned and walked towards Aryan. Mahir helped Daksh to get on his feet, and with arms around each other, they came walking towards Yash and fell on those seats. But they too forgot the pain when Aadhaya reached the punching range with Aryan.

"Now, you. Why were you not picking up my calls?" said Aadhaya, looking down, then at him.

Aadhaya took a few steps forward. It was an unforeseen thing that Aryan, by the looks of him, was not afraid at all. He had his normal calm expression with a sage-like smile.

"Tell me, why were you not picking up my calls?"

It appeared that Aryan was the only one who took notice of her tone. He sighed and came forward. This action made the rest of them lean back in fear. Ruhi and Oviya were watching them keenly.

"I am sorry," said Aryan, softly. "And let me finish," said Aryan as Aadhaya opened her mouth, "I know, of all the people you hang around with, I know, how you feel when you get left out or don't get the answer you need—"

Everyone sat straight in their seats. Aadhaya was looking nowhere except into the speaker's eyes.

—I know you get furious, especially when one does it purposely, which is what we did today! I am sorry, Aadhaya. I know that these little things matter to you the most. I must know that—but as dumbass as I am—I forgot, again. Long ago I paid a price, very costly of which I am paying it still, for this very mistake. I am not denying the punishment...I am accepting it. So go ahead, but please forgive me."

Aryan's eyes did not flicker at all while saying those things. Ruhi and Oviya muttered "wow" under their breaths. The boys were looking stupidly at them, waiting for Aadhaya to punch him.

Aadhaya did nothing she just stood there looking at Aryan.

Please forgive me, Aadhaya, for all my mistakes.

Aadhaya came forward Aryan did not move. She hesitated but she did it, just a little push. Aryan walked back a few steps, but no harm was done to him.

"Hey, what the hell?" said Yash getting up with his hands at the front.

"What the hell was that?" said Mahir, displeasingly.

Daksh did not say anything, but turning his face, he did smile.

"Oh, shut up," Snarled Aadhaya walking towards them.

She walked straight towards Sam and hugged him. Ruhi and Oviya were the only ones who saw her rubbing at the corner of her eye.

Whosoever wrote that time is the best healer was indeed correct. They forgot the pain and started to talk, amuse, and even abuse each other, playfully, of course.

"Ok, I have to ask," Said Daksh looking at Aadhaya, they were seated in a pattern, boys were in the middle row facing those seats at the edge in which girls were seated, "What did you bring in your bag, a house?"

Aadhaya's bag was the bulkiest; of course, it was Sam who was carrying it around.

"Oh, God, I almost forgot," said Aadhaya tapping on her head.

She slid her bag towards her and opened it. She took out two big tiffin boxes. A delicious aroma spread between them, carried by the ocean breeze. They all sighed, closing their eyes.

"I brought sandwiches," said Aadhaya, happily.

"Dibs on the largest piece," said Daksh.

As the tiffin got opened, everyone fought for the largest piece, but in the end, Oviya got it as she skillfully pinched everyone away.

"Ya, I am not eating any," said Yash, leaning back on his seat.

They did not pay attention to what Yash said. They were busy taking pieces out of the tiffin box and choking them down. Mahir picked up two pieces and nudged Aryan, Aryan nodded. They both turned, Yash looked at them, Aryan came forward and opened his mouth by force, Mahir came and jammed those two sandwiches inside his mouth. Yash muttered some curses, but the sandwiches inside his mouth pacified the effect.

Again, the conversation began, a gentle breeze momentarily kissed their visages. Aryan was enjoying all this wholeheartedly. He looked at Aadhaya, Aadhaya looked at him and smiled. Then he wondered about Ekta and what she would be doing now.

Mahir, from the corner of his eye, saw Daksh sneaking his way towards the other tiffin, which was still untouched. He turned and saw Daksh picking up that tiffin and walking towards the bow of the ferry. There was a sort of cabin, Daksh went behind it, and there were seats there too.

"You sneaky animal," said Mahir, as he came in front of Daksh.

"Whoot?" said Daksh, his mouth full with those sandwiches.

Mahir sat beside him, to their back was that cabin thing, so others were not able to notice them. They started to enjoy those sandwiches together.

As they were in the very front of the ferry, the wind was tapping on their faces constantly. Just then, a very forceful wind came, making their heads lean back. It went away in a second; they both looked at each other and shrugged their shoulders. Suddenly, Daksh saw Mahir going all stiff, he was looking somewhere at his back. He turned slowly and got frozen, just like Mahir, he wanted to scream, he wanted to cry, but could not.

"There you guys are!"

Aryan came in between, Daksh and Mahir walked back into the present. Both got up and peeked behind Aryan.

"What are guys doing?" asked Aryan, curiously.

"Did you see that?" asked Daksh, hoarsely.

"See what, Daksh?"

Aryan turned he saw nothing, just another ferry at a distance, matching its pace with theirs. Daksh and Mahir also gazed over there, but the thing they saw a few seconds earlier, which made the back of their hair stand, was gone.

"Hey, you guys took that," snarled Aryan, pointing at the half-eaten tiffin. Aryan got taken aback as no response came from Daksh and Mahir they still had their confused looks. "Let's go, guys. Guess what...Yash brought a Bluetooth speaker, and it is on now. Come on, they started dancing."

Daksh and Mahir followed Aryan, surely, they were dancing. Yash was dancing, as his partner was the pole that made his head go coo-coo. Aadhaya, Ruhi, and Oviya were just beside him dancing in their own space like there is no one to judge. Sam was close to Yash moving his upper body he cannot dance like Yash was with his lean body.

The rest of the people on the upper deck didn't mind them dancing, some were embarrassed.

Aryan beamed and went towards them hopping like a rabbit when he sees a carrot. He joined in just beside Yash they started to move their bottoms as per the beat, and even Sam was trying to.

Daksh and Mahir stood there looking at them the scene truly messed up their joyfulness. Suddenly, there was a shrieking noise, and some four to five girls, about their age, came from the lower deck.

"Do you guys mind if we joined you?" asked one of those girls, who was wearing an orange t-shirt and light blue jeans.

"Not at all," said Ruhi.

So, they all started dancing. Daksh looked at Mahir and then turned his gaze to the front.

"Ah, what the hell."

Saying that, Daksh hopped like Aryan and joined in the dance. Mahir sighed, shook his head, hoping he joined too.

Chapter 7

The Town

The ferry was starting to slowdown, their carefree dance came to a halt. The boys were dancing like some local mountain tribe—beautiful, but bizarre in front of the town people. The engine sound, which our lovely ferry was making, was now soft. All of them realized that in a matter of minutes, their destination would be in front of them.

Sure enough, there came an island, entirely made up of a bunch of colossal four-legged concrete stones. Obviously, the ferry didn't stop there. She moved further, passing it behind. Yash went to the seat where his Bluetooth speaker was making noises. Pressing a button, he stopped it. He then realized he could do that with his phone.

On the upper deck, there was the sound of people getting up, packing their bags. That was the clue that they are here, almost. The group of girls, which came from the lower deck, said their goodbyes. One of those girls eyed Yash, but our friend replied to her with a simple smile and nod.

"What the hell is wrong with you?" barked Daksh, as those girls went out of sight to the lower deck.

"What...I can't, I already promised someone," Replied Yash.

Ruhi and Oviya beamed playfully, which took the rest of their attention and came in front of Yash.

"So, who is the mystery girl?" inquired Ruhi.

"Oh, now, don't be shy," said Oviya.

The rest of them came in front of him, too and formed a semi-circle around him. Yash was now cornered, but as he was the tallest of them all, he saw an opportunity.

"Hey, look, the port."

Everyone turned and saw the port approach. The port's base was made of colossal four-legged stones, and above it was a smooth base that would lead them to stairs moving upwards towards the skywalk, as the island's ground was above sea level.

The crowd started to move down to the lower deck, and the ferry came to a halt right in front of the port. There was a murmur of people unloading themselves. Just like others, our group pulled their bags over their shoulders and went down to the lower deck. Daksh's camera was hanging around from his neck.

Yash stopped them when they were about to move further with the people in front of them, as he saw those girls. Yash had no will to talk to them. As they moved out of sight, they all came out of the ferry carefully, as there was a gap between the ferry and the port. Aadhaya's bag had surely lost some weight, as she was the one carrying it, not our Sam.

They started climbing those stairs, and finally, they were on the smooth floor of the skywalk. Oviya almost slipped but Ruhi got her back. Both sides were open, allowing them to see the endless ocean and hear the sound of water splashing on the port. Their ears didn't need any music, as the lord of the wind was singing for them. It was good to see everyone having a beaming smile, the smile that shows no regret, the smile that our destroyer has in his kindness, the smile of curiosity about what is ahead.

The skywalk led them straight. They walked to the end of it, and they felt the heat of the sun. At the end of the skywalk, on their left was a huge map of the town.

"Here is the map," said Mahir, looking at it.

The map provided them with all the details a tourist required for the journey. The blue highlighted parts showed the beaches, the hillsides were marked with brown highlights, and the black highlighted spots represented forts. The forts were numerous but at surprisingly long distances from each other.

Daksh quickly clicked a photo of the map. However, Aadhaya coughed and took out the same map, a mini version, from her bag. Daksh sniffed and looked away as his smartness got wasted. They continued walking, passing many fast-food shops and ice cream parlors at both edges, but they didn't stop at any of those and came out onto the road.

The road was crowded with tourists and locals. The locals were walking swiftly, putting the rest of the crowd behind, heading straight towards the bus stand. The bus was on the right side of the road, and there was a queue for it. They saw many familiar faces from the ferry as they moved to the left. On the left side of the road was another vehicle stop, which locals called a *tum-tum*.

Colored like a taxi, black and white, but a tum-tum is somewhat ochre in color. It has three tires, one in front and two at the back. It makes a distinct sound when the engine starts, a sound that, if you are traveling in it for the first time, will ring in your ears for minutes after you take the exit from it. It can easily carry eight people, promising a happy ride, provided you don't mind the ringing sound and can endure a rough ride even on plain roads. But overall, it will be a blissful ride after all, what is life without some hiccups, eh?

"There is no way I am going in that," said Mahir, looking at the queue of *tum-tum*.

"What?" snarled Aadhaya, putting away the map.

They were talking loudly as the cacophony of people had surrounded them.

"I am with Mahir," added Daksh.

"What is wrong with that?" questioned Aryan, glancing at the *tum-tum*.

"Oh, it makes me go—belch," explained Daksh. "And after we ate that Sambar and the sandwiches—"

"I got the point," interrupted Aryan.

"Well, that leaves us only the bus," sighed Oviya. "Hope you don't feel uneasy in that too?" Oviya sniggered, looking at Daksh and Mahir.

"Who are you sniggering at?" said Daksh, elevating his eyebrow.

"Seriously, Oviya, you are taunting us—you know what happened last time we went together in that?" added Mahir, looking at Oviya and then at the *tum-tum*.

Everyone turned their heads to Oviya she looked perplexed. But her expression changed quickly. Her eyes got wide open, she gasped, and covered her mouth with her hands.

"Oh my God! You guys still remember that?" said Oviya, in a tone that suggested she just got exposed.

"Yeah, we do," said Daksh and Mahir together, and they laughed.

"Remember what?" asked the rest of the people together.

"Well, it happened when—" Daksh was talking enthusiastically, but Oviya let out a little squeak.

"Please don't—oh please, I beg you," pleaded Oviya.

Daksh and Mahir looked at each other, then at her, with not even a pinch of mercy.

Oviya's face went red; she stomped her feet on the ground, turned, and marched towards the bus stop. Daksh and Mahir laughed out loud. Ruhi went after Oviya, but she turned and said,

"Tell me later, ok."

Then everyone walked towards the bus stop and lined up in the queue. A bus came but got packed with people further in, so they waited for the second bus. Time passed by, Aryan broke from the line and walked further to inquire about the next bus Daksh joined him. There was a man who seemed like a local, he was short, and his hair was turning white.

"Excuse me, sir, when will the next bus arrive?" inquired Aryan.

The man looked at him, smiled, and said, "In about ten minutes, the bus will be here, but if you had arrived like an hour earlier, there might have been cabs available."

"Ok, thank you, sir."

The man nodded. Aryan and Daksh walked back towards where the rest of them were standing.

"Don't let Aadhaya hear about that," warned Daksh.

"Yep," replied Aryan, nodding.

Now the people in front were moving towards the *tum-tum* as the bus was taking time to arrive. There were a few of them now. Aryan saw Ruhi telling something to Oviya, to which she shook her head. Some more people diverted their way towards the *tum-tum*.

"Here comes the bus," informed Yash.

They all climbed inside and took the seat two rows further from the back door. Oviya and Ruhi sat on the left row, to their back, Sam and Aadhaya. On the right row just opposite Ruhi, Aryan and Daksh sat down, with Daksh taking the window seat. To their back, Yash and Mahir sat down. There were many empty seats behind them and some in front.

The engine made a sound, and the bus started moving. The town was simple and unique in its own way. The buildings here had only four floors, no more than that. The place was surrounded by tall palm trees and coconut trees, their height surpassing the buildings. Sun's rays were not blocked by any building, and the roads, the sidewalks, were illuminated by it. No big buildings meant no blockage for the wind, which came and went as she pleased. The gentle breeze never left their trail, touching them now and then. The place was bright and blessed with no darkness.

"This place is peaceful," sighed Yash, gazing out of the window.

Aadhaya took out the map again, and they all turned to face her. Oviya and Ruhi went on their knees above their seats, turning back to face Aadhaya. Aryan and Mahir turned their heads left, and Yash peeked behind Mahir's shoulder.

"Hmm, let's see. I think we should go here first," said Aadhaya, pointing her finger at a blue highlighted area.

"A beach," said Oviya and Ruhi together.

"I thought we were going to one of those forts," said Mahir, looking at Aadhaya.

"Do not worry, Mahir. There is a vast fort right at the shores of this beach," said Aadhaya, informatively.

Mahir smiled and patted on Aryan's back.

"This bus will stop right in front of the hotel, or at a distance?" asked Daksh, revealing his head from behind Aryan's shoulder.

"As per the research I did, this bus's last stop is not far from our hotel, we can go there on foot," said Aadhaya.

"We will walk then, if you guys agree. My legs are tired from sitting," said Sam.

Everyone agreed to go to the hotel on foot. Aadhaya put away the map in one of the many pockets in her bag, then turned towards where the boys were seated.

"About that Oviya and the *tum-tum* thing—"

"Aadhaya!" said Oviya, coming back on her knees above her seat and looking at Aadhaya in disbelief.

Ruhi also came above her seat and looked at Aadhaya, she turned to Oviya.

"I am sorry, honey, but I got to know," said Ruhi, impatiently.

Oviya opened her mouth, Ruhi closed it with her fingers and acted to kiss her. Oviya was already irritated, she moved her hand away and frowned.

"So, it happened when we were in the tenth grade, our last year in our dear school," said Daksh, just like Ruhi and Oviya, he too got above his seat.

Oviya made an "argh" sound under her breath, she turned and folding her hands sat back on her seat, gazing out of the window. Others turned back to Daksh, Mahir was already grinning.

"As you all know," said Daksh, "that Mahir and I used to live at a distance from our school. So, most of the time, we came together by walking or sometimes in a *tum-tum*. His parents—just like mine—didn't give us that much money, so the *tum-tum* option suited us. One day at school, I think it was break time when Oviya approached us and said she wants to come with us to the school by *tum-tum*. At first, I thought she was joking; I mean, her father had a car; she always came from that, fancy as she was—"

"It was a wrecked car," cried Oviya, in her defense.

The bus echoed with laughter, and Daksh continued.

"So, Oviya reached school by her father's *wrecked* car. We said yes, she can come with us. The next day arrived, she was jumping with excitement to go to school by *tum-tum*, weird isn't it? Anyways, when we were about some minute distance away from school, our Oviya here gave an almighty belch."

"NO!" breathed Ruhi "she puked!"

"Not just that", said Mahir "as I was sitting right next to her, she emptied all that she ate in her breakfast onto my lap."

The bus trembled by their outburst, Aryan was breathless, Yash was rolling on his seat, Aadhaya had to clench her stomach, even Sam was laughing in mirth.

"I hate you guys," said Oviya, hurt.

"Aw, don't say that. This doesn't make me like you less," said Ruhi. She sat down and wrapped Oviya in her arms.

"Hey, is that the same day you guys arrived insanely late, and Mahir, your pants were weirdly loose?" asked Aryan, looking at Mahir.

"Yes," said Mahir, "the guard saw me and my pants; it had that yellowish-green—"

"Eww, Mahir, that's enough," said Aadhaya when a mental image came in.

"You know that pant still stinks of tea, and God knows what she ate," exaggerated Mahir.

"Hey, I didn't mean to," said Oviya standing up. "I just wanted to experience that bloody *tum-tum*."

"It's okay," said Daksh.

"Daksh is right," said Aryan, "It was like—let's see, we are now twenty-eight—fifteen to twenty years ago, Oviya, relax."

With some more laughter and amusement, the journey in the bus went ahead. The bus stopped at her last stop, they all got out, and pushing back their bags over their shoulder they started walking.

Aadhaya was leading the way, besides her were Oviya and Ruhi, three of them were in deep conversation. Boys were at the back, walking beside each other, talking about beaches and trips they had together before this. Mahir was keenly focused on the forts he appeared to know a great deal about them. The road they were walking on was quiet with tourists like them walking around in shorts, very few vehicles passed by as the road was narrow. There were many shops on either side of the road. The building's height was the same as before, Aryan checked his watch, it showed that it was almost half-past eight.

"Hey, look at that!" said Mahir, pointing to the opposite side of the road from which they were walking.

There was a wine shop on square-shaped premises.

"Wine shop looks good," said Yash.

"No trip goes well without some alcohol," said Daksh, rubbing his hands.

"We will buy, but not now," said Aryan.

"You are right," said Sam looking at Aryan.

"Those girls have the nose of the hound," said Mahir.

"HEY...DREAMY HEADS."

They turned and saw Ruhi, gesturing for them to move their feet. They waved their hands up and started walking. After ten more minutes of walking, they arrived at their hotel.

The hotel, like every other building, had four floors although it was widely spread. They went inside, a flowery smell touched their nose. The hall of the hotel was big, few people were walking here and there, most of those were workers. Aadhaya and Oviya were talking with the woman in the reception. Aryan saw three canapés, all three of them facing a coffee table in between. At every corner of the hall, there were plants of some strange flowers. Behind one of the wide couches was a glass wall that overlooked the garden of the hotel. They put their bags on the couch and waited for Aadhaya and Oviya to return.

They came back with them a man dressed in a black and red outfit the man took their luggage. Aadhaya and Oviya thanked them, then Aadhaya turned to them.

"Ok, now listen," said Aadhaya, "I am giving you all exactly an hour to freshen up and meet right here. I don't want anyone to be late, we have to start by going to a beach, which is not far from here. And now you idiots, if any of you comes even a second—"

"We won't," said Yash.

"I promise we will not be late," added Aryan.

Aadhaya then turned to Daksh and Mahir they were silent for a minute. Then Daksh remembered her nut-kick and nodded, so did Mahir.

Chapter 8

The Crow Talk

"So, what is it like to be a gym trainer?" asked Yash to Sam.

Yash and Sam were the first ones to arrive back at the reception. They were seated on a couch, Yash in a soft chair placed in the corner of the couch in an L shape. Yash picked up a magazine from the coffee table in the middle, but it was not to his liking, so he started a conversation with Sam.

"Oh, it is a dream work for me," said Sam, rejoiced. "I love to train people, and you have no idea how good I feel when I see a certain-- even minute--change in them. It is good to be part of something like this."

"Wow, so do you have your own gym?"

Sam laughed, "No, not yet—that is what my goal is though."

"Do me a favor and call me when you begin this Gym project of yours...I would seriously like to invest in it," said Yash, sitting straight.

Sam smiled humbly and nodded.

"Hey, you are a professor, you must also have that experience of "change" in your students, right?"

"Yes, of course, Sam. But, no offense, mine is a little harder it is a lot to do with mental change. Plus, you know how moody teenagers are. Some students have shown me that change, and surprisingly most of them are boys—I know, but girls are also effortful."

"Can I ask you one more question?" asked Sam in a serious tone, leaning forward.

"Go ahead."

"What do you do for that chiseled jaw of yours, I mean there has got to be something you do?"

"Uhh—"

"Hey, freaks."

Aryan came walking, and he got seated beside Sam on the couch.

"So, what you guys were discussing?" inquired Aryan.

"Nothing, just stuff about jawline, change, and gym," answered Yash.

"Well, those knuckleheads better come soon," said Aryan.

"Don't worry," said Sam "I mean, girls are not here yet."

Aryan nodded looking at Sam. Just then there came a sound, the sound of someone in grave conversation, or argument. Aryan and Sam tilted their heads left, while Yash turned back. They saw Daksh and Mahir approaching. Aryan sighed in relief, as they showed up before any of the girls did. They were really in deep conversation, Daksh was speaking and Mahir was nodding then shook his head, and that surprisingly made Daksh disapprove of him.

"I am telling you it was not a—"

"It was, you idiot."

"Knuckle-heads finally showed up," sneered Yash.

"Say that again and I will surely mess up your jawline, Professor," Barked Daksh.

Yash gave him a cold look and turned away.

"What were you guys arguing about?" asked Aryan.

Daksh and Mahir came in front and sat on the coffee table so that they could face them while talking.

"It was about what we saw... back when we were on the ferry," said Daksh, gravely.

"On the ferry?" asked Aryan and Yash together.

"What did you see?" asked Sam.

Daksh looked at Mahir, he nodded, Daksh sat straight and took a deep breath.

"When I took that other tiffin and went behind that cabin thing to eat—DON'T YOU DARE DISTURB ME!" said Daksh as Yash spoke a half word. "As I was saying, I went behind it, thus I was in the very front of the ferry. Then came Mahir, and we shared the tiffin, but then a strong wave of wind made us tilt our heads backward. And then our eyes got directed to the right, where another ferry was keeping pace with us..."

"That's it?" said Aryan after a minute of Daksh's pause.

"No," said Daksh, plainly.

"What's the big deal? There was another ferry, what is wrong with that?" said Sam, bewildered.

"See, that's the thing, we didn't mind the ferry at all. What we did mind was..." said Mahir and went silent.

"What we're trying to say is," said Daksh, "that we saw a crow on the roof of that other ferry."

"What is wrong with a crow resting on the roof of that ferry?" said Aryan.

"Everything, Aryan," said Mahir and looked away.

"The thing is," said Daksh, "that was not a normal crow. It was…it was huge. I mean, I have never seen that huge bird in my whole life. And the place where we were watching that crow, by the looks of it—it had a blue eye."

Aryan and Yash looked at each other, turned, and laughed.

"Ni-nice one, you two," said Yash, controlling himself from not falling from the chair.

"See, didn't I tell you before that they won't believe us," said Daksh to Mahir.

Mahir clenched his teeth and looked away. Sam was looking at Daksh.

"Let me get this straight," said Yash, "you guys saw a huge crow, which had a blue eye?"

"YES," Cried Daksh and Mahir.

Aryan and Sam snorted.

"See, that is exactly why I told you guys not to eat that much when you are traveling on the ferry."

"It was a nice prank, didn't work though," said Aryan.

"We are not joking around, Aryan," said Mahir standing up from the coffee table, some magazines fell.

This sudden reaction of Mahir made everyone lean back, it also increased the tension between them.

"When did I ever joke around with this loony?"

"Hey!"

"Sorry, but we are serious guys. We did see that blue-eyed vulture."

"I thought it was a crow?" said Yash screwing up his face.

"It was a crow," said Daksh.

"I don't believe this," said Yash, placing his hand on his head.

"Oh, you will, when you will receive a punch from me."

"Yeah, and it was a vulture," said Mahir.

"It was a crow, you idiot."

"You both are lunatics."

"Say that again, I dare you."

"Oh-yeah—"

"CUT IT OUT!" yelled Aryan, he also got on his feet. "You dumb-heads, we are on a trip—do not create any hell." Aryan took a deep breath, "Look, because of us, this trip was on the edge of getting messed up. Everything is going fine now, and I would like to keep it that way. So, let's not make Aadhaya or Ruhi—or Oviya—unhappy again, good?"

Daksh and Yash looked at each other, one more nudge, and the quarrel began. But they tore their eyes away from each other and looked at Aryan.

"Okay."

Aryan turned and saw Sam; he was still seated on the couch looking at him. He sat beside him, Sam leaned forward.

"Do you believe them?" asked Sam with a note of worry.

"I don't know, at first I thought they were looking at some cute girl on that other ferry's upper deck."

"Here they come," said Yash.

Aryan turned and saw that Aadhaya, Ruhi, and Oviya were approaching. The reason for the delay was cleared as they had changed their attire. Aadhaya was wearing a sandal-colored, full-sleeved t-shirt with black jeans and matching sneakers. Oviya was wearing a rose-red shirt tucked inside her blue-washed jeans and a pair of boots. And Ruhi was wearing a brown leather jacket over a white t-shirt, with dark jeans and boots.

"That's why you girls took so long," said Daksh.

"You look amazing," complimented Sam, looking at Aadhaya.

"Thank you" said Aadhaya, smiling.

"Ooh-la-la, Oviya, you look enchanting," said Yash cheerfully.

"Thank you, Yash," said Oviya, giving Yash a flying kiss.

"You sure look like a person you must not mess with, Ruhi," said Aryan.

"Aw, thank you, Aryan," said Ruhi, beamingly.

There were many amusing comments on Daksh's throat, but he was controlling them to keep it inside. He wanted to comment, but then he saw their heavy soul boots and chose not to, letting out a squeak.

"What were you guys arguing about so loudly?" asked Ruhi, looking at Aryan.

Aryan said nothing he just turned to Daksh.

"Nothing," said Daksh quickly. But the answer didn't satisfy her or others, "Err, I told you, it was nothing, just talking about birds—doing stuff with—other birds."

"What?" cried Oviya, narrowing her eyes at him.

"You know—"

Mahir didn't let Daksh finish by patting hard on his back.

"Just overly excited about the trip," said Mahir with a fake smile.

Everyone nodded in agreement. Daksh nodded while massaging his back. It was not enough to satisfy Aadhaya and others, they still looked suspiciously at them. Daksh took notice of it.

"THE TRIP BEGINS!" cheered Daksh, which made others startled.

There was silence for a minute or so, making Daksh embarrassed as his fist was still raised, but—

"YEEHAW!" cried Aryan, Yash, Mahir, and Sam, raising their fists.

Without looking back, they walked and hopped out of the hotel. Aadhaya, Ruhi, and Oviya stood there, surprised, confused about what just happened.

"Is it just me, or are they *really* getting crazier as they are growing up?" said Ruhi.

"They are, aren't they?" said Oviya.

"I think they are hiding something," guessed Aadhaya.

"Forget it."

And by putting arms around each other, they moved out of the hotel.

Chapter 9

The Last Bliss

"Yes—Yes! I did it—I did it!" exclaimed Oviya, jumping in joy as she exited from the *tum-tum*.

They asked many travelers and some locals about how to get to the beach, and the only answer they received was through the tum-tum. They considered walking, but one of the locals strongly suggested they should go by tum-tum. Oviya hid her face and stayed back, growing anxious as no other ideas popped into their heads. With no other option, they took a *tum-tum* towards the beach.

Daksh and Mahir sat beside the driver, not wanting to take any risks. Meanwhile, the others were at the back, with Oviya at the corner beside her and Ruhi and Aadhaya in the seats. In front of them sat Aryan, Yash, and Sam. Oviya's head was down with nervousness.

Oviya didn't puke, and the journey was quiet and pleasant, even though many speed bumps came along the way. At one point, Oviya burped, making Aryan and Yash almost jump out of the vehicle. Ruhi and Aadhaya burst into laughter at this little action, and Oviya went all red with embarrassment. Meanwhile, Daksh and Mahir were engrossed in a conversation with the driver about other places to visit. The driver knew a great deal of it, of course as this was his vocation, and both Daksh and Mahir listened keenly, making mental notes of what he said.

Aryan gazed out, observing a change in the climate. The breeze touched him, but the sun's heat was relentless this time. Aryan knew that the beach was nearby. On either side of the road, palm and coconut trees lined the way. Many tourists were walking around in shorts. Aryan shook his feet in excitement, realizing that soon they would be touching the soft sands of the beach.

Ah, the sound of the water approaching the land was like a long-lost dream that, upon reaching her goal, regretted it and walked back. That sound filled them with a tremendous amount of bliss.

The *tum-tum* stopped right in front of the beach entrance, and Oviya was the first to step out.

"See, I told you it was just a one-time thing," Ruhi said, coming out of the *tum-tum*.

Soon, everyone exited, and Oviya was on top of her spirits with joy.

"That, or she just didn't want her outfit to get ruined," Daksh commented to Mahir, who had a good laugh, earning them cold looks.

"Let's go, what are we waiting for!" Aryan exclaimed with enthusiasm.

Ruhi put her arms around Oviya, and they walked towards the beach. The rest of the group followed, stepping onto the land that sank when you pressed your feet on it. Palm trees surrounded the back part of the beach, swaying with the wind.

What a perfect word *beach* is; no one can regret coming there, even a person filled with sorrows. They walked towards the shore, and there it was, in the middle of the waters—it was so vast that it had its own huge island. The fort gleamed with the rays of power provided by the lord of light, featuring wide walls taller than twenty feet—a true presentation of strength.

"I want to go there," sighed Mahir, gazing dreamily at the fort.

"Everyone does, Mahir," said Ruhi, patting him on the back.

They were all standing a little back from the border where the ocean was annoying the beach.

"Hmm, the boats have not yet begun," observed Daksh, gazing around.

"Boats?" asked Aadhaya, turning to Daksh.

"Of course, what are you planning to go there by swimming?" replied Daksh, sarcastically.

Aadhaya's lips twitched with irritation, and Daksh immediately turned his face away.

The beach was quiet, with only a few people wandering around. Some were walking towards the back, where the jungle of palm and coconut trees awaited them. Others were seated on the soft sandy beach, gazing at the horizon.

"Hey, until then, we can take some pictures on this beautiful beach," suggested Ruhi.

Ruhi's sparkling eyes and pleasing expression convinced them to say yes. Daksh took off his camera, which was hanging around his neck, and got ready.

"No, over there, where the water is touching the sand, and give me a good pose."

Ruhi ran, and Daksh started clicking pictures. In a few seconds, Aadhaya and Oviya joined them. Aryan smiled, not because of this joyful scenario he had his own artifice ready in his mind.

Aryan walked back, and soon the rest of the boys joined him. They formed a crescent moon shape around Aryan.

"Sam, Mahir," said Aryan, in a tone of urgency, "you two go to that wine shop we saw and buy a small bottle that can fit in your pocket."

"Ok...but what about them?" said Mahir, looking at the three girls posing together in front of the cameraman.

"Yeah, won't they notice us?" asked Sam, worriedly.

"Don't worry about that," said Yash optimistically. "That's a thing about our Ruhi, Oviya, and Aadhaya They usually get oblivious when they start posing for that perfect picture."

Yash was right. The girls were so into posing for that perfect picture that they didn't notice Mahir and Sam leave. The index finger of Daksh started aching, his memory filling up with photos of Ruhi, as she was the one more keenly observed. Aryan turned his gaze towards the entrance and saw Mahir and Sam return. Soon, they were beside him, and Mahir showed him the crystal bottle hidden behind his flannel jacket. Aryan and Yash grinned, tapping them on the back. As Aryan turned his gaze back to the front, he saw Daksh running towards them, it was a hassle to run on the beach.

"I've had enough of this," exasperated Daksh, standing beside Aryan.

Shortly, Ruhi came in the same manner. She approached and grabbed Daksh's hand, pulling it towards her.

"Please, only a few more pictures. Only few, I promise," pleaded Ruhi.

"No, Ruhi. I cannot because I brought only one memory card," said Daksh.

Ruhi frowned and let go of his hand.

"He is lying, I saw him with more than three of those back on the ferry when he was taking out the camera," said Yash.

"You son of a...."

"You liar!" said Ruhi.

The quarrel began again, and Ruhi started to pull his jacket now.

"Hey, not my jacket."

Aadhaya and Oviya walked towards them, not bothering to yell at them to stop.

"Hey, the boat has started," said Mahir, rejoiced.

The quarrel came to a halt. They turned and saw two men pushing a motorboat into the water. One after another, many men came and started pushing their boats. There was no doubt they were there to drop them off at the fort.

Aadhaya and Oviya rolled up their jeans and went towards them. They started talking with one of those dark men, with a swimmer's physic, who was pulling most of the boats. Aadhaya then turned towards them and waved her hand.

"Finally!" said Mahir.

They all ran towards them, folding their jeans and taking off their shoes. They climbed inside the motorboat, which was made to carry ten people at a time. Seeing eight people boarding, the man decided to take off immediately. It had seats in the corners, five on each side.

"There is a lot of water traveling here," said Daksh.

Ruhi and Oviya took the very first seats of the boat. Behind them, Sam and Yash settled, and to their back were Aadhaya and Daksh. Finally, Aryan sat beside the driver.

The man pulled the string, and with a thunder-like sound of the engine, the boat started. In a matter of seconds, the boat gained so much speed that Ruhi and Oviya's hair flowed back. Yash and Sam leaned back as their hair brushed their faces. The boat hopped momentarily, and they enjoyed it by making noises.

"Whoa, it is getting bigger," said Aryan, looking at the fort.

"It will take us the whole afternoon to go inch-by-inch," said Mahir, rather happily.

The faded ocher walls of the Fort gleamed even brighter than before, so much that the water was reflecting it with joy. Its thick, tall walls were so big they had to tilt their heads up to see the edge of it. There was no doubt that this Fort unveiled power.

The engine went off, and so did the heavy sound of it. By floating, they reached the shores of the Fort Island. Mahir, most excited, jumped out of the boat without thinking.

"Ouch!"

There were many stones and shells on the ground; the stones were rounded, but the shells were pointy. So, when Mahir jumped, they welcomed him with pain.

"Don't wear your shoes now," said Aadhaya, warningly to Oviya and Ruhi. They saw what happened to Mahir and decided to wear shoes.

"You are right...the water will get in and destroy them," admitted Oviya.

Aryan, Daksh, Yash, and Sam walked out of the boat carefully. Their shoes were in their hands. Aryan looked at his feet, the water was coming and going when it touched the land. The water was clear. He observed it when a wave came over those shells and stones, but still, he could see them. Mahir was standing on his right leg, massaging his left leg.

"Clumsy!" said Daksh, passing by him.

Then they started their inclined walk, as the Fort was above sea level, towards the entrance. Ruhi squeaked when a shell touched her naked feet. They arrived in front of the vast entrance, Aryan and others got a royal feeling seeing it. In front of the entrance, on the right was a sort of cabin. There, they had to pay entrance fees. The entrance fee was seven rupees each they paid the man and sat there, starting to pull their shoes and push down their rolled jeans.

Passing the entrance, they went inside. At first, it was a narrow way the ground was made of some sort of unknown bricks, it looked old but had no cracks on it. At the edges were wildflowers. Then it became wider, and they were in an open space now. It was a strange view at first as the garden had many weeds growing on and wildflowers.

Further, they went and saw people wandering around, some were locals judging by their attire. They approached one of those locals and asked him about this strange garden.

The man smiled, not surprised, or hurt. "The garden is like this since the fall of this fort. The caretaker of this fort believes in reality. They don't want to change anything or fabricate some parts of the fort. It is as it is. It shows the visitors, like you, young people, how old this fort is, on the other hand, it clearly represents the power it still holds."

Everyone thanked the man and went further the route turned right, leading them to a temple. The man informed them that there were many temples in this fort, which is why he was there – to pray. They continued walking further, looking around. The fort did not miss any chance to surprise them and make them wonder. There were walls everywhere, but most of them were broken.

"My God, there must have been a fierce battle that took place here," said Mahir, looking at those broken walls.

They went where most of the people were moving. The scene coming up made them start. Here, the walls were not just broken but burned. The walls had turned into charcoal black.

"I am so thankful that they keep it as it is...it feels historic," said Yash, thankfully.

They were able to see the blue Ciel. It was the reason for the brightness inside the fort, as it was open. Mahir and Yash were the only ones who had the admiring approach to everything they saw, hence they got separated. They were now in an open space the sun was above their heads, and they didn't mind the heat. Both were observing a tall, thick wall in front of them the ocher color on the top had turned black.

"What do you think made these strong walls burnt?" asked Mahir.

"There must be a battle, of course—in that battle, there must be some cannons involved, judging by those broken walls. But that is not the strange part," said Yash, keenly observant.

"What is the strange part then?"

"Mahir, you can see that those outer walls are unharmed, but the inner ones are the most damaged. It is very unusual because the enemy obviously had come from outside, but then these walls are burned from inside. Something devilish must have happened here."

Mahir nodded and turned back to observe the wall.

"Mahir—Yash."

They turned and saw Sam running on the open space towards them following him were Aryan and Daksh.

"You have got to see this…" said Sam, panting.

"See what?" asked Mahir.

Aryan and Daksh came close.

"Girls have found something really interesting," said Daksh.

Mahir and Yash looked at Aryan he nodded in reply. At once, they ran towards that place. Their boots made noises on that strange bricked floor. Now in front of them were some stairs, they climbed those, and Aadhaya, Ruhi, and Oviya came into view. They had their phones out and were clicking pictures of a temple in front of them.

"Wow, which God rests in this temple?" asked Yash.

"Well, we don't know," said Aryan.

"Actually—we meant that," said Sam, pointing aside towards the right.

There was a big, about six-foot-tall, black marbled wall on it, there was writing in golden letters. It read—

This Fort was the naval base

Of the

Maratha Empire

"Cool" beamed Yash and Mahir together, their eyes sparkling as they read those words. They continued reading further information about the fort.

Aadhaya, Ruhi, and Oviya joined them.

"Let's keep it moving, boys," said Aadhaya.

"Yes, there is a lot to see," added Oviya, excitedly.

But Mahir and Yash didn't move a muscle they continued reading the information about the Fort on the wall.

"I overheard someone on our way here" said Ruhi, coming forward, "she was saying that there are actual and live cannons over here."

Yash and Mahir immediately turned their faces to her.

"Cannons?"

"Did you say alive?"

Ruhi nodded, and in a blink, Yash and Mahir disappeared into thin air. They were already running far away from them.

"HEY, WAIT FOR US!" screamed Aryan, and he too started running.

Sam looked at Aadhaya, she nodded, and he disappeared. Daksh yawned and stayed there.

"I also overheard her saying that there is a temple which has a square-shaped pond behind it" added Ruhi.

"Oh, how beautiful! I wonder how the pictures would come out," said Oviya.

"Hey, where is Daksh?"

Aadhaya looked around, and the three of them saw Daksh pacing ahead, far ahead to be called back forcefully.

Chapter 10

The Hoax

The sky had turned orange, the sun was pulling his ocean blanket on, his face turned yellow-red like a child going to sleep. The waves were getting higher, soon when the sun would completely get hidden behind the horizon, it would be their time of the day.

All eight of them were back in the motorboat coming back from the fort towards the beach. Daksh was seated in the front of the boat. Beside him was Yash. The rest of the boys were behind. Aadhaya, Ruhi, and Oviya were seated at the back. The girls had their eyes closed, enjoying the gentle wind, and listening to the melodic sounds of water. The boys were talking about the big cannons they saw on the fort and discussing something about water sports.

"The fort was awesome," said Aryan, lazily, his eyes slightly open as the wind hit his face.

"It really was," agreed Mahir, turning towards Aryan.

"I am really thankful to you, Daksh," said Yash.

As Daksh was in the very first seat of the boat, he turned, his eyes half-closed because of the wind.

"Well, what can I say? Everybody is my friend, and I have always been a giver," said Daksh, suddenly comparing himself with God.

"No, you idiot," said Yash, admonishingly.

Mahir, Aryan, and Sam laughed.

"Then why are you thankful?" asked Daksh.

"Because you brought that beautiful camera of yours," answered Yash.

"Yes, it captured many moments in his little brain," joked Aryan.

Mahir and Sam nodded, agreeing with Aryan. Daksh smiled beamingly.

"My Senorita always gets me compliments," said Daksh, lifting his camera and kissing it.

"Senorita?" said Aryan, chuckling and then turned to look at the rest of their expressions.

Mahir and Sam laughed heartily, grabbing their side of the edge so that they didn't fall out, as they were still at a distance from the beach.

"Hey, ladies, do you know Daksh's camera has a name!" said Yash, with a mischievous look.

"Huh?" said Ruhi, opening her eyes.

"Ha-ha! Seriously?" said Oviya, looking at Daksh.

Daksh sighed and gave a bemused look to Yash, to which he replied by dancing his eyebrows up and down.

"Yuh-uh! What, people can name their pets, and I cannot name my *brand-new* camera?!"

"Yeah, just for your information—dogs are living creatures," said Yash.

"You—piece of shit—"

Everyone screamed as Daksh stood upon his legs, and the boat tilted a little. Mahir took hold of his collar and sat him back down. Yash was almost out of the boat if Sam hadn't been around to grab him.

"You imbecile," snarled Yash, breathlessly.

Daksh was ready for a rebellion, but Aryan hissed looking at him. Daksh gritted his teeth and looked away. No one spoke a word or suddenly jumped on the boat until their feet touched the warm sand of the beach.

Ah, the evening time at the beach sure brings out the romantic vibe in one. The beach was quiet with a countable number of people around, walking, some seated, looking at the horizon—usual things. The whole milieu was turned into an orange-bluish blanket because of the blushing sun. They all sat down on the soft sand of the beach and started to pull their shoes back on, without caring what the sand would do to their pants. They all got back on their feet one-by-one.

"Hey, guys," said Daksh, "let's not go anywhere else…just sit here and relax."

"I cannot believe I am saying this," said Oviya, dramatically, "but Daksh is right, let's sit here and watch the sunset."

"I cannot believe I am saying this," mimicked Daksh in his own version of Oviya's voice.

Oviya narrowed her eyes and teased him by letting out her tongue.

"Daksh!"

"What? She started it," cried Daksh, looking at Aryan.

Everyone agreed to just sit here on the beach and look at the sunset. They all sat back down, boys on the left and girls on the right. Aryan leaned back, supported by his hand, his eyes fixed on the orange-yellow ball. On the far ocean, he saw some silhouettes, unsure whether they were a boat or something foreign to him.

"The sunset has his own charm, eh?" said Aadhaya, dreamily. She then turned her gaze towards Aryan, but quickly shifted it to Sam.

"No doubts," Sighed Oviya.

Ruhi stood up in a whoosh, and Aadhaya had to lean back as she started to tap on her back to clear the sand. She walked towards the boys line, with Sam on the right and Aryan on the left, and Daksh in the middle. She came right in front of him.

"Daksh, take my picture with the sunset," Said Ruhi, hastily.

But Daksh stayed put, not moving a muscle, his eyes having no focus at all.

"Come on, please, I promise this will be the last one, please," said Ruhi, begging.

Daksh didn't even look at her; his mouth was pursed, and the rest of them were enjoying this soft quarrel. Ruhi walked towards him, about to grab him—

"That's enough, Ruhi."

It came as a great, sad surprise to her that it was Aadhaya who stopped her.

"You have already taken more than a hundred photos... now come and sit back down."

Ruhi gave Daksh a cold look, to which he replied with his teeth-less smile. She grunted and walked towards Aadhaya, this time she didn't sit beside her, she sat beside Oviya. Oviya rested her head on her shoulder.

Minutes passed by, this time Sam got up, Aadhaya too. They both walked away towards the left, holding hands, and sat down facing the horizon. Sam's legs were stretched out, while Aadhaya rested her head on his shoulder.

The sky would start to turn dark very soon, the sun was now a tiny reddish-yellow dot. Aryan didn't know when the rest of them changed their position by forming a circle. He also was perplexed about how the topic broached to Aadhaya. He observed everyone's expression and chose to speak first.

"Look, guys," said Aryan calmly "You don't have to feel uneasy or awkward, or give me that look."

"What look?" said Daksh, quickly.

Aryan laughed, he sat straight, "I know that you all feel uneasy when Aadhaya and Sam are—you know."

They smiled and nodded.

"I also noticed nervousness in Sam, back at the Fort, I was standing beside him, and Aadhaya came close. He took a hold of her hand but instantly let go seeing me around," said Aryan.

"So, you are ok…with this?" asked Ruhi.

"Ok? Ruhi, I am married."

"Yeah, but…," said Oviya.

"First of all, I love my dear Ekta," said Aryan, doubtlessly. "And there is no one in this world to change that fact. So, act normal from now on, you too, boys."

Mahir smiled and patted him on the back, Daksh put his arm around him. Yash screamed the word "agreed".

"Answer me this then," said Ruhi, not willing to give up, "Why did you guys break up?"

Aryan heaved a sigh, he looked back up towards Ruhi.

"Ruhi, I promised Aadhaya that no matter what, I will not be the person to tell that story," said Aryan. "Even Ekta does not know about this."

There was silence, and they heard waves coming and going.

"Why all this?" said Ruhi "When you know that she was the one who broke up with you?"

"Believe it or not," said Aryan, his voice shaking a little. "I will always have a little space in my heart for Aadhaya because she was my past. And without the past, how can we know what we demand from the future, even though we all know that the future is unpredictable."

"I wish Aadhaya had heard that," said Ruhi in a hushed voice.

She turned and saw Oviya was already looking at her she heard what Ruhi said. They both looked down and smiled.

"Oh, please, somebody change the topic or—or I—girls will cry right here," said Daksh, hiding his face behind the space between his biceps and forearm.

Everyone laughed, which brought back the cheerfulness. Aryan was so glad to be on this trip.

"I almost forgot," said Oviya "Why didn't you bring Ekta with you?"

"Oh, there is a—well, let's say it's a surprise—and I will tell you later, don't anyone dare to soften me."

"This trip is really turning out to be a different one, isn't it?" said Yash.

"Yes, better than our last trip," said Daksh, with a corner of his eyes, he looked at Ruhi.

"What are you looking at me for," said Ruhi, annoyed.

"Uh, Hello, because *you* were the cause of it," said Daksh in an accusatory tone.

"No, I was not," said Ruhi, startled with such an accusation. She looked at Oviya, hoping for support.

"I am sorry, Ruhi, but they are right," said Oviya.

"Oh!" yelped Ruhi.

"You know how much fun we were having in Kerala," said Daksh, with a note of sadness. "But your fear about your father, we stayed there only for a day."

"And when we came back," said Yash, partnering with Daksh, "your father was surprised to see you came back that early."

"Hey, don't put all that blame on me," said Ruhi, exasperated. "Aadhaya's mother kept calling her like every second."

"Yes, but—" said Daksh but stopped as Ruhi clenched her teeth.

"I love this group." sighed Aryan.

"You don't blame me for that, do you, Oviya?" said Ruhi, looking at Oviya.

Oviya knew by her looks that if she agrees with Daksh, Ruhi will sob right here.

"No, of course not," said Oviya, Ruhi got relaxed. "It was like many years ago."

Ruhi smiled, she turned towards Daksh and Yash, and she gave them a cold look.

"I need something to drink," said Oviya, as she felt her voice dry.

By that "drink" word Aryan sat up straight, he looked at Mahir and Yash, they were already looking at him.

"And I need to go to the bathroom," said Yash standing up.

"I will join you," said Mahir.

"I will too, Daksh, you want to come?" said Aryan, looking at Daksh.

"I would, but I have no power to get up," said Daksh, lazily.

Ruhi and Oviya were eyeing them suspiciously. Aryan gave a bemused look to Daksh, it was then he realized that Daksh didn't know about the alcohol. Aryan looked at Yash.

"Hey, look over there," said Yash pointing towards the horizon.

As Ruhi and Oviya had their back to it, they turned and started searching for what Yash was trying to look at.

"Where, Yash?" said Oviya, looking at the horizon.

By that time Mahir shook his flannel jacket, Daksh saw what needed to be seen by him.

"On second thoughts," said Daksh, sounding casual, "I think I will join you too."

Daksh, Mahir, Aryan got up clearing sand from their back. Ruhi and Oviya also got up.

"What are you guys up to now?" said Oviya.

"Oh, grow up, Oviya," said the professor. "Why do you always have a suspicious eye on us?"

"Because you are like that, you all are," said Ruhi waspishly.

They all muttered something together and turned. They all started to walk towards the jungle of palm trees, at the back of the beach.

"Where are you all going?" asked Oviya, loudly.

They stopped and turned, looking at each other searching for some answer.

"She's right, the hotel is all the way over there," Said Ruhi, pointing towards the opposite direction from where they were heading.

Daksh smiled, as a cunning man of the group he got just the thing to say.

"You girls will never understand the pleasure of releasing the pressure inside of your body open in the woods," said Daksh in a satisfying voice.

Oviya and Ruhi looked disgusted, Aryan laughed softly. Without looking back, they started marching towards the woods.

"Something is definitely fishy," Said Ruhi.

She saw them turn left, they ran into the woods and disappeared.

"Where did Sam and Aadhaya go?"

"Nice one, Daksh," Said Mahir, patting on Daksh's back.

Him and Daksh were walking side by side, Aryan and Yash were a step behind. Here and there were only palm and some coconut trees. They went deeper as it was Yash's idea so that no one sees them.

"I didn't know that this area has a slope," Said Aryan.

The land had a little slope over here, which made them walk inclined. They walked further in, it was quiet. As it was sundown no birds were singing their respective melody. A cold breeze touched Aryan's face, he felt different. The palm trees trunk was so thick and wide one could hide behind them without others realizing it.

"How did you come up with that wood and pressure thing?" inquired Yash.

Now four of them were walking side by side, at the corners were Yash and Mahir, with Aryan and Daksh in the middle.

"To be honest, I wasn't lying," said Daksh, he walked right while Aryan left as a palm tree came in the way. "I knew that you guys will agree with me about that."

They walked further, now the ground had a very thin layer of beach sand.

"I think this will do," Said Mahir, he stopped.

They were now in a plain area surrounded by tall palm trees, the east side of the sky was already darker, and the west was about to. The only thing bothering Aryan was this silence.

"So, who will drink the first sip?" asked Daksh.

"Now, now, before you start to fight—yes, I am looking at you both. I think Mahir should, as he bought the bottle," said Aryan.

"Fine," Said Daksh, rolling his eyes.

Yash nodded looking at Mahir. Mahir came and tap on Aryan's back, he took out the small bottle of wine. The crystal glass sparkled when it touched the open air.

"To this trip," Said Mahir, raising the crystal bottle. The top of it touched his lips,

"Aaaa!"

A high-pitched feminine scream echoed in the woods, which made the bottle slip from his hand and shattered on the ground like a cursed mirror.

Chapter 11

The Blue-Eyed Crow

The wine was already consumed by the land, leaving a dark patch as proof of it. Those pieces of crystal lost their shine as that shriek echoed in the woods. All of them were now facing where that shriek came, and it came from the beach. Now there was nothing but silence, this silence was not ordered by peace but chaos.

A breeze touched their hair and visage, bringing them back to the present. They looked at each other in the utter wilderness.

"Wh—what was that?" said Daksh, panic-stricken.

"Who's scream was that?" asked Mahir, cold sweat visible on his forehead.

They all looked at each other, and no one had an answer for those questions.

"I—I think it was…"

"You think what, Yash?" asked Aryan, walking close to him.

Yash was horrified to say what he was thinking, and even more so if it proved to be the truth. He looked at Mahir and Daksh, then turned his gaze to Aryan.

"I think it was Ruhi," said Yash in a hushed voice, but the silence spoke it out loud.

Aryan stayed motionless; it was not the scream you make when someone is trying to catch you in some sort of play.

It was a scream of a horrified person or the scream of pain. With that thought, Aryan shut his mind, and he looked at Yash, who already had his eyes fixed on him.

"This is stupid…how can you be so sure?" said Mahir, "I mean it could be anyone, there are other people on the beach."

"Yes, I am with Mahir," said Daksh, trying to hide his frightened tone.

Yash shook his head and looked back up, glancing at Aryan.

"I am like seventy percent sure that it was Ruhi," Said Yash, "I have heard her scream before, and I remember it quite well."

"You are wrong," Said Mahir.

"Yes, it was not Ruhi," said Daksh.

"It was—"

"It doesn't matter who screamed," said Aryan, loudly, "What I am saying is, let's go back to the beach and check for ourselves, that will give us a clear answer."

"Yeah—yes, you are right," Said Mahir, "The bottle is shattered anyway."

"And the mood," said Daksh.

They turned, walking beside each other towards the beach. Aryan was gazing here and there, unsure why he was doing that. Maybe because his mind was telling him that a grave danger lies here, at this place.

Oh, God! Ruhi, please be okay. No, it wasn't Ruhi.

Aryan shook his head and continued walking. The silence persisted, accompanying them all along. The only sound they heard was their own footsteps. It was odd how it only took them a matter of minutes to come this deep into the woods. Aryan and the others realized it when the beach was nowhere to be seen.

"Argh! Screw this, let's run," Said Mahir, impatiently.

Increasing their pace, they began to run towards the beach. Aryan looked up, and in a matter of minutes, darkness would fall upon them. Huge palm tree leaves were waving as a gust of wind passed through them. They were all running at the same speed, except Mahir, who was pushing forward. Aryan turned and saw a look of grave concern on Yash's face, with Daksh beside him.

Aryan stopped in the middle. Seeing him, Yash and Daksh stopped too. Mahir glanced backward, seeing them he also halted and walked back towards them.

"What is the matter?" asked Yash, panting. He was just beside Aryan.

"I don't remember coming this far into the woods," said Aryan, after taking in some air.

"My thoughts exactly," said Daksh, putting his hands on his knees.

"Call them—yes, call every one of them," Suggested Mahir.

"Yeah, I think you're right," said Aryan.

Yash was the first to take out his phone from his pocket, he looked at it.

"What the—stupid piece of shit!" scowled Yash, and he started slamming his phone on his lap.

"What are you doing?" asked Aryan.

"The junk won't work," said Yash, frustrated.

"Huh!"

Everyone turned to Daksh, he too had his cellphone out.

"Mine neither, even though I remembered that it had almost sixty per cent battery."

"Okay, what the hell is going on?" said Mahir, panicking.

Aryan was afraid to tell them that his phone too was dead. He gulped and put his phone back in his pocket. Aryan looked at the rest of them, they too were as perplexed as he was. The fact that the beach was still at a distance was arcane. He didn't let his feelings decide his expression, he took a breath and looked up.

"I think we should keep moving."

Aryan continued running, Yash, Daksh, and Mahir looked at each other and ran after Aryan. Soon they were matching their pace with each other, to Aryan's left was Mahir, and to his right was Yash and Daksh. Yash turned to look at him, Aryan knew he was trying to form a smile but failed successfully.

All of a sudden, when Aryan looked down at the ground, he saw a huge shadow passing over them. Instantly, they stopped right there; the shadow covered them and some trees around them easily. A coldness swept through their bodies. Together they looked up at the sky, too late whatever it was, it flew away. The trees stopped moving, and the noise of them moving stopped, bringing back the silence.

"Okay, was I the only person—"

"NO," answered all three of them to Yash.

Aryan looked at Mahir; their chests were rising because of heavy breathing.

"I admit," said Aryan looking away, "I admit that something definitely doesn't feel right here. And I agree with Yash that it was Ruhi who screamed."

It did alarm them, but their real emotions were covert. Daksh took off his camera and wrapped its strap around his hand. He grabbed the camera with the same hand. The surrounding was quiet, or hushed up by someone? This embraced dysphoria in them.

Thud!

The voice came from behind, the sound of a landing, something or someone landed with such force that made the ground shake with fear. Aryan's heart was pounding so fast he felt that it would come out of his body. What got into him, he didn't know he dared to turn and look.

He was now breathing with his mouth, his rubatosis increased the thing was right there some yards away. The image he would never forget in his life. There, in front of them, its feathers darker than the empty space, its size like a mini truck. The crow was looking straight at him, its face turned to the left, its right eye fixed on Aryan. The crow was standing in a space between palm trees, the same place where the bottle shattered. Aryan was not able to digest all this: how could a crow be so huge? He wanted to speak, he wanted to scream, but sadly his own body was not in his control anymore. He tried to direct all his will to move at least his finger but failed to do so.

Move. Damn it, move.

It didn't matter how hard he tried his body wouldn't move. Just then he heard something, voices of breathing from the mouth just like him. Aryan only knew how hard it was to turn his head. The struggle was worth it he saw Daksh, Yash, and Mahir, their eyes open in shock, directed towards the crow. They also turned like Aryan did and were stiff like him.

The crow moved a few steps further, and the ground trembled while trees shook with each heavy footstep. His movements echoed in the woods. Maybe because Aryan knew that his friends were with him, facing this monster, his legs came back to life, or perhaps it was the extreme fear. As the crow moved, Aryan took two steps back. He turned and saw Yash, Daksh, and Mahir doing the same.

Daksh and Yash squeaked when the crow faced front, and now his long, dark beak pointed at them. His feathers were not the darkest part his right eye was. To Aryan's surprise, he gazed at the crow's left eye. It wasn't visible properly, although it was a shade of blue. The crow only had to take two or three steps to be very close to them. To their relief, the crow didn't move any further.

Everyone screamed in horror as the crow opened its beak. They thought this was it the crow would eat them alive, but—

"Welcome," came the cold voice. The crow was speaking to them.

They all shuddered at the harshness of the voice, moving back two more steps. If the crow didn't eat or kill them, Aryan was sure he would die by himself, as his heart was beating rapidly.

The crow wasn't pleased by their moving back step by step. The crow opened its dark feathers, which were twice the size of the rest of its body. It pointed those feathers to the sky, and just like that, the sky went instantly dark. The crow turned its head to the right, revealing the left side of its face. It was clear now its left eye was gleaming blue.

"RUN!"

Daksh screamed at the top of his voice with vocal power. Aryan obeyed, just like the others. He didn't know how, but he was running now. He was thankful that even though it was dark, he was able to see a further way. Trees were moving behind, their footsteps echoing in the woods. Panting, Aryan was putting all his power into his legs. He still couldn't feel his legs, but he had no choice but to run.

Daksh was on his left, just like others. He was running with all the power left in him. Mahir was expressionless, and to his side was Yash pacing forward. Suddenly, the ground started to shake, and a sound—it sounded like,

Thump...thump...thump

Echoed all around them. Aryan looked back without stopping his feet. He was wrong about the never-forgetting image this was the most horrific scene. The crow, its feathers behind, was running towards them. Aryan's hand shook as he instantly turned his head back to the front, focusing only on running away. The echoing of those heavy footsteps stopped.

"Caaaw!"

The crow's shriek pierced through the air, and they screamed in pain as the sound pinched their ears. Daksh was about to lose control of himself but gained control.

"THE BEACH." Called out Yash.

He was right they were able to see the beach. The problem was it was still far away from them. There was another shriek from the crow, and this time they buried their hands in their ears to block out the troubling noise. Aryan was the only one who noticed that the shriek came from a distance, which meant the crow had stopped for some reason.

Aryan immediately turned to his right, remembering the huge trunk of palm trees at this site. He ran towards one of them and hid behind it, shortly came Daksh and Yash. Daksh stood beside Aryan, and the trunk was able to hide them both. Yash had hidden himself behind the tree on the right.

"What the hell?" screamed Yash.

"Sshh," Hissed Aryan.

"Keep quiet, or that monster will hear us," said Daksh in a low voice.

They had their back to the beach, able to see each other as they were close by. Aryan couldn't take this, so he banged his head on the trunk of the tree the pain didn't bother him at all. Daksh was beside him, drawing breaths, Yash was hidden behind the neighboring tree, his face covered by his hands.

"Why is this happening to us?" asked Yash in a wobbly tone.

Daksh was speechless, his eyes wide open, staring forward into his mental picture he was trembling from head to toe.

"You were right," said Aryan, moving his head back, which was touching the trunk, "I should have believed you."

Aryan was looking at Daksh, who, like him, was also shaking. He turned to Yash and saw him sitting down on his knees, his face buried in his hands as if there was no hope, everything they do will be hapless.

Daksh came to his senses, he slapped himself, lightly, on his cheek, shook his head. He grabbed Aryan by his shoulder, and Aryan turned. Even Yash got back on his feet.

"We have to do something…otherwise, that crow will kill us," said Yash, gravely.

"Those heavy footsteps are still ringing in my ears," said Daksh, his voice shaking.

Aryan's whole face was hot because of the running or fear he did not know. He ran his hands over his face the past few minutes were still abstruse for him.

"There is no point going to the beach," said Aryan. "It is open, and we will get caught instantly. If we decide to swim, that crow will grab us out of it with those long bird legs."

"Correct, at least here we can hide," said Yash, trying to sound optimistic.

Aryan knew this was dubious judging by the size of the crow and its long, strong feathers, it could knock these trees right off the ground.

"Hey…Where is Mahir?"

Chapter 12

Amber Eye

"Mahir is gone!" Those words hit like a dagger stabbed in their already damaged heart. Yash slumped down on the ground, those soft meadows pacified the movement. Yash put his hands over his head and went in deep, gloomy thought. Like Yash, Daksh too sat down on the ground, feeling helpless, his eyes closed, his hand rubbing his forehead. For a moment, Daksh thought that it doesn't matter now let that monster come and take him, but he shook off those hapless feelings. Aryan had his forehead touched on the tree he was hiding behind his eyes were down, looking at his foot.

"Why I mean, why is this happening?" said Aryan, "What did we do that made the gigantic crow follow us to our death?"

Daksh had his back to Aryan he looked up and shook his head. He felt like his callowness was long gone and may never come back.

Yash looked up and muttered some words under his breaths. Daksh took notice of it; he looked towards him.

"What?"

"Signal…" said Yash, looking at Daksh, "It was a signal for us when you and Mahir told us about that…that…we should have got out of here at that moment—if we would have believed you—and Mahir."

It was hard, but he did it. Daksh brought back his normal tone and his sense of confidence.

"Listen here, Yash," said Daksh, "I know that this is going to sound fatuous, but don't put more pressure on your brain."

"How do you know that "fatuous" word?" said Yash, absurdly.

"Seriously, that is important right now?" snapped Daksh, "Anyway, at first, I also considered that my mind was playing games with me that time because honestly, I ate too much back there."

Aryan turned seeing Daksh back in spirits took a gram of load off of him. A zephyr touched them all at once it was not any good. That is when Aryan realized something, that thing was very awful that he couldn't bury inside him, so he groaned out loud.

"What happened?" asked Daksh, alarmed.

Daksh walked close to Aryan Yash too got up on his feet but didn't leave his tree.

Aryan looked up, straight at Daksh. He didn't want to say it, but he knew he has to, no matter how much dark those words might be.

"Do you think—that is why—Ruhi—because that crow got…"

Their hearts were already empty this time it was the soul that got stabbed with a strange, dark, object known as feelings. It was bad enough already that a huge crow is after them to take their life. Now they realized they are the only ones left.

Melancholy! There was not even time to feel the melancholy! That is when a CRACK echoed in the woods, the sound came from their front. They knew the crow has now come close to them.

Aryan shook his body to get ready. Yash stood up straight with alertness he looked at Aryan. All three of them at once peeked from behind their trees. As Aryan and Daksh were sharing a huge trunk, Aryan peeked from the right while Daksh from the left. Channeling their inner power to one single wish, hoping it to be something else! Ah, but their will was already damaged, they were able to see that crow, a few trees away, his blue eye glinting.

The sky went even darker, as the crow pointed his long beak at the sky, his feathers wide open. Aryan was confused as a yellow light came from his back. They turned their gaze to back, at the end of the beach, from where the end of the wood was, a bamboo with fire conjured. Aryan turned his gaze to the left and saw the whole place light up by those bamboos at a certain distance, there were more of those bamboos with fire dancing on top at the start of the woods.

"Boys," said Aryan.

They turned.

"I think we should get back to the beach," said Aryan, appealingly.

"You are right," said Daksh, looking at Aryan.

"I think you are right," Said Yash, "There is no light here like on the beach, I can see sand glowing."

"But—what about the openness?" asked Daksh.

"That's the risk we have to take," said Aryan, "exit is on the beach, we will straight go to the hotel from there."

Daksh and Yash nodded. They peeked again to locate the position of the crow. It was itself a task as the crow changed his position.

"There, on the right," said Yash, in a low voice.

The crow was moving to the right, he was turning his head momentarily, that is when Yash caught a glimpse of his blue eye.

"Now listen carefully," said Aryan, "we will not go straight to the beach, we will go to the left. We will hide ourselves behind those trees at the start of the woods. Careful not to make any noise—one sound and we are done for this life."

"CAAA!" shrieked the crow.

Aryan was the first to move he turned towards the beach and started walking. When he was on the end line of trees he started to walk towards the left. He took right and hid behind it, then to the left where a huge trunk was ready to hide him. Aryan looked back and saw Daksh following the exact same pattern. Keeping close behind him was Yash. Aryan was aware of a sudden change on the ground it got sand now, difficult to run.

Daksh, breathing heavily, tip-toed from one spot to another. He turned left, waited behind a tree, and in a swift motion, turned right. He was careful about choosing trees with wide trunks, aware that Yash was close behind him. Daksh and Yash shuddered behind a tree when the crow shrieked again. They looked at each other, gave a nod, and continued walking.

"Everything is fine," Daksh muttered in his breath while changing his position, "just a normal day—nothing to worry about. Everything will be fine because it is a normal day—just a freaking huge crow who wants to take the life out of me—blue-eyed demon—"

Daksh waited behind a tree for Yash, turned his gaze to the front, and saw Aryan pacing ahead like a cat. They kept moving forward, and now Aryan was like two trees away from them. The ground was now clearly visible, and the bamboo at certain spaces from each other helped them. It was an effort to move now, as their feet pressed into the sand.

"Oooof!"

Daksh fell on the sandy ground. Yash stepped on the back of his shoes, which imbalanced Daksh, and he fell with a soft thud. Yash slapped himself on the head, Daksh looked up, his face masked with sand. Aryan ran towards them, and they lifted Daksh up, hoping it didn't attract the crow—

"Do you think you can hide from me?"

It was that harsh voice that came out when the crow opened his beak. Daksh was limping, Yash caught him, Aryan waved his hand back and slapped him hard. Daksh came back to reality. There was no time as those heavy footsteps echoed again.

"Run!" hissed Aryan like an angry serpent.

Avoiding those rumbling footsteps, they kept running forwards. The beach was on their left, and those dancing flames were helpful.

There is no way we can outrun that crow.

Aryan was in the middle, Yash to his left, and Daksh at his right. Now nothing was in their favor, and the sand below their feet was not helping them in any possible way. They were trying their best to keep up the pace.

Aryan's ears were playing drums or was it his own heartbeat he didn't care. It was like they were putting all their power into running, but jogging was all they could do. With each passing second, each footstep they took, their spirits were going down.

An ironic zephyr flew past them, and trees bent behind. The crow flew from above and landed behind them. The three of them stopped, sharing a look of horror. No, it was the look of boldness, even if it might be their last expression. Without any other thoughts, they all kept moving forward, and now they were able to hear the sound of water. Ekta came into Aryan's mind he wanted to cry out her name, he wanted to think more about her, but he didn't. He brought back his focus to running.

To his right, Daksh was taking heavy footsteps, almost jumping. The noise of those footsteps was heavy, but Aryan didn't mind them at all.

He knew that the crow was just behind them. Yash was also putting all his energy into practice.

Now, the wind blew from the back, and trees were forced to bend forwards. They all felt a push on their back, a powerful push. Again, the crow flew above them, but this time he landed right in front of them. They had to protect their eyes so that sand didn't go in them. They stopped, breathing heavily, and they looked at the monster.

Their bodies betrayed them as their legs were frozen. Facing the crow, they saw it didn't move for a minute. Its tail was visible to them. Then it turned, its sapphire eye gleaming. The crow took a step closer towards them, and sand bounced with the land. It was now two trees away from them.

Aryan knew that this was the final chapter his legs refused to move, and his friends shared the same look of abysmal.

"I don't want to die like this," said Daksh.

The crow opened its wide feathers, and it turned its face towards the beach. The blue eye was visible, something was moving inside it. Aryan was oblivious to the fact that his attention got fixed at that eye. Suddenly he felt the strangest feeling he had ever felt. It was like his own soul was getting pulled out of his body. That blue eye seemed to be doing it, the crow's weapon.

Just then, out of nowhere, Aryan saw a yellow shadow come in between them. It happened in an instant the crow shrieked loudly as it got banged on one of those trees. The tree broke from its roots, and with the crow, it rolled onto the beach. Aryan and Daksh's ears were ringing after those shrieks and bangs. It took a second for them to realize what just happened. They turned to see what saved their lives.

Where the crow was about to take their souls away, it was knocked out by an eagle. The eagle was the same size as that of the crow. Its ocher feathers were shining with the yellow light produced by those bamboo fires. Its feathers had some black spots, scattered everywhere except its face and front body. Aryan looked up and saw a strong beak he turned down and saw pointy legs. It was him that knocked out the crow and saved their lives. The eagle was looking at them with his left eye, which was completely dark.

Aryan saw Daksh he was looking up at the eagle's face, his mouth was wide open seeing such a huge creature. Aryan glanced back at the eagle, and the eagle turned its face. Its other eye was glowing amber. Without taking their eyes off him, Aryan tapped on Daksh's back. They both looked at each other, smiles appeared on their faces.

"Thank you," said Aryan to the eagle.

"Thank you very much," added Daksh, bowing to the majestic bird.

The eagle remained stoic, gazing up at the sky.

Daksh nudged Aryan and pointed toward their backs. Aryan turned and saw the crow lying flat on the beach.

"Where is Yash?" Aryan asked Daksh.

Daksh scanned the surroundings, moving his head in every direction.

"YASH—YASH!" Aryan called out desperately.

Aryan turned back and continued forward, Daksh trailing behind. As they moved ahead, Daksh kept glancing back at the eagle, but the majestic bird showed no response.

"YASH...YASH...YASH!"

Anxiety etched their faces. Aryan looked at Daksh, who had his hand over his head.

"Your friend is gone," said a totally new, fruity voice from behind.

Aryan looked back in a jolt at Daksh. Daksh wore a bewildered expression, shrugging his shoulders. Together, they turned to the place where the eagle was resting.

To their surprise, there was a slight change. Instead of a huge eagle, a man now stood at the same spot. His face was hidden behind a bushy beard, and his lush hair flowed sideways in the breeze from the shores.

Aryan and Daksh slowly walked towards him. As they approached, they observed that his hair was going grey. The man stood straight, hands joined together in front. Up close, they saw that he was taller than Aryan, dressed in full dark-maroon clothes reminiscent of a warrior's costume, complete with heavy boots. His arms indicated strength, with wide shoulders and a well-built chest. The man's right eye was shining amber, and the left one dark. However, there was a calmness about him that set him apart.

"How in the—what the—who are you?" Daksh gaped.

"What do you mean by gone?" asked Aryan, avoiding the arcane events. "Is he—like my other friends…?"

"No, he is not dead," said the man calmly. "Just like your other friends, he is also alive."

Aryan really felt the happiness he thought was gone from him. He looked at Daksh, and they immediately turned back to the man.

"Then where are they?" asked Aryan impatiently.

The man said nothing he just stared at him in the eye, perhaps observing his character.

"First, you have to answer my one question," said the man.

"Aryan!" said Daksh.

Aryan turned and saw Daksh had his back to him. Aryan matched his gaze, and he was looking at the beach. They both shuddered the coldness came back from the toe and stopped at their hearts.

"The crow is gone!" said Aryan, horrified.

"You didn't answer my question," said the man.

They both turned and faced the man.

"You didn't ask one," said Aryan.

The man smiled behind his bushy beard,

"I apologize for that. My question to both of you is—tell me, what did you take from the Tomb?"

Chapter 13

Back to the Fort

"Excuse me?"
"Take?"

The man raised his bushy eyebrows and heaved a sigh his mustache flew forward. He looked at both of them with strange curiosity. For a second, Aryan thought he was a book and the man a reader.

"Of course, you don't know," said the man calmly.

"Don't know what?" said Aryan, impatiently.

"Are we in—"

Daksh stopped as the man showed his palm to him.

"Before you two confused boys shoot your questions like a rain of arrows," said the man. He then faced all his fingers towards the beach, with his palm facing the sky, "let's go over there and sit…you both look exhausted to me."

Saying that, the man turned and started walking towards the beach. Aryan and Daksh looked at each other.

"Hey, I am not going anywhere unless you tell me what the *hell* is going on?"

The man turned in a swift motion when he heard what Daksh said. He flashed his amber eye at him, and Aryan and Daksh both moved back a few steps.

"OKAY, got it!" said Daksh, putting his hands in front.

The man turned and continued walking, passing by two trees, and entered the beach.

"Hey, why did you hit me?" said Daksh, rubbing his shoulder.

"What is wrong with you?" said Aryan, "Didn't you see his eye? He is probably friends with that eagle that saved our lives."

Daksh's eyes got wide, and he gave a nod, looking at Aryan. Aryan patted his back, and they also walked towards the beach.

The beach was quiet with no one around but themselves, obviously they knew that. The way they screamed and those of the crow might have alerted people by now. Aryan looked right there were a number of those bamboos, making the sands glow. Ah, there is nothing more I hate than a moonless night, it was a moonless night! When they looked at the horizon, there was nothing but emptiness.

They walked forwards, and the kind sea greeted them with her melody of going up and down, giving them kisses like they were her own children. Aryan felt drowsy as those breezes kept touching him on his visage. It was silent, with only the shores making noise, gorgeous. He closed his eyes, and such was the milieu that no man can resist thinking about his beloved such sly is the beach. He kept wondering about Ekta and her soft touch on his face. But then his mind changed to Aadhaya and his friends he trembled and opened his eyes.

They stopped a few steps away from where the water was teasing the land.

"Oh, my buttocks!" said Daksh, as he sat down.

Aryan laughed it was wonderful to sit on this soft layer of sand after all that running for their own lives.

"Where is that man?" asked Daksh.

Aryan had his eyes closed, so he didn't know. They both looked back by moving their heads and spines. The man was standing beside one of those bamboos. They observed him the man took a tight grip on that bamboo with his left hand. And in one swift motion, he extirpated that bamboo off the ground. Aryan and Daksh's heads tilted back when they saw what the man did.

"Woah!"

"Not a person to mess with."

They turned their faces forward as the man started to walk towards them. His footsteps came close, so they acted as a normal person would. The man came in front, looking grimly at them. He tossed the bamboo to his right hand, and the flame on top flickered. His right hand moved upwards and strongly came down, digging the bamboo into the sand. All this he did without taking his eye off them.

Aryan and Daksh gave him a pursed lips smile. The bamboo was now at Daksh's side, and the place brightened up. Aryan observed that the man was wearing an attire that was familiar, but he couldn't recall what it was called.

The man sat down facing them, with the sea and the horizon behind him. He assumed a meditation pose, his spine erected, and his hands on his lap. Seeing him in such a composed posture, Aryan and Daksh straightened themselves up and mimicked the man's pose.

"So, did you remember now what you stole?" asked the man, politely.

"Stole?"

"What—I told you, we didn't steal anything," said Daksh, outraged.

"That is a serious accusation," added Aryan.

"Answer me this: What is the last thing you remember?"

"Hello! A crow, the size compared to a truck, with a blue eye, chasing us to our death," said Daksh, coolly.

"Huff," sighed the man in disbelief. He rubbed his eye and looked up suddenly, "the Fort—what is the last thing you remember about the Fort?"

Aryan blinked; he almost forgot about the Fort. He turned his gaze towards the right at the ocean. There it was, but for him, it looked like a huge silhouette, although those top walls were glowing.

There are bamboos like these up there too?

"How do you know we went to the Fort?" asked Daksh, puzzled. "I am begging you...please—please for the love of God tell us what is happening. And more importantly, WHY?"

The man raised his eyebrows, observing Daksh's desperation about the situation. He glanced at Aryan, who was still looking at the Fort. Daksh straightened up as the man turned to him.

"When you find out about the *why* part, all the things that have been happening to you will be cleared out—instantly," said the man, as if discussing something while having a meal.

"And how are we going to find out?"

"By recalling things about the Fort."

"Something definitely arcane happened in that Fort, right?" asked Aryan, facing the man.

The man smiled and nodded. Aryan began to think. He clearly remembered taking Mahir and Yash to that black wall with descriptions and history written about the Fort. He also remembered climbing those thick stairs that led them to the top of the Fort. He recalled the feeling of excitement in his heart when he saw those cannons so close to the parapet.

"Strange!" said Aryan, suspiciously. "I don't remember anything that we did after seeing those cannons."

Daksh's head was between his hands, resembling someone who had just licked a lemon.

"Nope, me neither," said Daksh, looking at Aryan.

At the same time, they turned to look at the man. His dense beard failed to hide his satisfying smile.

"Why are we not able to recall the rest of the trip?" asked Aryan.

"I know we were there until sundown," said Daksh.

"Our brain is a fascinating part of our body and life, Aryan and Daksh," said the man, smiling.

"How do you—"

The man raised his hand, signaling them to say no more.

"We have no time, and I have no power. Just like I told you, your brain, if you focus, will give you the answer you need."

Aryan obeyed, closing his eyes and trying to focus. However, the situation was a strange ball, and his mind was prone to diversion. Ekta took over his thoughts—some were happy, but most were gloomy. When the thought of his unborn child crossed his mind, he went adrift.

Would I be able to see Ekta again? Would I be able to see my child?

"I just remembered something..." said Daksh.

Aryan opened his eyes and looked at Daksh. Daksh noticed those tearful eyes of his. He looked at him for a minute, then he continued.

"Remember when Ruhi started to annoy the soul out of me?"

Aryan raised his head, remembering something. He closed his eyes, took a deep breath, and then opened them, looking at Daksh.

"Yes... so you handed her the camera."

"Indeed."

"Wait a minute—that is how we got separated because you both fought."

"She told me that I am not a good photographer—me—how can she say such preposterous things, that old—"

"Now, from where you got separated," said the man, "start the story from there. I can bet that the answer you need is at the end of it."

Aryan was astounded by his behavior. He was so right about focus. Although it made Aryan scared a little, he hoped that the 'stealing' part might prove to be wrong.

"Remember every single detail, you will know eventually."

Aryan and Daksh both nodded in agreement.

It was around two in the afternoon; the boys got separated from the girls, except for Sam, who went with Aadhaya.

So, the four of them started to wander around by themselves. That is how they came in front of the vast second gate of the Fort. It was indeed a big one, and different, as it overlooked the ocean. The gate had many beautiful carvings and was made out of thick bricks. The second entrance was crowded with visitors coming and going.

On the outer side of the entrance, there was a rocky coast it was not widely spread, just surrounded the entrance area and stretched to the front for some distance. The constant sound of water banging on the coast soothed them greatly. A cold breeze was a constant visitor.

On those rocky shores, people were relaxing, clicking photos of each other, and some were having an outside look at the second entrance.

Aryan and Daksh were seated close to the end line of the rocky shores. Just beside them were standing Yash and Mahir, discussing keenly about something. Aryan heard some of it.

"I think this is the place where the boats and ships must halt, and the soldiers of the empire must relax," said Mahir, ebulliently.

"Yep, definitely," said Yash. "I was wondering about those carvings on the entrance...do you want to go back and have another look?"

"Who am I to say no, let's go."

Yash and Mahir ran back towards the entrance. Aryan and Daksh looked at each other, shrugged their shoulders, and continued staring at the ocean. To their left was the beach, people on there were tiny little dots for them. They didn't mind their heads getting toasted those winds were making things even, temperature-wise.

Daksh yawned loudly Aryan didn't mind as it was siesta time. After some minutes, Daksh picked up a flat surface stone and threw it in the water.

Tap...Tap...Tap...Splash.

"I got three!" said Daksh, beamingly.

"Pff, that's nothing—I can do much better," said Aryan teasingly.

"Oh-yeah? Prove it then."

"Find me a stone!"

Daksh looked around for a flat surface stone as he found it he passed it to Aryan.

"Here, now let's see what you got."

Aryan smirked and took the smooth-surfaced stone in his right hand. With his left hand, he rolled up his shirt sleeves this maroon shirt of his earned compliments from his wife, who always encouraged him to wear more colors. For momentum, he threw his hands backward, and with force, he brought them to the front.

Tap...Tap...Tap...Tap...Splash.

"Woo-Hoo!" Aryan jumped up and waved his hands upwards to exult in his victory.

Daksh stayed seated, looking bemused, his head rested on his hand. He too got up and came face to face with Aryan.

"Told you, didn't I?" said Aryan, grinning.

"Pff, that's nothing. You haven't seen me at my true potential," said Daksh, conceitedly.

"O-ho, so what is your true potential?" said Aryan, mockingly.

"I hit the target of seven once," said Daksh slowly.

"You mean your stone tapped seven times?"

"Uh-huh!"

Aryan narrowed his eyes at him, "No way you are that capable, you liar."

"I am not," said Daksh, acting as if he were hurt.

"Hey, what are you guys doing?"

Aryan and Daksh turned, and they saw Yash approaching them, a couple of steps behind was Mahir.

"Nothing, just Daksh whining because I beat him," said Aryan, smiling.

"What the—"

"Beat him? In what?" asked Yash, curiously.

"Well—"

"Nothing," said Aryan, cutting off Daksh, "It is just my stone got more taps than his."

"Hmm, how many?"

"Five."

"Dishonest, Bastard."

Mahir joined the group shortly he tapped on Daksh's shoulder but looked towards Aryan.

"Let's move."

"Where?" said Daksh, turning his neck towards Mahir.

"You guys are not planning to stay here all day, are you?" said Yash, screwing up the right side of his face.

"It is nice here," Argued Aryan.

"Yes, I know that," said Yash, as a matter-of-fact. "But there are other places to see."

"C'mon you guys, we can have our own tournament about who gets more taps," said Daksh, persuasively.

"Seriously?" said Mahir, indifferently.

"Oh, that's not good enough for you?"

Yash looked at them in disappointment he looked down scratching his head. Suddenly he looked up, straight at Daksh.

"What sorcery are you planning?" said Daksh.

Yash smiled mischievously he walked close towards Daksh. Daksh stayed rigid to his place.

"You really want Ruhi to tell you," said Yash, cunningly, "about how she took different pictures of various historical spots in this Fort. And that with your camera, she will show it to you, saying things like "well,

I took these pictures before even you reached the spot." I mean, that is really bad, don't you think, Daksh?"

Daksh went into deep thought, but his eyes remained wide open looking at Yash.

"You artless freak!" said Daksh. "I will come only if you promise me that *you will not* use that cajole nature of yours on me, on this whole trip."

"Alright, fine," said Yash.

Mahir smiled beamingly and led the way. Yash went after him. Aryan looked at Daksh coldly the coast was gorgeous, and he didn't want to leave this place. Daksh looked at him, tapped on his back, and nodded millions of times to look approachable. Aryan had no choice but to follow.

Yash and Mahir went past the entrance that opened up in an open ground with many visitors wandering around. Aryan and Daksh took a last look at the rocky shore.

"Remember this place, my friend," said Aryan, dramatically, "the place where—I beat you."

Saying that, Aryan ran forward before Daksh could react.

"WHERE ARE YOU RUNNING, YOU LIAR? I am going to kill him so dead!"

Yash and Mahir spent more than a minute getting things straightened out between them. In that running, yelling, and unspeakable curses, they forgot about the rocky shore. Every turn they took or went straight with the road, there was a surprise waiting for them. There were many broken walls, some had ancient carvings on them, and some had severe burns.

They arrived at an open place, surrounded by huge walls. To their left, a wall, which was obviously at a distance, had stairs to go up and have a view of the backside of the fort. They saw many people climbing those stairs lazily. At once, the four of them decided to go there, but just then, they saw a similar figure up there. It was Sam. Realizing girls would be close by, they turned their backs and marched away.

They all agreed to see those cannons one more time. Looking at those cannons certainly brought a warrior's feelings in them. They descended those stairs and turned right. The sun was making their shirts stick to their back, as it was behind them at half-past three.

"Hey, look!" said Aryan pointing ahead.

They were following some tourists to see where they led them. Now, in front of them were around four sellers, seated in the shade of a hut. The hut was made of baked bricks, and the roof was made of grass straws. The hut matched the color with the ground, brown. It was short in height, although it was much wider. Under the shade of the hut were placed wooden benches, and visitors came here to take a break and fill their stomachs with vitamin C.

Judging by the surroundings, Aryan thought that this may be the royal garden. To their left were many unknown trees and plants, some were wild, and others had beautiful flowers. Aryan, Daksh, Mahir, and Yash rushed towards those sellers. As they came close, they saw there was another hut, just beside the first one they saw, identical to the first one.

Those four sellers, all of them were women in their mid or late thirties, were selling already cut pieces of watermelon, tamarinds, fennel seeds that were still hanging on those little branches, and the most demanded thing: green mangoes which are red from inside.

Those cheery women had their own accent. They were all dressed in a sari, treating everyone with their cheerful mood. The four of them got friendly and approached them using the word *Kaki* instead of Miss or other informal names that people think are formal.

They observed that those huts were not for living purposes. A man came out whenever one of those Kaki called him. The man then brought watermelons, a basket full of tamarinds, those short branches of fennel, and mangoes. So those huts were sort of a warehouse. The man cut those watermelons with his big knife, and those *Kakis* plucked out seeds with their tiny knife. It was a somewhat HUF situation.

The heat was increasing so they ate everything those *kakis* had to provide. They enjoyed those half-moon-shaped watermelons. Not just that, as our boys had no timid quality since they were born, they talked a great deal with them. About the fort, some other places to visit. Those whole-hearted women replied to them with great affection.

Tack! Aryan made a sound by clicking his tongue on the roof of his mouth as he ate one of those tamarinds. Daksh and Yash made the same sound. Mahir was anxious to eat them, but they teamed up and force-fed Mahir those tamarinds. Seeing his face, all three of them, including those jolly women, laughed. The mystery about those mangoes which are red from inside got revealed. Those green mangoes, after they have been cut, *Kakis* dipped them into some pale pink powder, and it turned red. They said it helps with the sour part of those mangoes. They ate till their hearts were content. Their lips turned red because of that sweet powder on the mango. They said their goodbyes to the *Kakis* and moved ahead, chewing the little fennel seed branches.

"Now where?" asked Aryan.

"Let's see," answered Yash.

They walked back where they came from, although this time they took a left. Further, they went, and here the walls were glowing, matching their color with the charming sun. They were to the left from the second entrance of the fort that overlooked the rocky shores. They climbed up the sudden slope that came in front of them. That slope led them to some steps going upwards. They climbed those steps and arrived at a place where, in front of them, was a small, square-shaped temple. To their left, they were able to see the vast ocean. The wind was whistling as it passed by their ears. Continuing their curiosity for the place, they moved further.

They looked to the left, as they were on a height and wanted to observe the Fort from the top. In front of them, the place they were looking at, was like a maze. With walls here and there, some were broken in between. People were passing by them, some were, what appeared to be, playing. They walked down and went to that place instantaneously.

Here, the ground was crunchy with dry leaves and meadow carpets. Those trees came into view from everywhere, like from between the gap of those walls, in the middle, and on the sides.

The sun was shining in the west, and at any time, it would start to hide behind the horizon. The four of them were now walking in a narrow space, surrounded by walls and trees. Their footsteps were making crunching noises. They saw an entrance to their left and went towards it. Just beside the entrance was a thin tree that expanded from above. Yash entered first, and the rest of them followed as the entrance was not that wide.

"Wow..." said Daksh, impressed.

They were now in one of those many squares, which looked like a maze back when they were on the top. The cryptic part was that, unlike other places inside the Fort, this place had completely dark walls.

"Hey, guys, check this out!"

It was Mahir who spoke. He turned left while the rest of them turned right. They went close to Mahir to see why Mahir called them.

"God bless my soul!" said Aryan, happily.

"Mata Kali!" said Daksh.

Indeed, there was a carving of the most powerful Goddess, pardon me, the most powerful God, Devi Kali. The carving of the Goddess looked even more charming because of a charcoal-colored wall. Even though the wall had many cracks, there were none nearby Devi Kali.

"Do you think the walls here are charcoal in color because this may be the temple of Devi Kali?" asked Daksh turning to Mahir.

"Hmm, I don't think so, Daksh," Said Mahir, he moved his hand forwards and touched the wall in front with his fingers. "See, it's all powdery, definitely burnt."

"Look."

Came the voice of Yash from behind. They turned and saw Yash had his back to them, observing the wall in front. They walked towards him and as they got close another carving of Devi Kali came into view. However, this was different as Devi Kali was in one of her dance poses, this wall was the same in colour as the previous one, but at the top one could see that the black shade had hidden the ochre.

All together they joined their hands and paid their respects to Devi Kali. They moved further in search of more arcane places.

"What do you guys think this part of the Fort was?" asked Daksh curiously.

They were now walking in a wider space than before. Here the walls were much taller and thicker. They were in shining ocher in color. Meadows were everywhere, but very few wild trees. Their footsteps were not making crunching noises like before.

"I think room quarters," said Aryan, guessing.

"Yeah, I thought the same," said Mahir. "Oh, this may be the place where they used to hold their Sabha and some secret meetings."

Aryan and Daksh nodded.

"Or, maybe this could be the place where they kept all their weapons," said Aryan, ebulliently.

"O—that'd be so awesome," said Mahir, matching his excitement with Aryan.

"What is that place called where they practice with their weapons?" asked Daksh.

Mahir stopped walking and screwed up his face, seeing him like this Daksh and Aryan walked back.

"You alright?" asked Aryan.

"Yes...I just knew that," said Mahir, looking at Daksh.

"Mahir, it is OK if you can't remember what it is called," said Daksh, laughing.

Mahir said with great difficulty, "No...I knew—ah, well forget it."

Aryan and Daksh laughed, and Mahir also joined in.

"BOYS!"

It was Yash again, his voice echoed behind the huge wall to their right.

"When did he go past that wall?" said Mahir, puzzled.

"I was wondering the same thing," said Aryan.

"Yash is sure the sneaky one," said Daksh.

Together they glanced at the huge wall to their right. Mahir turned back from where they came.

"I think we left behind the entrance. Yash must have seen it and went inside."

Aryan and Daksh nodded. Together, they started walking back from where they came. As they walked on the sandy ground, they could see their past footsteps.

"Wow, we walked this far without noticing Yash, eh," said Aryan.

"Because nobody pays attention to that tall, high cheekbone bastard."

Aryan and Mahir laughed at this sudden comment of Daksh about Yash. Their laughter echoed in the open space. Here, there was no hustle of noise, as there were very few people around. The place was open and somewhat confusing, with tall walls here and there. Additionally, the powerful rays of the sun were not helping at all. They had a stomach full of vitamin C, which was the reason why they were so energetic.

After what seemed to be half an hour, they finally found an opening to go to the other side of the wall. The opening was not like a proper entrance it was a huge gap where those two walls were supposed to meet. It was wide enough for two people to enter at a time. Three of them entered one after another.

What they saw mollified their body and emotions. Here, the climate was also different, as it was mildly cold. In front of them was an open space, like a ground, but not big enough for a playing ground. There were many wild plants in the corner and some in the middle. There were no trees, just an open space. As they walked further, they observed that right in front of them, there was a wall, tall about half a foot, and stretched towards the right.

Mahir sighed, gazing at this place, just then he noticed something.

"This is odd!"

Aryan and Daksh looked at Mahir, who was now gazing up at the sky. It took a moment for both of them to realize, but they got it. Here, the surroundings were greyish compared to other places of the Fort, and the heat was not as intense as on the other side of the wall. A soothing breeze sighed past them. They wandered around and observed something else: in this place, they had no clue how the shining rays of the sun were effaced.

The land here appeared to be white, but when they turned their gaze to it, it somehow changed into greyish.

"Hmm, strange," said Daksh.

"Maybe we are surrounded by these giant walls, that's why it is like this," said Aryan, guessing.

Together, they hopped past that half-a-foot-tall wall and started to walk further.

"YASH!"

Daksh screamed so loudly that Mahir and Aryan were startled as they were occupied observing this mysterious place.

"YASH…YASH—WHERE THE F—"

"OVER HERE!"

The voice came from somewhere in front it appeared that Yash had gone further.

"Enough with the screaming, Daksh," snapped Aryan as Daksh drew some air in and was about to explode.

"Aryan is right, there is no one else here except us," said Mahir.

"There is no one around us," mimicked Daksh, in his version of Mahir's voice.

Mahir came forward, Daksh tried to run away, but Mahir grabbed him by putting his arm around his neck. They walked further Daksh was now behaving, one callow move and Mahir will squeeze his neck.

Turns out they were wrong Yash didn't call out from the front. They knew this as they saw nothing but more open space. So, this time Aryan called out his name, but softly.

"Over here!"

The voice came from a close distance it didn't come from the front though. The voice came somewhere to their right.

They turned their bodies right. They observed that some meters away was a wall, barely taller than a foot; it was stretched towards the left.

Daksh suddenly gasped, Aryan and Mahir matched his view. They saw Yash, the problem was only his head was visible to them. The rest of the body appeared to be buried inside the ground, behind that foot-size wall.

Without any further thoughts, they ran towards him. Yash wasn't buried he was standing. Aryan and Daksh shook their heads and looked again. In front of them were numbers of stairs going under the ground. Yash was standing on one of those stairs.

"W-what is down there?" said Mahir with mixed emotions of surprise and curiosity.

"Don't know," answered Yash. "I was waiting for you guys to show up. You thought I was going down there alone, no way."

"So, we are here now—let's go," said Daksh, excitedly.

"Careful though," said Yash, warningly, "these stairs are *insanely* uneven, like some are big, some are almost flat, so be careful."

Seeing Yash serious, they nodded. They all started to go down those stairs. At the front was Yash, to his back was Mahir, and then Daksh, at last, was Aryan. Seeing Yash almost fall, three of them placed their hands on their left wall for support. Aryan noticed that these walls were made of the same brick as those outer walls of the Fort. Those stairs were indeed uneven, some were to their knee size, two or three were the size of their toe.

Daksh and Mahir had spread out their both hands, as space was not that wide enough. After about ten to fifteen stairs, those stairs turned right. There was a square space in between. Yash and Mahir stood on that square space while Daksh and Aryan peeked from behind the wall.

Right in front of them was the view that gave them the feeling to move back immediately. In front of them was like only five stairs, at the end was around a six-and-a-half-foot tall entrance. Completely dark of what lay behind. Mahir tapped on Yash's back, they walked forwards. Now, they were able to see a wall behind the entrance. They climbed down the last step and that the wall was four to five steps away from the entrance. It gave the clear view that it turned towards the right or left.

"Take out your phones, guys," said Aryan, burying his hand inside his jeans pocket.

They did as Aryan told them to do, keeping their phones in their hands they looked forward. Together they walked inside the entrance, it was really dark in here, and for a second, they believed it was nighttime. As the entrance was below the level of the ground, shining rays of the sun were not able to reach here. They turned on their phones flashlights.

"What?"

"What sorcery is this?"

Even though four flashlights were on there was no reflection back. It stayed dark, they pointed their flashlights everywhere, but it was a hapless act. Those dark walls were not made to reflect blue lights.

"Ok, I am not getting a good vibe from here," said Aryan, his voice echoed.

"Likewise," said Daksh.

"Fine, why don't we do this," echoed Mahir's voice, they were not able to see each other clearly, "we go back up, call the rest of them and come back here. Seeing this place I am sure they will have their own ideas about…this."

"OKAY." came the mixture of voices.

They climbed back those stairs and came out in open. Mahir ran a bit further to call Aadhaya.

Aryan sat down on the very first step of those underground stairs. Yash was seated on the second, right below was Aryan. Daksh was standing on the third step, leaned against the left wall facing Aryan and Yash. Daksh was looking in front where Mahir was standing, screaming their location. With his rough loud noise, Aryan and Yash also turned to see his excitement.

"Yes, now go straight from there. Don't you dare stop anywhere! NO—NO! NOT EVEN IF YOU ALL ARE HUNGRY. NOW GET HERE!"

"Oof, I think after all this, we should go see caretakers of this fort," said Daksh, looking at Aryan and then Yash.

"You think…but why?" asked Yash.

"To find out who is the living heir of this Fort!"

"OKAY—but why would we do that?" asked Aryan.

Aryan knew Daksh was waiting for that question, as he had a punch-line ready.

"Well, we have to talk to them," said Daksh. "Without talking, getting to know each other, how can we set up the marriage between Mahir and this Fort?"

Even though Aryan knew there was something funny coming he could not stop his outburst. Yash's eyes were flowing with tears, Daksh also joined them.

"He is kind of attached to the history," said Aryan, controlling himself.

"History is amazing!" said Yash. "I also like to see and gain information on it. Although Mahir is very deep into it."

"Hey, I love history," said Daksh. "Don't give me that look Yash. I love History, unless I don't have to write eight points answers for *five* marks, I mean that is a total war situation, cruel."

This time they couldn't control themselves, Yash almost rolled down his stairs. Just like this, laughing, sharing some more amusing stories ten minutes went by. Mahir came shortly to inform them that the other half is here. They got up on their feet and went outside.

Aryan saw them approaching. Oviya and Ruhi were in front, Aadhaya and Sam, holding hands, were walking right behind them.

"So, what did you find?" asked Ruhi.

"Wait a minute, why are your lips red?" asked Oviya.

Mahir's eyes widened, he hissed at them not to stop at those stalls. Others touched their lips and then looked at them.

"Because of those red mangoes," said Daksh.

"Yeah, those were really good," said Yash.

"You-you ate there?" said Aadhaya, her voice trembling with anger.

"Not just ate, we had our lunch over there," said Daksh.

Mahir hissed at Daksh, Daksh stood there, puzzled.

"And you told us not to stop," said Ruhi, punching Mahir on his shoulder.

"Even though we were starving," said Oviya, she too punched him.

Mahir stood there rubbing his shoulder.

"Not cool, Dude," said Sam. "Seeing those full of vitamin C, and that juicy watermelon it brought a different kind of lust in me."

"Hey, don't call me *Dude*!"

"Don't you dare yell at my Boyfriend!"

"Oh, shut up!"

Everyone made a gasping sound. Mahir was startled. He saw Aadhaya boiling with rage. He turned back and saw Yash and Daksh wearing the look of *you-are-dead.* He immediately turned towards Aryan.

"Help me," mouthed Mahir.

Aryan came forward and stood between him and Aadhaya.

"We have already wasted enough time the Fort will close soon as the sunset time is getting nearer. So, please don't fight here like a bunch of teenagers."

He went on explaining everything they saw down there. Mahir looked thankful, girls and Sam's expressions changed instantly.

"You fools turned on your flashlights, right? I mean that would be very stupid of you if you didn't," said Ruhi, over-smartly.

Daksh gritted his teeth and was about to snap. Yash came to the rescue by placing his left hand on his chest and coming forward.

"Yes, we did that, Ruhi," said Yash, calmly.

"It had no effect at all?" asked Aadhaya.

"Come and look for yourself," said Mahir.

So, they walked towards those uneven stairs. Yash once again warned them about these stairs.

"Psst, like we don't know how to go down st—oo."

Ruhi screamed as her foot failed to find the ground and she fell in front. As Daksh was right in front of her, she got saved by placing all her weight on Daksh's back.

Daksh turned he helped her to stand straight while grinning.

"You were saying something?"

"Argh!" groaned Ruhi.

They all arrived in front of the dark entrance. Sam whistled, Ruhi and Oviya stayed motionless looking at it, Aadhaya had her curious look. As their curiosity aroused, they all went to the other side of the entrance. Again, it was dark, the only light was coming from the entrance, as it had no doors or anything some rays of the sun were coming in.

Four of them, like before, turned on their flashlights. And it gave them the same result as before.

"My God!" came Oviya's voice.

"How…"

Aryan was sure it was Sam. Like them, Aadhaya, Ruhi, Oviya, and Sam turned on their phone flashlights. They were barely able to see each other, and there was a sound of someone crying in pain.

"Who stepped on my foot?"

It was Daksh's voice, right beside Aryan. Aryan knew it was he who did it.

"This is incredible!"

Aryan noticed the sudden echo as Aadhaya spoke.

"There is nothing we can do here," said Aryan, disappointingly.

"Yeah, let's move out," came Yash's voice.

One by one, they all moved out. Those who were already past the entrance stood on those stairs. They noticed Ruhi didn't come. Oviya went further and stood at the edge of the entrance. She saw Ruhi, standing still.

"Ruhi, let's go, come out."

Ruhi stayed motionless, "Guys, come back in!" her voice echoed inside.

Oviya looked back at the others, all six of them shrugged and moved back inside.

"You guys still have those lighters which you use to light the smoke?" asked Ruhi.

"Yes."

"Light it up."

Aryan took out his lighter from his pocket. He assumed Daksh, Yash, and Mahir did the same as there were noises of skin rubbing on cloth. Aryan lit his lighter, and just after his, there were three more clicks!

Everyone sighed in astonishment as the darkness turned into gold. Those four little flames conjured by those lighters brightened up the place, just like the mighty sun presenting his first rays onto the dark world of ours. They were able to see each other clearly as daylight. Not just that, they were able to see some further distance ahead.

Aryan noticed the walls were made of stone, not baked stones. As he was on the corner, he touched the wall beside him. His hands felt the coldness, and there was also some texture on those walls. Aryan turned his gaze front they were in a passageway that moved straight ahead. It was not that narrow, as two people can stand side by side without rubbing each other on the shoulder.

"How did you know this would work?" said Aadhaya, smiling.

"Well, I read it in a book," went on Ruhi, "that back in the old days, Kings used to have their secret places. They used them to hide their valuables and secrets. These places were protected by some charms. Of course, the King had their ways, and they knew many people, including the Tantra people. As secrets are dark and cryptic, the King couldn't risk putting them like that. The person with Tantra Gyan is really a big deal. So, they cast a spell, a spell that only a pure form of light can show them the way, and that is—

"How did you get the idea of lighting those lighters?" Aadhaya completed.

Everyone beamed at Ruhi. She smiled and blushed,

"The way I see it," said Daksh, drily. "Something really good came out of us smoking."

Aryan, Yash, and Mahir laughed, and even Sam did. Aadhaya, Ruhi, and Oviya looked bemused. Aadhaya nudged her elbow into Sam's stomach Sam groaned in pain and stopped laughing. Others ceased their laughter and looked away instantly.

All of them looked backward the passageway was leading them forward for about five to seven steps and then turning left. It displeased them, so they looked back at the front. The passageway here was leading straight, and it pleased them, as everyone loves roads that have no turns and are straight, but dislikes the person who is straightforward.

"What are we waiting for? Let's move ahead," said Aryan, as his signature dialogue.

Everyone beamed, and Yash was surprised by such an outburst of excitement.

"WOAH—WOAH—hold on!"

They turned to see Yash sweating coldly.

"The Tantra people are involved," said Yash, emphasizing the gravity of the situation, "these people are really not the ones to mess around with for fun. I mean, even Gods keep an eye on them."

"So, you are saying that God doesn't keep an eye on me," said Daksh, seriously.

Everyone laughed, Yash looked at them disbelievingly.

I am surrounded by imbeciles, thought Yash, scratching his head.

"Let's go," said Ruhi, her eyes twinkling.

"I hope gold comes in our way," hoped Daksh, greedily.

"We must not—"

"Like piles of gold," said Oviya, jumping.

"Maybe, I guess."

"LISTEN TO ME!"

Everyone turned their heads towards Yash, his eyes expressing his rage.

"What?" said Daksh.

"Didn't you hear what I just said? Didn't you hear what Ruhi said?" said Yash, solemnly. "Dark power is involved, and *believe me* when I say this to your tiny brains, where secrets are involved, we must not unveil them thoughtlessly."

There was a momentary silence as no one had any comebacks after what Yash said. Those little flames only flickered when its respective holders hand shook, as there was no wind passing in the passageway. The passageway was indeed glowing yellow because of those four flames.

"First of all, I do not have a *tiny* brain," said Daksh, airily. "Second, did you see any board out there saying "KEEP OUT, DANGEROUS PLACE"? Did you see such a board?"

Yash thought for a moment, and as he had no answer, he remained silent.

"And third," said Daksh, "I want my camera back, Ruhi."

Ruhi screwed up her face and let out her tongue. Daksh took his camera from her and wore it around his neck, which was a few seconds ago on Ruhi's neck.

"Those in favor of moving ahead, where you can probably find actual gold, raise your hands."

All except Yash raised their hands in favor of moving ahead. Daksh sneered looking at Yash.

"So, you coming?" asked Daksh, mockingly.

"Like I have a choice."

"Move ahead, people!" said Daksh, directing his hand, holding the lighter forwards.

The formation was somewhat like this: Aryan and Daksh at the very front, leading the way. Just behind them were Ruhi and Oviya walking side by side, with a slight look of greediness. Second to the last were Aadhaya and Sam, holding hands and walking ahead. And at the rear were Mahir and Yash, using their lighter to spark from the back so they didn't get lost. It was, of course, Yash's idea, but he himself didn't want to volunteer to stay at the rear.

Their footsteps were echoing in the passageway. As they went further, the echoing sound increased. It would have been unmanageable if it weren't for those four lighters. With the lighters, they were able to see even a step ahead. As they got the lighters, they were able to see two steps further.

"Did she treat you right, my senorita?" cooed Daksh, looking down at his camera.

"What did you just say?" asked Aryan, turning to Daksh.

"What?"

"What…?"

"What!"

"Oh, we can do this all day," said Aryan, giving up.

The walls of the passageway were turning from pitch black to a glowing shade of yellow as they kept moving ahead. As they were walking, a curious thought ran into Aryan's mind:

Strange! There is no ventilation in here only air was coming from that door-less entrance. But we passed that, like, minutes ago. Still, I am not sweating like I was outside. I can feel no wind coming by; if there were any, these tiny flames must dance before air hit us. Hope we are going the right way! I just need an adventure, that is all I want.

"Your hair looks adorable today," complimented Sam, looking at his left.

Aadhaya blushed and tucked her hair behind her ears with her free left hand.

"Thank you," said Aadhaya, leaning against Sam's wide shoulder.

Aadhaya then turned her gaze forward. She saw Oviya and Ruhi looking at her, smiling.

Yash was talking to himself, *Don't any of these idiots read—or just watch a movie or something. I mean a place like this will not take you to heaven that I am sure of. God! Why did I find this place and call them!*

"Will you stop?" said Mahir.

Yash turned his gaze immediately at Mahir, making sure that he didn't say those things out loud.

"I can read your expression," said Mahir, "You are scared!"

"Scared?" said Yash. "I am just concerned, Mahir. I mean, look at this, Mahir, you know better than I do. These sorts of places are dark, and we are walking freely like we are in a heyday era."

"I know, Yash," said Mahir, plainly. "But don't you have that curiosity that is telling you to move ahead, just to have one look?"

Yash sighed and looked forward. His hand holding the lighter was steady, and he was looking at it.

"Hey, Yash," said Daksh in a normal tone from the front.

"Yes?" replied Yash.

"You know we are in a passageway," said Daksh.

"Yeah—so?"

"So, it echoes here, just like my voice is right now."

Yash bit his tongue and looked at Mahir, who smiled by elevating his eyebrows.

"We can hear you...bickering like a woman."

"Hem-ahem!" Aryan cleared his throat.

"No offense, ladies," said Daksh, turning back at Ruhi and Oviya.

"Yeah, none taken," said Ruhi, ironically.

The rest of the voyage was quiet. The only voice echoing in the passageway was their footsteps. They must have walked much further by now, as their legs started to ache a little. As there was nothing happening that would make the hair on the back of their necks stand straight, they moved ahead.

Those four flames were smooth and beautiful, making the further way visible. They walked for about five to six steps, then they realized that their footsteps were now echoing differently. It was like walking in a puddle, instead of on a hard floor.

Aryan and Daksh shared a look and directed down those lighters.

"Eww!" cried Ruhi.

"My boots!" yelped Oviya.

Surely it was an unpleasant sight. They were now walking on a ground filled with water. The water was barely coming up towards their ankles. Although, the disagreeable part was that the water was dark, almost black or dark brown in color they were not certain.

Yash and Mahir had their lighters directed down at the ground too.

"HA—HA! This is not someplace where you can find gold. This is the sewer system of the Fort."

Saying that, Yash laughed even louder. Mahir, Sam, and Aadhaya had the same look of disgust.

"Let's get out of here," said Aryan.

Aryan turned backward, people in front did the same. Now he was at the rear. After walking about two steps, Aryan looked at his side and saw Daksh wasn't there he turned.

"Daksh!" called out Aryan.

Daksh was standing at the same place as before like a statue.

"Let's go, Daksh, there is nothing here to see."

Now others turned too Aryan's words appeared to be unreachable for Daksh. He didn't move a muscle ironically, he took a step forward, and then another. His footsteps were making a sound that of stepping on a puddle.

"Daksh, what are you doing?"

Daksh was bending down, his right hand holding his lighter. And just like that, he buried his left hand inside the black water below. He took out his hand like ten seconds after and stood straight.

Bewildered by his move, everyone approached him by walking. As they all went further, Daksh definitely gave them a heart attack. In his left hand was a thick gold coin.

"OH MY GOD!" cried everyone, eyes fixed on Daksh's left hand.

Without wasting even a mini-second, they all put down their hands inside that disgusting water, just like Daksh did earlier. Ruhi was not feeling uneasy at all, nor did Oviya. The passageway was echoing with splashes and movement inside the water. Daksh was staring at the gold coin he found, like a child looking at his candy after a serious struggle.

"There is nothing!" screamed Ruhi.

Oviya too got back up with a look of annoyed disappointment. She stomped her foot onto the water, it splashed right at Mahir. Mahir yelled at her.

"I think we should go further," said Mahir, breathlessly.

So, they walked further, almost ran. Just like before, they buried their hands inside the water.

Suddenly, Ruhi jumped with joy. In her hand was a bluish-pink diamond, the size of a watch face. Oviya jumped as she got the same diamond as hers.

"Woo-Hoo!" Yash screamed in joy, in his hand was a gold coin, identical to Daksh.

Aryan too found a gold coin. Sam found a diamond, Aadhaya found a gold coin. Sam exchanged his diamond with her gold coin. At last, Mahir jumped holding a gold coin.

"I cannot believe this," said Aryan, beamingly.

"Me neither," said Ruhi, observing her diamond closely.

"I love this one," said Oviya, kissing her diamond, not caring where she took it out from.

Yash was keenly observing his gold coin.

"I am so glad you guys found this place," said Aadhaya.

"You don't regret coming here now, do you, Yash?" said Mahir, slapping playfully on Yash's back.

Yash didn't say anything he remained silent.

"Hey guys, what if we find some more of this further in?" said Daksh, greedily.

Everyone's eyes twinkled with greediness.

"There is one problem," said Aryan, "the fuel in this lighter is about to vanish."

"You are right," said Daksh.

Yash and Mahir checked their lighters and saw that the liquid in them was down to a few drops.

"What should we do now?" asked Mahir.

"I think we should go, head back out and come back tomorrow with some big lanterns," answered Aadhaya.

Everyone adored Aadhaya's suggestion. So, they turned, following the same formation with Aryan and Daksh at the rear.

BANG!

The sound was like something stony banging on even harder stone. The sound made Aryan and Daksh almost fall on Ruhi and Oviya both of them screamed like Aadhaya. Sam looked back. Yash fell sideways at Mahir, and Mahir caught him.

"Wh—what was that?" said Yash, standing up straight.

Everyone looked at each other with the same scared look. Yash was breathing heavily and then he groaned.

"I knew it—I knew it."

"There is not—"

BANG!

The sound came again, like something in the distance got closed... or just got open.

"Your back to the walls!" said Aryan, urgently.

Everyone obeyed they touched their backs to the right wall. The sound came from the back, where they found those gold coins and diamonds. Oviya was shaking, Ruhi was alert.

Right then, a cold wind passed through them, making those tiny flames dance and finally shut. There were four cries of terror, three of them were feminine. It was pitch black, Aryan took control of his hand, which was shaking badly.

Click!

Four flames conjured back, and the place brightened up. Aryan was aware that he was sweating now. His chest was rising and falling. He looked right as he was at the very end of the line, the rest of the others were at his right, their backs stuck to the wall. He saw they were as scared as he was.

Aryan looked at Daksh he was right beside him, trembling badly. His hands were shaking, and he dropped his gold coin. With great courage, he dared to bend down, directing his lighter. When he was about an inch close to touching the water, what he saw made him scream.

Others looked down and gasped in horror. The darkness of the water was flowing away. It was flowing towards where the sound came from, leaving the water crystal clear. They saw some more of those gold coins and diamonds they were half-buried inside the ground.

For a moment, there was silence, and they were only able to hear each other breathing heavily. Aryan looked to his right again. He saw Ruhi and Oviya with their faces looking down in shock. Then he saw Aadhaya, her expression was almost at the brink of crying. He was about to tell them to start moving towards the entrance, but—

BANG!

Everyone screamed, trembling from head to foot. The sound came from the left, where the darkness went. Aryan was sure something got opened.

There was again that silence of unpleasantness. Aryan was struggling to move his feet—

Their ears almost bled, hearing the focused high-pitched scream of the crow.

Chapter 14

A Real Deal

Realizing the reality and heaviness of what they did, Aryan and Daksh felt a huge bubble of guilt flowing upwards in their bodies. Their eyes were wide open, staring at the endless thoughts inside. The bamboo was now in three pieces, lying on the sand, with the fire on top of it. The flames danced whenever a breeze came to tease them.

Aryan felt a serious dislike for himself, for what he had done.

"How could I do this?" cried Aryan. "God has gifted me with everything, I mean everything, still... I went for that stupid gold—the freaking gold. I cannot believe this. I—I brought this upon myself. What would Ekta think of me? Wo—would I be able to see them again?"

Aryan squeezed his face with his hands and groaned out loud. Hearing this, Daksh came back to the present. He gave a little shake to his head and slid towards Aryan. Daksh rested his hand on Aryan's shaking shoulder. Aryan brought his face out from behind his hands and looked at him.

"It was actually my fault," said Daksh, slowly. "If I would have just turned like you guys did and didn't follow that shiny, cursed thing—and went there to bury my hands and pick it up…things would be a lot different by now."

Aryan was so tensed he opened his mouth, but no voice flowed from it. He looked up at the moonless sky, taking a breath he tried to calm himself.

"Thank you, Daksh, for taking the blame," said Aryan, "but I am as guilty as you are, my friend. I also put my hands down in search of gold," Aryan looked up and said in a hushed voice, "Sadly, I too got it."

Aryan felt such ignominy for what he did. Seeing Daksh beside him was assuring that he is not alone in this. Just then, he realized about the masculine man who was seated in front of them. How furious he got when the man asked them "What did you steal?" He felt even guiltier as the thing proven out to be correct.

Aryan was not able to lift his head up. What a strange situation life puts us in! He had no courage to look at the man. So, he faced Daksh. To his surprise, Daksh was facing front. Building up some courage, slowly, he looked front.

The man was seated in the same position, he hadn't moved an inch. His long beard and lush hairs were flowing with the wind without putting up any fight. His right amber eye gleamed as the fire was conjured in front of him. Ironically, he was smiling. His expression was peaceful, like a person enjoying the view from the top of the mountain. His spine—just like before—was erect. Aryan observed and saw that the man hadn't moved even his fingers were as they were. This made Aryan even more speechless. For like five minutes, only the noise of the shores and the fire between them was conversing.

I am feeling so guilty I can't even open my mouth to speak, thought Aryan.

The man faced the sky and laughed heartfully. Aryan looked at Daksh both shared the look of incomprehension.

I have never been this confused in my life, thought Daksh.

"Then let me clear out all your bewilderment, Daksh," said the man, looking straight at Daksh.

Daksh gasped in shock, surely taken aback.

"Well, I have to say that I am surprised by you, Aryan," said the man, facing Aryan. "You are one of those few who take full responsibility for what they did. Your contrite has impressed me. And that includes you too, Daksh."

Those words didn't help them to set low their confusion it got additional.

"Mr. Man—with…well-groomed-beard, can—"

The man stopped Daksh by showing him his palm.

"You can call me Aigile," said Aigile.

Aryan gave him a smile, which he graciously returned, Daksh nodded.

"So, Mr. Aigile—"

"Just *Aigile* is fine by me."

"Ok, Aigile…you can read minds?"

"Well, eyes, to be certain," said Aigile.

"Huh!" sighed Daksh.

Then Aigile's eyes met Aryan, he gave him a smile and then looked away. He was staring in the space between Aryan and Daksh. Aigile's both eyes appeared to be gazing far away, to their back, in the woods.

"You have answered my question truthfully and I appreciate it," said Aigile without turning. "Now it is my time to answer, and you will be, Aryan and Daksh, the ones to ask me questions."

Aryan and Daksh both nodded earnestly. Aigile looked at them, slowly changing his gaze from Aryan to Daksh, then he gave his hand a wave up.

"Aadhaya, Ruhi, Oviya, Yash, Mahir, and Sam, are they dead?" asked Aryan.

"I have told you before, and I am telling you again—they are not dead."

"So where are they?"

"You will know shortly."

"We—I mean us—stole those gold coins and diamonds, that is why that crow is after us, right?" asked Daksh.

"Indeed, Daksh."

"So, if we all get back all those diamonds and gold coins, and give it back to—it, it will not chase ever again, right?"

"Yes, that would be a wise activity to do," said Aigile, nodding. "Although let me make this clear that Corbeau—"

"Excuse me?" said Aryan and Daksh together.

"Oh—yes—please forgive me for my ignorance," said Aigile, formally. "His name is Corbeau."

"You mean that big, scary crow?"

"Yes..."

"That thing has a name?" said Daksh, disbelievingly.

"Correct," Answered Aigile.

Daksh gave Aryan the look of *how-in-the-world-is-this-possible*.

"Please continue, Aigile," said Aryan.

"As I was saying," continued Aigile, "Corbeau is beyond any powerful person—"

"A person?"

Daksh's mind was not willing to accept what he was hearing. Aigile looked at him but chose to continue.

"He was loyal to his king—still is—even though our noble king died way long ago. He is protecting those riches because he was given that responsibility."

"You mean his, what I meant is your king gave him that responsibility!" said Aryan, his face and body appeared to be hiding a strong emotion.

Aigile smiled looking at him. Aryan knew from this that something really bad has happened. They didn't just steal but committed something dark. The question he was about to ask he already knew its answer, but chose to ask it anyway.

"Who was your King?"

Aigile closed his eyes for a second, he opened them, his amber eye twinkled at Aryan. He turned his wide upper body towards the left. To Aryan, Aigile's body was blocking the view of the Fort for him. Aigile was now turned, his wide right shoulder was facing them. He raised his left hand, palm facing the dark sky, he pointed all his fingers towards the Fort.

"The Lord of this Fort!"

Aryan looked down and rested his head on his hand. Even though he knew the answer, his stomach lurched badly.

"Hold on," said Daksh, loudly, "the Fort is like thousands of years old, and the ruler—I mean—how—did we time travel?"

"NO, you idiot," said Aryan, still looking down. Then he looked up straight at Aigile. "Did we?" Aigile laughed heartfully.

Aigile laughed heartfully.

"Don't be preposterous time isn't something a mortal can play with. If a mortal did, the consequences will be beyond grave."

"So, you are immortal?" asked Aryan, loudly.

"Not exactly," said Aigile, shaking his head. "I died when my soul got separated."

"WHAT IN THE NAME OF GODS!" cried Daksh, dragging himself backward.

Aryan and Daksh looked at each other, speechless, even more horrified. Aryan knew that his emotions are now ineffable. Aigile looked at them, he read some of their thoughts. He got the feeling of digressing.

"Do you want to go back to the life you were living or not?" asked Aigile, straightforwardly.

Aryan and Daksh looked at him.

"Good," said Aigile. "Now answer me this: how are you both planning to return what you stole?" Aryan stood up on his feet, Daksh did the same. They both buried their hands inside every pocket their clothes had.

Aigile, again, laughed pitilessly.

"Oh, Aryan and Daksh, how humorous you both are!" said Aigile. "You think you will find what you stole inside your pockets?" He laughed again. "Now sit back down the information I am about to give you will surprise you gravely."

Aryan and Daksh slowly sat back down right in front of Aigile the wood was still making those cracking noises.

"This is a real deal," said Aigile, "the moment you step in that Tomb—"

"T—T—Tomb?"

"That is what I like to call that place," said Aigile. "If it is possible do not interrupt me," said Aigile seriously. "You were already trapped the moment you stepped inside that Tomb. Corbeau is artful in the matter of playing with a person's mind. He was the one who drew you in. All eight of you knew, deep down, that this is not the place even to lay your eyes on. And when you all picked up those lustful gold coins and diamonds, he trapped you inside right that very second. Yes, Aryan?"

Aryan had his hand raised.

"I want to ask—no, I had to ask this, can I?" said Aryan, desperately.

"You can, Aryan," said Aigile, calmly.

"I am curious about how— much I focus on my mind, my memory...I cannot recall the fact about how I came out of the Fort?"

Daksh looked at Aryan, he started nodding.

"Me too," said Daksh. "I focused, and the only close thing that comes to my mind is the boat we came back from."

"Why is it like this?"

"In the first place, when did I ever say that you people came out of the fort?" Said Aigile, he got relaxed as the question was coming from the direction he wanted.

"What do you mean by that?" asked Aryan.

"You, Daksh, including your other friends, are already inside the world that we created."

Chapter 15

Give in to Go in

Aryan and Daksh sat still with their eyes fixed at Aigile. They both looked like some artful statue figure, expressing a very strong emotion of bewilderment and horrification.

As usual, Aigile looked calm and satisfied. He momentarily closed his eyelids as a breeze touched his visage and then opened them again.

"What I am about to tell you," said Aigile, smiling behind his God-like beard, "will clear it all, additionally, it will give you an answer about what to do next. As I said earlier do not interrupt me—unless the question must be answered."

Taking a deep breath, his lips moved, it was a dance or a prayer, Aryan didn't know neither did Daksh.

"When you entered the Tomb," said Aigile raising his voice, "you were already at the mercy of Corbeau. I made myself very clear about that. But when you took those gold coins and diamonds, you woke him up… which is egregious. What made him act is when you all tried to take away what you took. That is when he came out and drew you inside our world. The world that we created. The world of Hoax."

Aryan knew, since Corbeau started to chase them, that because of their futile greediness they woke the unnatural, and now they are trapped. Daksh was aghast.

"Now you both said to me—and it seems like it—but it is not. You still think that you came out of our king's noble fort, am I right?"

From the corner of his eye, Aryan saw Daksh half nodded.

"This is the Hoax," concluded Aigile. "This is the place what you people call: level one. You have to go to level two. That is where you will find what you took, and let myself be clear, taking back is going to be hard…difficult than you can imagine."

"Can I ask you a question?" asked Aryan, nervously.

"Yes, Aryan."

"In that level two—there—I mean my friends are there, aren't they?"

"Finally, an answer!" Said Aigile, joyfully. "Yes, Aryan, your friends are there, in the second level. About to start their journey to give back what they took."

"I don't understand one thing," said Daksh, "Aigile, like you said that those gold coins we took are in the second level and that world, sorry, this world is created by both of you. Doesn't that mean that the gold we took is back into your, or in that crow's possession now?"

"A very wise question Daksh." Said Aigile. "You know how to impress a person. I have already prepared the answer to that. As you have seen, Corbeau, do you really think he is the type of soul that will just let it go? My thoughts exactly, Daksh. It is not in the nature of Corbeau to forgive, to let it all go away like love. Corbeau thinks that payback is a must. So, what he does is this: he transfers those who even try to take those riches out of the Tomb into the Hoax—"

Daksh and Aryan lower their heads.

"—There, I mean here, he forces them to do things as per his will, like some puppet. In order to return what you took you to have to give in and play as per his will and return what you and your fellow friends took."

Aryan pressed his head between his hands. Daksh was shaking with fear.

"Yash was right...he was right," said Daksh in a wobbly voice. "It was a bad omen to see that *blue-eyed crow* on that ferry."

Aigile instantly opened his eyes and looked at Daksh. His expression was not calm anymore.

"Can you be specific Daksh?" said Aigile, narrowing his eyes at him.

"We saw that Crow, I mean Corbeau, at the top of the other ferry which was keeping pace with ours."

"And that was before you entered the fort?"

"It was before we even took the bus that dropped us at the hotel."

Aigile opened his eyes wide and stared for a minute at Daksh. He looked away as he knew that Daksh was telling the truth.

"Corbeau will be here shortly."

Saying that Aigile got up on his feet and passed by Aryan and started walking towards the woods.

"HEY—where are you going?"

Daksh too got on his feet and walked towards Aigile. Aigile stopped right there he half-turned, Daksh saw his right hand shaking.

"Aryan knows what to do," Said Aigile, plainly. "At the end, I will say this: Keep trying—keep trying even if the time demands Dying. It is now a survival situation."

"What...?"

Daksh failed to stop him as he saw how fast Aigile walked and disappeared in the darkness of the woods behind those palm trees. Daksh put his hand above his left chest and felt the rapidness of his heart. He turned back and walked towards Aryan, he hasn't moved from his place.

"You heard him, Aryan, that demon is coming, we have to move," said Daksh bending down behind Aryan and placing his hand on his shoulder.

Aryan didn't respond, he didn't even turn to look at him.

"Aryan!" said Daksh, softly.

Daksh came to his right side. Aryan's face looked like there was no blood flow anymore. Tears were flowing down from his watery eyes. Daksh exhaled and sat beside him. He was worried from the start that Aryan will break. Daksh stayed quiet waiting for Aryan to speak.

"Ekta," said Aryan, after some minutes passed, "Will I ever meet her again?"

"Of course, you will," said Daksh, sliding close towards him.

"We are in a different world now, Daksh, how can you be so sure? Because of me—because of my *stupid* plan I dragged you all into this *hell hole*."

Aryan punched the sandy ground, some particles flew up. He looked away, some tears escaped from his closed eyes.

Daksh looked at him and exhaled, he directed his hand and grabbed the back of Aryan's head, where his second brain was. He shook it vigorously. That appeared to work. Aryan looked at him and actually gave him a smile.

"Your emotional brain has forgotten, but mine didn't," said Daksh. "We were *all* there together. We all came to this trip because we *all* agreed to. And we *all* tried to steal—well, you are smart, you know the rest."

"When did you get so wise, eh?" said Aryan, smiling.

"What do you mean when?" said Daksh. "I always was, has been wiser than you lot are."

"Don't exaggerate," said Aryan in a bored tone.

"I am now...just to be clear, wise and smart are both different qualities, right?"

Aryan laughed, "Yes, my wise friend Daksh, I think they are different."

"Now get up—move your butt, idiot."

Aryan didn't move a muscle, he just looked at Daksh, smiling. Daksh drew some breathes to yell at him—just then, a forceful wind flew past them. Aryan and Daksh placed their hand in front of their eyes as sand was going in them. The fire danced furiously and almost vanished. Daksh moved his hand away from his face and looked up at the sky. Something even darker than the sky was flying. Daksh shuddered when he saw a tiny blue ball, and the whole crow now appeared to be clear in the sky.

"Oh, no-no-no-no-no—not happening again, not..." Daksh turned to face Aryan. "HEY! WHAT ARE YOU STILL DOING DOWN THERE—MOVE YOUR ASS!"

"No, Daksh."

"WHAT?"

"Remember what Aigile said: We have to give in."

Daksh's body was not in his control. He was turning his head from Aryan to the sky, constantly.

"He also said "it is a survival situation now," and for me, sitting down does not count as surviving strategy, so move—"

The huge sound of *thud* came from behind Daksh. Daksh turned slowly and saw Corbeau standing at some distance, which was like two steps from his huge body.

"HEY—WHAT—YOU THOUGHTLESS CREATURE—WHAT ARE YOU DOING?"

Aryan put his hands under Daksh's armpits and grabbed him from behind.

"Sorry—I had to do this. It is for your own sake."

"You really want to die like this?" Daksh was putting up a fight to free himself, but Aryan grabbed him firmly. "Eaten by a crow, oh, what a worse way to die!"

Daksh was crying, begging to free himself from Aryan. But Aryan was surprisingly firm, like a father who wants his child to do the right things.

"Corbeau is not going to kill us."

"OH-REALLY?"

"Remember when Corbeau cornered us, and we looked straight at his blue eye?"

Daksh didn't listen, he squeaked as he saw with horror Corbeau moving forward towards them. Each footstep Corbeau took was like a heavy bounce on the sandy ground.

"Remember that drowsiness?" continued Aryan, gripping Daksh tight, ignoring Corbeau. "That feeling—like your soul is coming out of you—that is how we are getting to the next level."

Daksh tilted his head back towards Aryan and gave him a *you-have-lost-your-marbles* look.

"That is the only explanation, If you don't believe me, answer me: How are Yash, Mahir, and others already on the second level? You can't, can you?"

Daksh turned his gaze front and groaned. Aryan set him free. Instantly, Daksh made a move to run, but it was too late. Corbeau was now right in front of them. If they stretched out their arms and walked a step, they would touch his dark feathers.

Aryan observed his long, feathered body, and then he looked up at his face.

"Well-well, Aigile had a chat with you." It was that harsh voice again.

Aryan and Daksh shuddered, they were able to hear each other's teeth drumming. Just like before, they were unable to move.

"T-t-take us," said Aryan after a long, hard attempt.

Corbeau his beak upwards, and in one smooth motion, he flew upwards. The whole beach went dark as his blow blew away those sources of light. Daksh and Aryan fell backwards as they were right in front of him.

"OH-God, it is not like others."

"YOU THINK?"

They both got back on their feet. It was so dark they both appeared to be a shadow of each other.

Before Aryan or Daksh could say a word, Corbeau shrieked from above. They looked up and then back down. Right in front of them, a small tornado was forming and moving towards them. Aryan and Daksh started to walk backward keeping an eye on the tornado. They turned instantly, it was a bad idea, as the wind was flowing against them, and all of the sand was going inside their eyes.

The tornado expanded in a matter of seconds, sucking everything inside. Wind, which was heavenly, was now egregious. Aryan and

Daksh were putting a lot of effort into walking forward, they had their hands in front of their faces. The challenging part was to maintain balance, as they lifted up their feet, it appeared to be the tornado's sucking power got increased.

Aryan moved his hand away to look where he was going as a basket full of sand smashes at his face, his left foot was in the air, and he flew backwards, getting sucked inside by the tornado, which was now the size of those palm trees.

Aryan screamed in horror, Daksh turned to maintain his balance and grabbed him by his right arm.

"THIS IS ON YOU!"

Daksh lost his balance, and they both got sucked inside the tornado.

Aryan opened his eyes, it was like he was in the middle of some dark, cursed power. Aryan groaned as he got flipped into a very uncomfortable position towards nowhere. He was floating in the air still sand was still getting inside him from everywhere. He felt very ill when he got flipped again and then again.

"DAKSH—DAKSH!"

Again, Aryan was twisted in many flips by the tornado to a different side. He kept groaning, clutching at his stomach. Suddenly, he sensed behind his closed eyelids that someone was coming right in front of him. With great difficulty, he opened his eyes. He saw Corbeau right in the middle of the tornado. His torso was facing him, and so was his face.

Aryan blinked, and Corbeau was close to him. It appears that the tornado was not affecting him at all. He shone his blue eye right at Aryan's face.

"Aaahhh!"

Aryan screamed, he felt pain, unbearable pain in his head. It was like dying would be a much simpler option. He screamed, twisted, and turned. He opened his eyes, and again, he saw Corbeau's blue eye. The pain continued, and he got twisted.

The feeling he felt the feeling of his soul getting pulled out of his body. Suddenly, the pain got away; he was floating still. He almost felt that he was flying in mid-air. Momentarily, he noticed sounds of harsh wind piercing his ears, but he didn't mind.

Smoke was forming up in front of him. As he was about to think something about it, it got away. And a figure started to develop. It was a woman, she had her back to him. It didn't even take him a second to realize it was Ekta. She was holding something or someone. Aryan opened his mouth, but no voice came out. He was not able to speak, not even able to think what to say or think at all. It was like he was only allowed to watch.

A giggle of a baby came from the front of her. Aryan took a step forward, and Ekta disappeared. There was nothing in front of him now, just darkness. And his thoughts also got shut down.

Chapter 16

The Place He Most Feared

He felt the pain, the pain of guilt grabbing his pure heart. After a moment, he realized the left side of his face was touching the wooden floor. Minutes passed, and now he was able to feel his torso. Yash was laid flat on the wooden floor, on his abdomen. He felt the coldness of the floor. Yash didn't want to open his eyes, as it was a task itself, but he fought, fought with his feelings, and finally, his lids went up.

As the left side of the face was stuck to the floor, he was able to look at the right side without moving. He gazed, and without getting up, he took mental notes. Everything was black and blurry for him. The room he was in was also shady.

Yash blinked, and the blurriness was gone. He noticed that the only light was coming from somewhere around the back of his head. The room was surrounded by Yash's loud groan as he moved his head up. Feeling the penetrating pain, he moved his head back down, carefully, so he wouldn't get hurt.

Where am I?—what the—I cannot feel my legs—or hands—Aah, my head!

Yash was worrying about his hands and legs. No matter how he struggled, he was not able to move.

I must at least turn myself.

Yash drew some breaths, and particles of wood flew in front of his nose. He tried to turn by moving his torso, but it was hapless. Yash groaned very loudly. He was able to move his fingers and the whole hand. To test his sense, he directed his hand towards his face. He ran his hand over his face. He was now able to feel his legs too. In a push-up motion, he lifted his body. His eyes spun inside his head as he did that.

Yash immediately came into a sitting posture and rubbed his eyebrows and then his head. He opened his eyes, and everything was again dark and blurry.

"Oh!"

Yash's head started to spin. He saw flashes, flashes of him directing his lighter towards the watery floor and then burying his hand inside that dark water and taking out a gold coin.

"What was—"

His head spun again, another flash, and now he was running. He felt his wildly beating heart. He was exhausted and on the verge of giving up still, he paced forwards. Daksh was right in front of him, pacing forward. He felt something huge fly above them.

Yash opened his eyes instantly, he closed them again by force. The throbbing pain was back. He started to roll on the floor, his hands pressed on his head. Then he heard the voice, the penetrating shriek of the crow. It was so clear and uneasy that Yash felt the crow was right in front of him in the present. He saw the flashes of his dark feathers and his blue eye. He again felt that soul-sucking feeling.

Thud!

Yash fell, but he didn't know when he got up on his feet. That pain was insufferable. He screamed and pulled his hair with both hands. He then let his hair free from his grasp as the pain was gone. He was now normal, physically.

"I knew it, I knew it—that place was bad news," said Yash, his hands on his head, his voice shaking with fear.

Yash controlled his heavy breathing, and when that was done, he observed the place he was in. Everything was brighter than earlier. The room aroused negativity in him. He turned his gaze right, there was nothing but a three-foot-sized mirror at the edge where the two walls meet. The room was small and cubical in shape. He looked in front, there was a doorless entrance, and everything was dark behind it. He then observed the light, it was bluish-white. He turned back as the light came from behind him; there was a square window. The thing that made the room glow in bluish-white was the prince of the night. Yash got up on his feet and gazed out of the window. The Moon was reflecting its light graciously.

Yash was surprised by the size of the Moon. It was as if he jumped out of the window, and ran a few meters, and he might be able to touch the Moon. He dragged his eyes away from the Moon and looked around. It was just plain land, with meadows shining with moonlight.

Yash turned as he heard a sound coming from the other side of the entrance. It was as if someone or something had fallen down. Yash didn't move for a second. He did after a second. He walked slowly towards the entrance and peeked his head out. The corridor stretched towards the left. At the end of the corridor, he saw stairs going down. The same bluish-white light was coming from another room ahead, indicating two more rooms. Yash felt a certain nostalgia observing the corridor.

"Somebody there—please help!"

The voice came from downstairs, its volume low as it reached the last room from which Yash was peeking. Yash heard that voice, and he didn't know what he felt—anxious or joy?

"Mahir!"

Yash came out into the corridor at once. The corridor was narrow, and he walked forward. Another room to his left emitted a bluish light. Yash stood at the starting step of the stairs, which had no side support.

Was it really Mahir? The voice was clear, but what if it wasn't him?

Somebody groaned in pain, and Yash shuddered. The voice came from downstairs. He started to walk down the stairs, breathing heavily. Peeking out when on the last stair, he saw the stairs turning. They led him to a corridor identical to the one he came from. Yash walked down those stairs, and the corridor was lit up by the moonlight from the three rooms - two on the right and one on his left. They were identical with doorless entrances. The left one was closest, and the groaning sound emanated from there. Yash hesitated, but he walked towards the room anyway.

"Mahir!" cried Yash.

Mahir lay flat on the floor on his back, hands covering his face, mainly his head. He rocked left and right in pain.

Yash instantly came close and kneeled down to Mahir's left.

"Mahir...oh-God!"

Yash placed his hand on his chest. Mahir was screaming from behind his hands.

"It—the pain will go away—h-hang in there, Mahir."

Mahir stopped moving after some struggle. He moved his hands away from his face. Slowly, he opened his eyes. He looked up at the ceiling. Mahir's eyes then met Yash's, and for a second, he was just staring at him.

"Y-Yash, is that really you?"

"Yes- yes, Mahir."

Yash helped Mahir to get into a sitting position.

"You were right—you were right, Yash," Said Mahir, tears flowing down from his eyes. "You warned us about that place, still we...and that—that c-crow, my God, I—"

"It's okay, it's okay, Mahir," said Yash, placing his hand on his shoulder.

Yash hugged Mahir, and Mahir sobbed on his shoulder. Yash patted him on his back. After that, they observed the room, it was the same cubical, with moonlight coming from the window.

"Wait a minute," said Yash, surprised.

"What?"

"This room is on the left, the room I was in...right," he said with a puzzled expression. "How is the moon on both sides?"

Mahir observed the room, too.

"Why does this place seem oddly familiar to me?" asked Mahir.

"I know, right, the same feeling here," said Yash.

Mahir and Yash got up on their feet. They walked out of the room to the corridor.

"Oh-dear!"

"What?" asked Yash.

"This—we are in the Dodgy house."

Yash stared at Mahir with his eyes wide open. He didn't believe it for a second, but then reality slapped him.

"No way, we can't be in that place," said Yash in denial.

"Look around, Yash, this is the first floor."

Yash looked around weakly, finally having to accept that they were in that abandoned building.

"How the hell did we get here?"

"That blue-eyed crow, I knew it—we had touched something dark, something opposite of divine," answered Yash.

"Let's get out of here," said Mahir quickly.

Yash and Mahir started to walk downwards from those stairs towards the ground floor. Mahir was walking in front. Yash's expression clearly showed his dislike for this place.

"Dear God!"

Both were now standing on the second last step of the staircase. The problem was everything in front of them was dark. The whole area was pitch black, just like a bottomless chasm, identical to the almighty space without stars. Yash shuddered when he saw that.

"Let's go back up...we will jump out of the window," said Yash.

"O, just like that time when we jumped out when Oviya got mad at us and threw that geometric rounder at us," said Mahir, rather seriously.

"She sure gets mad a lot."

They both started to climb back those stairs.

"I am sorry I didn't listen to you back there," said Mahir, regretfully.

"There is nothing to worry about," said Yash. "I found that hellish place, and I must be the one to say sorry."

They came in front of the corridor.

"Hey, isn't it weird that the moonlight is coming from both sides?" said Mahir.

Yash looked at him, he exhaled as he realized that Mahir didn't pay attention when he was talking back there in the room.

"This place has been dodgy all along," said Yash. "Now, it is combined with something we cannot comprehend, my feelings...this isn't the real dodgy place. We are in something much darker."

"Wow, you professors always know stuff like this, eh."

They turned left and went inside the room where Yash found Mahir. They stood there for a second in front of the window.

"You know why I call Oviya Moody?" said Mahir. "It is because of that incident. If we didn't jump out of the window, that geometric rounder must have passed through my heart—or yours."

Yash laughed softly as he walked forward towards the window. He saw the ground, which was not that below from the window. He turned to look at Mahir.

"You go first," said Mahir quickly.

"What? Argh, fine—I don't like this place anyway."

Saying that, Yash put his right foot on the periphery of the window. He hesitated to jump, he looked back at Mahir. Mahir smiled and gestured to him with a thumbs up. Yash shook his head and looked front, he looked at Moon. Just like that, he jumped.

Mahir ran forward and moved his head out of the window. He looked down.

"What the f—"

There was no one on the ground below. It was as it is. Mahir looked completely puzzled. Suddenly, there was a loud Bang, and Mahir turned. He was terrified.

"HOW THE HELL..."

Mahir recognized it was Yash. He ran outside the room into the corridor. Yash showed his face from the very last room, on the right side.

"What—how—are you...?" said Mahir.

Yash walked slowly towards Mahir. He was out of words, and he stared blankly at Mahir.

"Are—we trapped?" asked Mahir in a terrified tone.

"I don't know," Answered Yash, honestly.

They turned their gaze to the right, Yash to the left as he was in front of Mahir, in the room. Yash's expression was hopeless about the fact that this room's window would help them escape.

"As per my memory—that room is the biggest, right?"

Yash nodded in response. They both went inside the room, passing the doorless entrance. Mahir was right. This room was bigger. It stretched towards the left, forming a rectangle that was unlike the square shape of others.

The window was a little towards the left and not directly in front of the entrance. They walked towards it. Yash observed that the right side of the room was completely dark. They came in front of the window. It had the same view of the Moon and the meadowland.

"This was the room where we made the plan for this trip, right?" asked Yash.

"Yep," Answered Mahir.

"Now you go first, I felt sick when I popped into another room."

Mahir opened his mouth to argue—

"Gggrrrhh !"

It was not Mahir; the voice came from the right, where the darkness flowed through their bones with that inhumane sound.

Chapter 17

The Quiet City

When, in that state, Aryan opened his eyes, he found himself flat on the floor, his nose nearly touching the ground. Slowly, he pushed himself up and sat down on his knees, feeling a slow ache in his head. He shook his head to clear his thoughts and took in his surroundings.

Directly in front of him was a glass window with a balcony beyond. Aryan gazed at it, realizing that the room he was in was at a considerable height. He then looked down at the floor and noticed shattered glass scattered everywhere. Turning left, he saw a brown couch just a step away from him, dirty and stained with various liquids. Glancing back at the window, he felt the warmth streaming in.

Aryan got up on his feet and turned. The view in front of him made him squeak. The room stretched forward, and it didn't take Aryan even a second to realize that he was in a high-priced apartment. The walls were ocher in color, and the ceiling looked like the owner must have invested millions in it. From the coffee table to everything that must have been fine glass art was broken. Objects that were not shattered into pieces were furniture.

Where is Daksh?

Aryan began to walk forward, crushing many pieces of glass under his footsteps. He turned his neck here and there, observing details like a rectangular-shaped tan on the wall, which Aryan guessed must be the television. As he walked ahead, the room appeared to be quite spacious.

This might be the living room.

Continuing forward, he spotted a door. To his horror, the door was half broken from the top, allowing him to see a flickering light behind it and a metallic surface or something. He turned his head left and saw an entrance.

"Might lead me to the bedroom or kit—"

Aryan felt something below his feet, and he slowly looked down.

"Daksh!"

Daksh was laid flat on the floor. His face looked like he was in a deep, peaceful slumber. His legs and hands were both spread at the sides as if he wanted to conquer the place. Aryan gently lifted Daksh's legs from his hands, then went on his knees and started patting on his cheeks.

"Daksh—Daksh…Wake up!"

"Hmmm."

With a last hard blow on his cheek, Daksh finally woke up from his peaceful sleep. Aryan helped him into a sitting position. Daksh didn't speak a word for a minute. He inhaled and then exhaled, looking up at the ceiling where a broken chandelier dangled from a hook. Then, he fixed his gaze on Aryan, who gave him a smile.

"YOU STUPID TWO-LEGGED ANIMAL!" cried Daksh, taking hold of Aryan's collar.

"What are you doing?"

"Give in? *Give in?*" said Daksh, outraged, shaking Aryan back and forth. "Give in my butt! Do you have any idea how badly I got twisted in that horrific tornado—because of your stupid oooo..."

Daksh turned his face to the right with a disgusting *Blaargh. He* puked all his inside out.

"Oh my God!" said Aryan, backing off.

Daksh looked up, panting, and fixed his gaze again at Aryan.

"Don't you dare give me that tone," said Daksh waspishly. "This happened because of you and your oolluuu..."

Daksh turned his face again and puked with loud, groaning noises. Aryan, unwillingly, came forward and patted on his back.

"There-there, take it all out."

Daksh lifted his head again, slapping Aryan's hand away from him.

"Feeling better?" asked Aryan, caringly.

"Ehhh, all that sandwich came out!" said Daksh, looking directly at what came out of him.

"Er, Daksh, you still have... vomit on your lips," said Aryan, trying not to screw up his face.

Daksh looked around, to his right, beside where he emptied his stomach, was a table. On that table, there was a piece of cloth, definitely not a napkin, more like a rug. He took it and wiped his face with it.

"God, you are nasty!" remarked Aryan.

Together, they got on their feet and faced the half-broken door.

"Woah! Did you eat the rest?" said Daksh, amusingly.

Aryan was in no mood to reply or snap. He pushed Daksh aside and went first towards the door. Aryan opened the half-broken door, and the door completely came off the wall, hitting the floor with a loud noise. Daksh came and patted on his back as if showing pride.

They were in the building corridor; the light above was indeed flickering. There was no place where sunlight could come in. To their left, they saw endless stairs going downwards and up. The metal wall Aryan saw was an elevator door.

Aryan and Daksh sighed in relief when the door opened, and they walked inside the elevator.

Apparently, they were on the eleventh floor. The elevator helped them reach the ground, and all along, it was a smooth ride. They came out of the building; the hallway was made of marble floors, and the walls had some paintings, which now looked like somebody had purposely destroyed them. Aryan knew that this building was decorous. The gate was broken, so they passed it and came onto the street.

The street was oddly quiet, but they shared a look and started to walk in silence. Their bodies were attentive after seeing all those broken things, they knew something terrible was waiting for them. The road was clean, not a single soul—apart from them—was there. So, instead of walking on footpaths, they were walking right in the middle of the road.

There was no sound at all; Aryan guessed it must be because it is siesta hours. No vehicles were to be found zooming on this clean, long road. On both sides, there were tall buildings.

Aryan turned his gaze front, gazing at those buildings. Looking at those buildings, he felt a strange feeling. Up ahead, Aryan saw that the road they were walking on was forming a "T" shape. The sun was at the top, spreading its burning gaze.

They kept walking forward. And at last, the time came to turn, either right or left. Before they were able to decide or think about it, the view upfront staggered them.

"Are we in—"

"Mumbai."

To their front, passing the road, was the ocean. Aryan and Daksh took the left and were now overlooking the concrete jungle. The buildings here were so high that they touched the clouds.

"Not just Mumbai," said Aryan, gazing around, "we are in...South Mumbai."

Daksh showed his agreement by nodding. Without any further words, they started to walk straight.

"There's something strange about this place," said Daksh suspiciously. "There is something here that makes me feel that we are not in South Mumbai."

"The traffic and people, Daksh," said Aryan. "I mean, look around...there is no one here apart from us. I mean, look at the road we are walking on. This is the highway. I remember getting trapped in traffic for hours on this very road."

"And the cacophony of people walking on the street, teenagers bragging about the place they're walking...this is indeed strange."

"Something is definitely wrong here," said Aryan, expressing his fear.

The rays of the sun had been pacified by charming breezes coming from the ocean to their right. Aryan and Daksh kept walking forward. Not even for a second did they let themselves relax. Here and there, they were able to see high-priced shops. Then, of course, those sky-touching buildings, the rent of which was so unaffordable that one could buy a house somewhere else.

That feeling of uneasiness never left them. It was a boon and a curse. Aryan remembered coming here with his beloved wife. He laughed softly as he recalled the fact about how both of them got annoyed stuck in the traffic.

The road ahead was turning left, and both of them were still walking in the middle of the road. If it were a normal day, they might now be at the bottom of some high-priced vehicle.

"Oh my, look over there," said Daksh, turning his body to the left.

Aryan turned to match his gaze with Daksh. He saw the road was turning in an arc towards the right. Although Daksh wasn't looking over there, he had his eyes fixed on a lavish car showroom. It had its shutters down, but one could clearly see the entrance door open.

"What are you planning?" asked Aryan skeptically, looking at Daksh.

"Nothing, I swear I am planning nothing…let's just go over there and have a look," lied Daksh.

Aryan sighed, closing his eyes. He prepared a lecture to snap on Daksh. He opened his eyes and saw Daksh running towards the car showroom.

"HEY, WAIT FOR ME."

The showroom was shady from the inside. It did not present the lavish environment when they got inside. At the entrance, there was supposed to be a sliding glass door, which was shattered in pieces on the ground. It was dark inside, but still, they were able to see some area of it as there were windows up on the wall, and sunlight was passing inside from those. The area was wide, and it had no stairs or additional floors.

"OH, COME ON!" said Daksh in disappointment.

The showroom was empty and clean, with no cars, and not even a tire was to be found. Aryan came in shortly. He walked towards Daksh and stood beside him. Aryan himself was disappointed a little to see the showroom empty.

"Come on, Daksh, we must not stay in one place for long," said Aryan. "Besides, if there were any cars here—what—are you planning to steal them?"

"That is the exact thing I was planning to do," said Daksh, turning to face Aryan.

Aryan heaved a sigh.

"Aryan...we are in the Hoax."

This macabre information Aryan was oblivious of. That this world is the Hoax. Aryan's expression changed into a tense look.

How in the hell did I forget that? Oh Lord, how can I be such an ignorant? What has got into me?

Daksh came close and tapped on Aryan's shoulder, bringing Aryan back into reality.

"It is OKAY," said Daksh, pacifyingly. "Even I was unaware...until now."

Aryan nodded, giving a smile to Daksh. They did not exit the showroom. They stayed there and observed some more. Aryan examined those white walls and, at the far end, towards the left, spotted stairs leading to the sitting area of the showroom.

That must be the booking area.

Aryan then turned right. There were wide spaces over there, in walls closed down by shutter walls. Aryan confirmed his thought that this might be the area where those high-priced cars were put on display. The shutters get opened, and the passersby will fix their greedy looks on these cars. Close by, he saw a lever right beside the closed shutter. Because of that thing, the shutter could be opened. He observed some more areas to the right, then turned back to where Daksh was standing. Aryan's right eye got teased by some reflection, and he instantly, as a reflex, turned to look.

"Daksh!" called out Aryan slowly.

Daksh came quickly and looked in the direction where Aryan had his finger pointed.

A minute later, something happened, and the shutter got dragged up, and A breathtaking black convertible car with a red strip in between came roaring out. Her body reflected the shine of the sun.

"Woo-hoo!" screamed Daksh joyfully.

Aryan was the one driving the beauty. Her engine roared like a fearless tigress. The blow of winds teased their hair as there was no roof on the car.

"What a smooth thing!"

Aryan's hands were trembling with joy. He had never driven such a lavish car. The way this smooth beauty was gliding on the road made them dance with excitement.

"Huh-ha! I knew it—I knew it—that we were going to find something in that showroom," said Daksh.

Daksh went up on his feet and spread his hands like a free bird, enjoying what the Hoax had given them. Daksh's face leaned back with the force of the wind, which he didn't mind.

They zoomed left and right on the road carelessly. The sound of the engine was the only thing echoing in the air, except the momentary beaming of Aryan and Daksh. As they were the only ones with a vehicle and the only people around, they didn't stop their—stolen—car at any point.

It was a blissful time to drive such a smooth car and without even traffic. There was nothing in this quiet city to stop their voyage. Aryan saw that the road ahead was a four-way. He decided to take a left.

While turning the steering wheel, he slowed down and had a good look to the right.

"What the hell!" said Aryan, horrified. He even stopped the car.

Daksh almost hit his head at the front, but his hands saved him by bringing them forward.

"You idiot. I almost died—"

Daksh stopped abruptly as he saw towards the ocean. There, in the middle of the ocean, was a sea link that connected the land of South Mumbai. The problem was the bridge was broken in the middle of the ocean. Only a small part of it was visible, it was a terrible view to look at.

"This isn't real, Aryan," said Aryan out loud to himself.

"Nuh-uh, not real—it is a hoax—a le-level...*Drive the damn car.*"

The engine roared again, and they paced up front, taking the left. They maintained the speed so they were far away from the bridge. As they took a left turn, it was already behind them, just like the ocean.

Now they were surrounded by corporate buildings, just like other areas, this was also dessert-like. Despite being the most visited area by tourists, the place was quiet. Aryan noticed that Daksh was singing a song, and *the world was sleeping.*

"Somebody is in a good mood," said Aryan.

"Sorry?"

I said, "somebody is in a good mood that is why you're singing, right?"

Daksh didn't answer, he exhaled and turned his face towards the left. His eyes saw many apparel shops, more showrooms, and a building he did not know what it was for.

"Can I ask you a question?" said Daksh, facing Aryan.

Aryan was so about to give an amusing or sarcastic reply for it. But seeing the gravity in his tone, he chose otherwise.

"Yes, Daksh," said Aryan, looking ahead at the road.

Daksh waited for a second, although he kept his eyes fixed on Aryan.

"You and I both know that this is the Hoax," began Daksh, "but still...looking at that bridge, seeing this, not even a single person on these streets of Mumbai. This shuddered my spine—hell, it was still shaking badly. My question to you is...how—how are you Okay with this and moving-on on this stupid, void road? I mean, we are in a *different* world...doesn't it sound ludicrous to you? Doesn't it seem like someone is playing tricks on us? How in the name of the world is this happening?"

Aryan stayed silent. He did not see that coming from Daksh. He believed for a second that Daksh was about to tell him a joke or something about girls. Aryan stayed quiet, battling his own thoughts. He also wondered that the fact they are in a different world indeed sounded farcical. Finally, he gave up the thought of fabricating his reply for Daksh, and he spoke about what he really felt.

"The thought is, Daksh, that I am not OKAY with this, not comfortable at all. It is like my worst of the worst nightmare is moving in front of me. Ever since this all started, I am avoiding closing my eyes. Why? Because whenever I do, I see Ekta crying or crying in rage. It is a horrific-horrific view to look at. I have to use a totally different will to keep myself together; otherwise, I am as good as dead—"

Daksh was listening keenly to what Aryan had to say, he watched him changing his emotions.

"—And yes, I know all this about a *different* world sounds ludicrous, I don't believe it either. Although, I am now."

"And why is that?"

"Why? Look around, Daksh. Just observe where we are. I mean, since the beginning, have you ever seen Mumbai this empty, without people? Have you ever seen or read in a book that the sea-link bridge broke in the middle of the ocean? If we all seven put together our yearly income, I think we might only be able to afford the down payment on the car we are driving right now. My mind didn't believe a word of what Aigile said, but now it is. We have to find the gold we stole. Then find the rest of ours and get out of this nightmare."

Aryan looked ahead and focused on his driving. He was smiling, adoring the fact that, given the situation, Daksh was incisive instead of inane. Buildings here were shining, reflecting light from their glass-finished outer body. Hearing no sound, except their car's engine, gave them the feeling that something bad was covert somewhere, and at any moment, it would show itself as a surprise.

"I didn't want to bring that up," said Daksh, slowly speaking his thought.

"I am glad you did," said Aryan reassuringly.

They both gave each other a warm smile. Aryan had no idea where he was heading. As the car was smooth and had enough gas, he didn't mind just hanging around. Aryan looked at Daksh as there a sound came.

"What was that?"

"Oh…it was my stomach."

"You are not going to projectile again, are you?"

"NO."

Daksh turned his face. Aryan knew Daksh was hungry. He drove the car forward and took a right. Aryan, ahead, could see a shop where the road was turning right. The shop was at the corner.

"Hey, look, it is a café."

The café was at the corner, covering the area in an L shape. Aryan slowed down the car and started to park it at the corner.

"What the hell is wrong with you?" barked Daksh.

"What?"

"You are giving an indicator and parking in the corner. Aryan, there is *nobody* around."

"Sorry—old habit—God."

Aryan parked the car right where the road was turning right. It completely blocked the road. If someone else was around, there would be a smooth curse word quarrel.

Together, they exited the car and walked towards the café. As they noticed earlier, the café was in an L shape. It came as a great surprise that the glass walls of the café were not shattered, although they had many cracks. Besides the entrance, on the glass wall, there was a sort of spider's net structure.

Daksh went in first by pushing the door inside. Aryan followed him. The view inside the café was ironic compared to what they saw outside. It was like a war was practiced here. Tables and chairs were broken on the floor, and not a single piece of furniture had minimum damage. As they walked a step forward, they noticed cups and glasses were also shattered on the floor.

Aryan noticed the walls. They were blue with many stains and splashes here and there. He turned his gaze front, and he saw the counter. The wall behind the counter was painted yellow, perfectly matching the other walls. Behind the counter, the shelf was empty. Aryan had no hope when he stopped the car to find any food. He cursed his own will for being right.

Daksh's face turned red with anger. He said each word by kicking broken tables and chairs in front of him.

"I—hate—this—stupid—place."

Aryan knew this was coming. Hunger always turns people impatient, let alone Daksh, who has a tenuous line of patience.

"Stop...stop it," said Aryan.

Aryan walked close to him and hit hard at his spine. Daksh moved forward with the blow.

"What was that for?" said Daksh, sullenly, rubbing his back.

"We should spread out and search for some food. You go over there behind the counter. I will search somewhere around here."

It was a hapless thing to do. Aryan knew that clearly, but he wanted to play against his own will. Daksh sniffed, giving a cold look to Aryan. He walked towards the counter.

Aryan turned and observed the place keenly, hoping he might get some answers about why there were no people around. His eyes went on a board at his front wall. The board was supposed to have listed the specials or some reviews of customers. Now, there was only random scribblingif,e someone had closed his eyes and tried to write something.

What a jolly place this might have been.

Aryan turned, and his footsteps crushed some glass below, towards the counter. Daksh wasn't there.

"Daksh...Daksh."

Aryan walked forward and came behind the counter. It was a disaster here. Those cups and glasses which were supposed to be on the shelf were lying on the floor. The floor was completely hidden behind those broken mugs. Aryan was thankful that he was wearing boots. There were many shelves down the platform. Aryan opened them to see whether or not Daksh was hiding behind them, he was not.

He got back up and observed that the further way was turning left. His instincts were telling him not to go over there. Boldly, he started walking, and he took a left turn. Instantly, there was a door; he pushed it and went inside.

It was the back alley of the café. Right in front of him were four huge dustbins. The alley was narrow compared to the roads. Aryan screwed up his face as he smelled something very bad, and he heard a very unpleasant sound. He turned right as the noise came from there.

"There you—"

To the right, Daksh was standing, rigid like a statue. Aryan stopped as he saw from behind Daksh's shoulder what he was looking at. Aryan added one more view to his *Never-Will-I-ever-forget-this* memory. There was a massive bull weighing about tons; his tail was facing them. The bull's head was turned right, and Aryan saw something dangling from his mouth. He didn't want to focus, but he did. It was like an internal organ. The bull bent his head down again, that unpleasant sound, and the bull got back up with blood all over his mouth.

Aryan grabbed Daksh by his back jacket collar. He dragged him back inside the cafeteria, pushing the door slowly.

"Did you—did you see that?" said Daksh as they got safely back to the counter of the café.

"Yes."

"That bull was eating a man." Screamed Daksh.

"Sshh, no, that bull was not eating a man," said Aryan confidently. "I saw the legs of it, it was not human."

Daksh closed his eyes and sighed.

"We have to get out of here," said Aryan.

Daksh nodded. They both ran out of the cafeteria and got inside the car.

"Wait-wait, hold on," said Daksh, grabbing Aryan's hand to stop him. "What if we start the car, and because of the roar of the engine, that—that bull will get alert and attack us."

Aryan immediately took off his hands from the steering wheel.

"Let's go over there," said Daksh, pointing at the building on the opposite the café.

"You are right. That building is right in front of the alley. We will stay there, at the window, until that bull goes away."

Hence, they exited the car and ran towards that sky-touching corporate building.

Chapter 18

Action in the Moonlight

Mahir"s face was fully exposed to the moonlight coming from his left through the window. Yash was to his right, his face from the nose up shrouded in darkness. Both of them faced the side from where the angry grunt emanated.

As the only light in the room poured through the window, darkness clung to the corners. The grunting noise persisted from the right side of the entrance. Hearing the inhuman voice, Yash and Mahir tensed.

"Wh—what was that?"

"How would I know?" replied Yash.

Eyes fixed on the corner from where the noise emanated, they began moving backwards, step by step, to the left side of the entrance where the room stretched. It seemed like both of them had forgotten how to blink.

"Grrr!"

Yash and Mahir jumped, letting out a squeak. The noise sent shivers down their spines. They continued moving backwards, Yash lagging half a step behind Mahir.

Yash halted, causing Mahir to nearly stumble into him. Mahir turned back to see why Yash had stopped. Complete darkness now loomed behind them, the light unable to reach. They quickly shifted their gaze forward. Both of them ceased breathing as they saw a figure emerging from the corner. Yash closed his eyes, praying.

The figure emerged into the light, positioned in front of the window. Yash cautiously opened his eyes and saw a large, brown-furred dog. Its black eyes locked onto them, its size nearly that of a wolf. There was nothing friendly about the dog's appearance.

Both of them remained motionless, staring at the formidable canine. Yash felt a change in his heartbeat as the dog revealed its sharp, pointy teeth, which were capable of breaking through wood. The dog emitted a soft growl, followed by a bark. Yash and Mahir jumped in fear, their bodies trembling at the thought of the dog's savage bite. Yash took a step back—

"Don't make sudden movements," cautioned Mahir, never taking his eyes off the dog. "Trust me, I've escaped from many street dogs. I have to warn you, though…they weren't this big."

Yash nodded, he screwed up his face into *why-in-the-name-of-God*. Yash then gave an angry look to the dog, which responded with a loud bark.

Controlling their heavy breaths and taking slow, low steps, both of them started to move back a step.

"Don't you think we should head for the entrance?" said Yash.

Mahir nodded. Both of them had not taken their eyes off the dog. They started to move right, keeping their bodies facing the dog. Both of them stopped as the dog started to move, too. To their bad luck, the dog stood right in front of the entrance.

"Dog is right in front of the entrance!"

"Yes, Yash, I can see that."

They moved backwards and stood right beside the window.

"Jump out of the window; we will be in the next room," said Yash.

"Yeah, that is a—"

"Oh God!"

In a blink of an eye, the dog jumped right at them. Yash fell to the right to save himself. Sadly, the dog got Mahir, as he was not that quick. Mahir fell on his back, hitting hard on the floor, with an ear-deafening scream. On top of him was the dog, covering his whole upper body. Yash got up in an instant and came to the back of the dog. Yash grabbed the dog from behind and tried to take him off of Mahir, who was struggling to do the same. It was surely no easy task. The dog got angry, and with his back legs, he kicked Yash. It was not that hard a blow. But then Yash saw the dog turning; he looked at him. Yash froze, not knowing what to do. He shook his head and boldly took a step forward. Yash kicked right below his neck. But the dog was built differently; he pointed his nose down at the floor, and before Yash could make a move, the dog jumped and buried his head right at his stomach. Yash fell a distance away from where the dog showed his menacing face.

Mahir got into a sitting position as the dog went off him. He saw Yash fall with a great blow that shook the whole floor.

"YASH!"

The dog turned to face Mahir. Mahir gritted his teeth and got up on his feet. But by that time, the dog had already made his move. It jumped right at him, making Mahir fall backwards again. The dog's two legs were placed on his chest; where the rest were, he didn't know. Mahir could feel the weight on his chest as if a pair of heavy dumbbells were about to be put on him. At that moment, the dog looked down at him and tried to bury his sharp teeth in his neck. Luckily, Mahir grabbed his mouth at the right time. Mahir screamed in pain as the dog stomped his feet on his chest. The dog was shaking his head to free himself from Mahir's grip, but Mahir was not giving up that easily. He struggled hard to keep his grip competitive. Mahir screamed again as the dog stomped his legs on his chest. Now scared for his life, one more of that jump, and he would be forced to let go. Just like that, the dog would bite off his neck.

Suddenly, Mahir heard a sound as if someone was running heavily towards him. In that very second, the dog cried in pain and was thrown off his chest towards the left side into the darkness.

"Are you okay?"

Mahir looked up and saw Yash holding a thick part of wood, which he had pulled out of some furniture. Yash offered a hand to Mahir, and Mahir got back on his feet.

"Did you see that? That dog tried to kill me."

"Yes, I saw. It almost had me."

They both looked towards the left and saw the dog's tail, stable on the floor.

"Where did you get that stick?" asked Mahir.

"Oh, this. I pulled it off that bench in the corner," said Yash, looking at the place he fell.

Mahir was still panting, and Yash patted him on his back.

"Let's get out of here."

"But where?"

"We can go upstairs," said Yash. "There are three rooms. It will be hard to jump from there... but my gut says that we can get out from one of them."

Yash and Mahir reached the entrance, and Yash went out first. Right then, there was a heavy rumbling noise. Mahir and Yash turned and saw the dog just a split second away from them. Mahir had no time to react. The dog came close to him and sank his teeth into his right foot.

The whole corridor echoed with his agony. Mahir fell down on his bottom. Yash's hand shook, seeing this horror. At the same time, anger flowed through him. He grabbed the wood tightly in his arms, swung his elbows backwards—

"Aaargh!"

Yash put all his anger into that blow. He swung the stick forward and hit the dog right above his eye, on his forehead. The dog cried in pain and went motionless right there on the floor.

Mahir kicked the dog with his left foot, and his right leg got free from its teeth.

"Go-go-go."

Yash passed the wood to Mahir. Yash then came back and passed his hands from Mahir's armpits, starting to drag him backwards.

The stairs were not that far; Yash started climbing one step at a time carefully. He had lifted Mahir a couple of inches. Yash kept looking backwards, and checking the steps. On his front, he was dragging Mahir.

"That looks bad," said Yash, looking at Mahir's right leg.

"Hmmrrgh,"

The air was stinging his injured feet.

Yash noticed the smell of blood but didn't say anything. He continued dragging Mahir up the stairs. It took all his power to do that, as Mahir was heavier than himself.

At last, they were on the second storey. Mahir was holding the wood firmly. It was a clever strategy, as Mahir was facing forward, and if the dog came back, Mahir would hit him with the stick while Yash would continue dragging him backwards.

"Go to the last room," said Mahir. "That way, we will have some time if that bastard creature ever comes up."

Yash agreed, and both of them reached the last room. The room in which Yash had opened his eyes. Yash thought, and he helped Mahir move. They both got seated on the right side of the entrance. Just beside the entrance was Mahir, to his right was Yash.

"Good thinking; this way, we would be able to hear him coming without exposing us," said Mahir, looking at Yash.

"Let me have a look at your wound."

Mahir rolled up his jeans. It stung, and he let out a soft groan. Right above his ankle, behind the arch of his right leg, below the calf, there were teeth marks. Blood was flowing profusely out of them. Yash's hand started shaking in his life he had never had to deal with blood.

Yash started to have some negative thoughts. Right then, he raised his right hand and slapped himself hard on the right cheek.

"Good-God! What are you doing?"

Mahir got scared by Yash's sudden reaction. Yash did not answer, and started to rub his face.

"Think, Yash, think," said Yash to himself from behind his hands.

He took off his hands and buried them inside his jeans pocket.

"I am sorry, Mahir, but there is nothing more I can do."

Yash took out his handkerchief and tied it around the wounded part of Mahir's leg. It stung badly, but Mahir stayed quiet. He was in awe of how, like a soldier, Yash was handling the situation.

"Do you have a handkerchief?" asked Yash, looking at Mahir.

"No."

"What man does not keep a handkerchief with himself? Unbelievable," said Yash, disappointed.

Yash started thinking again, as that handkerchief he tied was not stopping the flow of blood completely.

"Your jacket is way too big and thick to tie up on your leg," said Yash. "Oh, I have an idea, although it is going to be disgusting."

"Do whatever you like to stop the bleeding, Yash."

Yash pulled off his full-sleeved t-shirt over his body. He was wearing a white inner, and he took that off, too.

"You have abs?!"

Yash looked at Mahir in a confused sort of way.

"Seriously, is that important right now?"

Yash wore back the t-shirt and rolling his inner, he came close.

"Can't you just pull off your sleeves and tie them around my legs, just like in movies?"

"First of all, this is not a movie. Second, my inner is thick. It will stop the bleeding. Third, I cannot just pull off my sleeves and walk around sleeveless—I will look like a lunatic."

Yash tied the white inner on the wound.

"Thank you for saving my life," said Mahir warmly.

Yash gave him a smile and got up on his feet. He then went to the other side of the room. As he recalled the fact there was a big mirror, he lifted that mirror and put it a somewhat north-east direction from the entrance. Yash walked back towards Mahir and sat beside him.

"Nicely done, Yash."

Surely, Yash did a remarkable job. Now, from where they were seated, they were able to see the corridor.

"If I had access to water, I would have cleaned your wound with it," said Yash, looking nervously at Mahir's feet.

"Shut up, you dragged me all the way to this room. You slapped yourself to come out of panic, which would be way amusing if the day was normal. Although tying your inner on my foot was a bit disgusting, but I think it is doing the work astoundingly."

Mahir slapped Yash hard on his back playfully. He rolled up his jeans up to his knees. There was a big red dot on the cloth tied on his legs, but no blood was flowing down. Yash was looking at the window and noticed the light coming from it.

"Yash, I think I noticed something when we reached this floor."

"What?" said Yash, turning himself completely to face Mahir.

"You know that this floor has three rooms, just like the first floor?"

Yash nodded.

"And there is only one room on the right, at the end of the stairs. That room took my attention. See, the thing is, downstairs, all the rooms were passing that moonlight on the corridor. This room, the one and only on the right, was completely dark. Some odd glow was coming from it."

"So, you think that room is our way out?" asked Yash earnestly.

"It is a long shot, but—"

"It is the risk we have to take."

Both looked ahead and exhaled. Mahir looked at Yash, he was already looking at him. Nodding earnestly, they both got back on their feet. Yash helped Mahir by taking his arm over. His right foot was some inches up from the ground. Suddenly, Yash pulled back Mahir.

"What are you doing?"

Yash, as an answer, pointed at the mirror.

The dog was back on his feet, looking crazier than before. The whole corridor was ringing with his constant groaning.

Mahir looked back at Yash. They quickly swapped their positions, with Yash coming in front and Mahir going back. Yash thought himself lucky, as they were to the right side of the entrance, and the mirror was giving them a clear view of the corridor. The dog was coming close, putting his nose down, sniffing his way. Yash knew that the dog would smell the blood. He grabbed the wood tightly and got into position by already lifting both hands and elbows behind. With that, he could land an even harder blow swiftly.

Their eyes fixed on the mirror. They saw the dog go into the first room on the left. He immediately came out from there.

They stopped breathing, in case it might alert the monster, as the dog appeared bigger in the mirror, indicating he was now close. Yash noticed that the dog was about to turn right and enter. But the dog took a step back and looked right at them, no, he looked at his own reflection in the mirror. Yash and Mahir didn't know what to make of this.

The dog waited for a second, staring at his own reflection. Then he barked angrily. Yash and Mahir trembled. Just then, very unusual, that even beat the term unusual, happened. The dog went back some steps and jumped forward. Yash had already predicted this, and he was ready to land a hard blow. Surprisingly, no one came inside from the entrance. Right then, the mirror shattered, and out came the dog. He landed on the floor, facing them, showing his sharp teeth.

"THIS IS UN-REAL" Screamed Mahir, shocked.

Yash didn't say anything; he grabbed Mahir with his trembling hands and pulled him to his back. Mahir was now behind Yash, eyes fixed on the creature. The dog was not moving forward; he was hesitating, seeing Yash in front. Was it the stick?

"Turn and stick your back against mine," said Yash commandingly. "And start walking towards that room. This bastard is hesitating seeing the stick in my hand...now, move."

Mahir turned and touched his back to Yash's. Mahir forgot his pain; all he cared about was getting to that room. He started walking, his wounded leg touching the floor lightly with each careful step. Yash was also attentive to keep his back touching Mahir's, although he never took his eyes off the dog.

They came out of the room following that same position, and with them came the dog. Mahir was leading the way and was able to see the room on the right. Yash faced the dog, who came close. Yash rolled the stick in the air and then banged it on the floor. This made the dog move back a couple of steps.

Taking each step carefully, Yash felt on his back that Mahir was taking a turn, which meant the room had arrived. He noticed the darkness, something from the back, and the wooden edge of the entrance going above him. They went inside, still with their backs against each other. The dog barked angrily when they entered; he attempted to pound on Yash. But Yash banged the stick again on the floor. The dog stopped but barked angrily, looking at him.

Yash noticed a very odd glow in this room. It was obviously dark, but he was also able to notice some kind of faded yellowish light coming from somewhere. He had a desire to observe the room, but the dog was now barking constantly at him.

"I can see the window. It is right in front of me," said Mahir.

"Now, Mahir, go with all the energy you have and jump through it."

"But what if it does not work? And I am back in some other room?"

"Well, then we have no other choice but to kill this sweet thing," said Yash, again banging the stick.

"Oh boy,"

"Yeah."

"What about you?"

"I am just behind you…on my mark, jump no matter what. Do you understand?"

Mahir hesitated but said, "Yes."

"One…two…GO!"

Yash felt air touching his back as Mahir's back left him. He turned his head, seeing Mahir limping his way towards the moonless window and finally jumping out. Yash looked ahead; the dog tried to grab his stick, but Yash stepped back a few paces. He waited for a second to see if Mahir came out through another window and landed in another room. That didn't happen.

"Ha-ha, it worked," said Yash to himself, happily.

Yash noticed that a faded yellowish glow was coming from the left. He swiftly turned his head in that direction. He did not know whether he felt guilt or happiness; on the left side, hovering in the air, were two gold coins gleaming.

The dog barked and twisted in frustration. Yash turned to look at him. In that second, he thought of a plan.

Yash took a deep breath, closed his eyes for a moment, exhaled, and fixed his gaze on the dog. The dog was outraged. He was constantly jumping and barking. But that wasn't affecting Yash at all, ironically, he was smiling.

"It is just you and me now, you son-of-a-bitch."

At that very moment, Yash grabbed the wood horizontally. The dog stopped barking and made himself face him straight. Yash then threw that stick right at the dog's mouth. The dog caught the stick in his jaw. Yash already made a run towards those gold coins still floating in the air. With his two long hands, he grabbed those gold coins. With his long legs, he turned and ran towards the window. The dog broke the stick in half with his strong jaw and ran after Yash.

It was too late. Yash had already made the jump and was out of sight down the window.

Chapter 19

Tribe of Mumbai

"Look! There he goes!" said Daksh loudly.

Aryan and Daksh both were on the fourth floor of the building. Aryan got the air when they entered that this building might be some huge organization's headquarters. It was now a habit to see soulless and messed-up places. Desks were upside-down, and telephones were laid on the floor broken.

Both were standing in front of the glass wall that overlooked the further Mumbai. It took them some time to find this exact spot. At first, the elevators were not working. That's how they decided to take the stairs. The first three floors were useless as there were many things broken down there, and it was shady. The fourth floor was compatible.

Daksh informed us that as the bull turned and came out of the alley, he started walking away from their car. Aryan sighed in relief and wiped the sweat from his forehead. He looked at his *stolen* car happily. Then, his eyes were directed towards that bull. He was now out of the alley, shook his head, and went right where the road stretched further.

Both of them pressed their noses against the glass wall and observed the bull. They didn't want to take any chances, as the bull was four times bigger than them.

"He is going away," said Aryan, placing his hands on the glass.

"Let's go back to the car," said Daksh, turning.

Aryan turned and again saw those rows of upside-down desks and countless broken things. Everywhere they went, it all looked similar – broken glass and clutter everywhere. Everywhere, the mess was common and looked like a war ground. It was blissful to see that instead of bodies, there were just things broken apart. The office was long-stretched and good-looking if you ignore the mess.

It was common that it took them a minute to reach the stairs from where they came. Right in front of the stairs was some sort of counter, possibly a reception.

"Let's go up," said Daksh, smiling.

"What? Why?" asked Aryan.

"I always wanted to have a view from offices like this, especially in South Mumbai," said Daksh, excitedly.

"You are unbelievable," said Aryan, giving Daksh a bored look. "We have to find those gold coins we stole. Then we have to return them. Then we have to find our friends. And then get out of here. Seriously, Daksh, is this the time to be childish?"

"Please…please…"

Aryan looked away and started to walk towards the stairs going downwards.

"Aryan, Aryan, please… just one floor up, I promise. For the sake of the view," pleaded Daksh.

Aryan turned, and saw Daksh with his hands joined above his head, his eyes watery. They went to the fifth floor. Daksh was hopping with excitement on the stairs.

As they turned to face the office, they were totally unaware of such a view. Here, there was the same situation – rows of desks, a huge office area. Although everything was in place, not even a scratch was on them. Aryan and Daksh shared a look of blank expression and went ahead. The glass wall overlooking Mumbai was further ahead. As they reached there, Daksh did not stop for the view. Instead, he turned and wandered around.

They saw those cubicle areas where employees of the organization do their work, which was to their left. Their hearts almost stopped beating as they turned their gaze right.

"P-p-people!"

To their right was a glass wall, and behind it was a long room that looked like a conference room of the company. In that room, there were people – actual people. In between them was a long, wide table. There were around twenty to thirty people in there, dressed in formal attire, including women. Some were on chairs, while some were on the ground. They did not appear to be conscious.

Aryan and Daksh walked close and stopped when their noses were an inch away from the glass.

"Hello?" said Aryan, gently tapping on the glass.

No response came from those people. Aryan was sure they were alive as he observed the rise and fall of their stomachs.

"HELLO?"

Daksh knocked hard on the glass, the whole fifth floor echoed with that sound, but those people remained motionless.

"This does not look good," said Aryan, facing Daksh.

"What is wrong with them?" said Daksh, looking at those people.

"What if we woke them up... and they jump from their seats and attacked us? I mean, Aigile said there would be challenges," said Aryan anxiously.

"Oh God, I am out of here."

They both ran towards the stairway and paced down until they reached the ground floor. They came out in the open and started to walk towards the car.

"I told you not to go, and yet we went there anyway. Because of you, I added an unhappy scene that I will never forget in my memory. Oh, this will haunt me every night."

Daksh was walking beside Aryan to his right, listening to what Aryan was screaming at him. Daksh grabbed him by his shoulder, and Aryan turned to face him.

"I am sorry, Aryan. I thought going a floor up and looking at the view might turn your mood. Turns out it was horror... why is your face so stiff?"

Indeed, Aryan's face was stiff. He wasn't even looking at Daksh. He was looking behind him, where the road went further and further. Daksh turned, and he saw, right in the middle of the road, some meters away from them, a tall, lean silhouette of a person looking at them.

Daksh slowly turned to Aryan. Aryan looked at him and shrugged his shoulders. They both looked in front of the person.

On this hot afternoon day, a cloud came to save the day. The silhouette darkness went away, and now they were able to see the person. It was a woman, surprisingly tall. Aryan had never seen such a tall woman. Her hair was tied in a bun behind her head. She was wearing a saree in Kshatriya style, which involves Dhoti draped in a pattern above the blouse. Her blouse was ocher in color and her dhoti white. Her skin was dark, and her eyes bloodshot red.

Aryan was scared in some way as he looked at her bloodshot eyes. She took a step forward. Aryan noticed her hands, which were slim but did not appear to be weak.

"I'll go talk to her," said Daksh airily.

"No—hey—wait."

Aryan couldn't stop Daksh. He walked boldly towards her. The woman stayed there, waiting, and she let Daksh approach her. She looked at Aryan, but Aryan had his eyes fixed on Daksh.

Aryan stayed still in his position. Aigile was constantly coming into view in his mind since he saw that woman. He was right. When Daksh got close to her, the woman grabbed him by the neck and lifted him above the ground with one hand. Daksh made a series of choking noises, struggling in the air to free himself from her deadly grip. Finally, he went silent, his hands fell down, which were gripped by that woman's hand, and his body stopped moving.

Aryan was trembling from head to toe. He was only exhaling, not inhaling air. His eyes were fixed on the woman.

What—h-how—this isn't happening.

Aryan wanted his body to move, but he was back in that freezing state, just like the time when he first saw Corbeau.

MOVE BASTARD—your friend is over there—probably—

Aryan cursed himself. He had put so much pressure on his already troubled brain that it got twisted, or perhaps it was due to the sudden, unbearable pain at the back of his head that knocked him out.

He found himself seated on a mat in the park, enjoying the daylight. His legs were stretched forward, left over right. Turning to his left, he saw his beloved Ekta. Her shoulder was touching his, and her face was glowing like the sun's reflection on the water. She turned to look at him, then cupped his face in her gentle hands. Suddenly, she slapped him on his left cheek, and again, and again, and—

Aryan opened his eyes, his left cheek was hot from those hard blows. He closed his eyes again; it was as if he had no power left in him.

"Wake up, you piece of filth."

Aryan heard the voice clearly. It was bold, loud, and rough at the same time. Despite keeping his eyes closed, another hard slap on his left cheek forced him to open them. Initially, everything was blurry, but after another slap, he could see things clearly.

Seated about a hand's distance away from him was a woman on a wooden chair. She was big and wide, with a round face and bloodshot red eyes. Her hair was tied in a bun at the back, and she stared at him with those deadly eyes.

Aryan realized that his hands were tied behind his back, and he was kneeling. As he attempted to bring his hands forward, his legs also lifted, almost hitting the woman's knee. In response, she grabbed his face and pushed him back into the kneeling position. Aryan understood that his hands and legs were tied together in some unknown knot.

"Who are you?" asked the woman in a heavy voice.

However, Aryan was too preoccupied with analyzing the room. Behind the woman was a wall with a small window near the top, seemingly the only source of light. To his right stood a door. As he began to turn left, the woman groaned and slapped him even harder, causing Aryan to cry out in pain as his face fell to the right.

The woman forcefully grabbed Aryan's face with her right hand, giving it a vigorous shake. Aryan screamed, feeling unbearable pain on his left cheek.

"Who are you?"

"A-A-Aryan," panted Aryan.

The woman released his face and leaned back in her chair. After a moment, she leaned forward again, her dark skin glowing as sunlight touched her. Her face was now inches away from Aryan, who breathed heavily with fear.

"How did you wake up?" asked the woman.

Aryan narrowed his eyes with uncertainty. He was clearly puzzled about what the woman asked him. Aryan's attention was constantly going towards his tied hands and legs. In his life, he had never felt such discomfort.

"Aah!"

Aryan screamed in pain as the woman slapped him again. He opened his eyes and looked straight at the woman. He was in rage now, his left cheek burning with pain.

"I DON'T KNOW WHAT YOU ARE TALKING ABOUT," screamed Aryan at her face.

The woman gritted her teeth. Aryan saw her closing her fist, and he knew what was coming to hit him.

"Oooof!"

Aryan smelled his blood. It had escaped from right below his left eye, where the hard part of his face stayed.

"I really—please—I do not know what you are talking about," Aryan pleaded.

The woman raised her fist again and moved backward for momentum.

"Wait—wait—please," begged Aryan pitifully. "I was in that building; I-I accept that. I was there with my friend Daksh. We were finding—"

Memories came back, like how Daksh was grabbed by the neck by that tall woman. He was choked until he stopped moving.

"Finding what?" asked the woman.

"I am not telling you."

He received another punch, landing right above his left eye, where his left eyebrow ended. Blood escaped from that wound. Due to the painful irritation, Aryan wanted to rub that part so badly, but his hands were tied. He shook himself because of this irritation he was feeling. But it was a futile struggle. He looked down and cried. With drops of tears, blood touched the floor. Aryan was confused about why he was crying, because of the pain or because he couldn't help his best friend.

The woman lifted his head up. Aryan opened his eyes and looked at her. She was smiling mercilessly.

"I am not—I am not speaking," said Aryan in rage. "I will not tell you a *shit*—unless you tell me where my friend is."

"What did you say, you *filthy man*?"

She raised her fist again, and Aryan closed his eyes. Her fist swung forward—

"That's enough."

It was a totally new voice. Aryan opened his eyes, the woman was leaning back on her chair. He turned his head left. There she was, that tall woman seated on a chair cross-legged. Aryan's rage piled up as he saw her. She did nothing; just stamped her leg on the floor lightly. Aryan gazed down at her foot. A person was lying on the floor in a prostrate position. His hands were tied at his back along with his legs. It formed a triangle as Daksh's hands were tied back with his legs.

"Is he dead?" said Aryan, looking directly at the tall woman.

"Sadly, no," said the tall woman boringly. "I am not allowed to kill strangers. So, I didn't squeeze that hard."

"Roti, can I hit him now?" asked that other merciless woman.

Roti gave no reply. She was looking, more of scanning, Aryan. And Aryan also had his eyes fixed on her.

"So, tell me, man," said Roti, adding that "man" part as if speaking about a disgusting thing or animal. "What were you searching in that building with this friend of yours?"

"Nothing... actually, we were hiding... hiding from that bull," said Aryan, honestly.

"I knew you were lying," said the woman in front of Aryan.

"How did you wake up?" asked Roti, looking at Aryan.

"I—I—seriously don't know what you mean by "wake up"—wait—I see—I am not one of those persons who we saw lay motionless in the office."

Roti leaned forward; the chair was comparatively small in the case of her tall, lean body. She looked at Aryan.

"This leaves me only one conclusion," said Roti. "That you and your friend here are spies, hired by the men tribe."

Aryan had no clue about what she was talking about. Although he knew he would have to say something otherwise, another opening would be created for blood to flow out from his face.

"I have no idea what you are talking about," said Aryan, trying to keep his voice calm. "Daksh and I, we did something... so Aigile—I am sorry—Corbeau—"

Aryan saw Roti go frozen. Her eyes were fixed on him, not blinking. He turned to look at the woman in front, and she had the same expression.

The woman raised her fist and punched hard on his face. Aryan spat blood on the floor to his right side.

"How dare you say his name!"

"STOP IT," barked Aryan, looking at her. "I am telling you the truth," he looked at Roti, "Daksh and I, including my other friends, tried to steal gold from that *tomb*. Corbeau caught us and cursed us by sending us into his Hoax. I looked into his blue eye." Aryan inhaled some air. "The next thing I knew, I woke up here with my friend Daksh."

He screamed out those words. Aryan tasted his own blood while speaking. He still had his eyes fixed on Roti. Suddenly, Roti looked at the woman who hit Aryan till he bled.

"Praan, go and bring a bucket full of water," commanded Roti. "And also bring Sundra here. He is telling the truth."

"Are you sure about this?" said Praan, doubtfully.

Roti nodded, and Praan got up and went out of the room. Aryan watched her leave. He instantly turned so he could face Roti. After some seconds, Roti got up from her chair and started to walk towards him. A wave of fear curled in Aryan's stomach as Roti took out a sharp, shiny knife from behind her back. She came close and went on her knees, still, she was tall. Aryan's head was facing her flat belly. She bent down, she was so close. Aryan was able to smell her. They both stayed there looking into each other's eyes. She had a scent of blood and forest. It was this time Aryan noticed her eyes; they were indeed bloodshot, but her eyes explained the details he had read in many books about Matsya women. Aryan shook his head as Roti went to his back. To his relief, she was cutting the knot.

Roti walked away and sat back on her chair, which was above Daksh's head. Aryan, with a soft groan, brought his feet forward and stretched them. Roti didn't free his hands. Aryan looked at his left shoulder. His red shirt now had dark stains, he knew it was his blood.

Shortly after Praan arrived, in her left hand was a metal bucket filled with water. Aryan took notice of the clothes she was wearing. Praan was wearing the same Kshatriya draped saree pattern, her blouse was faded orange, and her dhoti was ocher in color. Then Aryan looked at her right hand. There was a little girl, dark, but strong looking. Wearing the same type of clothes. Her hair was tied at her back. Aryan's attention quickly went to her ears. As for earrings, she was wearing a tiny red chain. At the bottom of those chains, like a magnet, were placed those two gold coins, hanging vertically.

"Those are the gold—"

"I know," Interrupted Roti. "Corbeau came to me. He gave me those gold coins, saying a person named Aryan would come looking for them."

Roti went on her feet and walked towards Praan. She took the bucket and walked back towards her chair. She splashed all the water on Daksh's head.

Daksh came into consciousness with heavy breathing noises. Roti grabbed the back of his t-shirt and pulled him up. Daksh came into a kneeling position, just like Aryan was before. He looked here and there empty-mindedly. Then he fixed his eyes on Aryan.

"Aryan, My God! What happened to your face?" said Daksh hurriedly.

Aryan's face, especially the left side, was badly injured. There was a purple patch right below his eye, and from above, where his left eyebrow ended, blood was flowing like tears.

"That's all the confirmation I needed," said Roti from behind Daksh.

Roti cut the knot, and Daksh brought his feet front. Roti walked in front of him.

"YOU!" gasped Daksh. "Did you do this to my friend YOU FILTHY BIT—"

Roti kicked Daksh right in the stomach. Daksh screamed and fell backward.

"Praan, pick these creatures up and follow me," Commanded Roti.

Praan nodded and walked towards Daksh. Aryan was looking at that little girl, Sundra. He was not looking at her earrings but at her. Aryan smiled, and Sundra turned her face away. Shortly came Roti and picked her up, and she walked out of the room.

Praan came and picked up Aryan. She was surely the strong one. Praan was so tall that her neck was the height Aryan was able to reach. In one pull, she picked Aryan up on his feet.

They were almost thrown off from the stairs. Praan was messing a lot with them. Momentarily, Aryan and Daksh shared an anxious look. Praan had grabbed them from behind, clenching Daksh's black t-shirt and Aryan's back shirt collar. Roti was leading the way. She was four stairs in front. Aryan noticed that Roti was even taller than Praan but slim. In her arms was Sundra. Sundra was giving them angry looks from behind Roti's shoulder.

That is how they reached the last step, but the surprise was yet to come. Aryan saw the exit, he heard some movements and noises of people playing and laughing. They came out into the huge compound of the building. Aryan and Daksh were surprised to see more than fifty women walking around. In the middle of the compound was a beautiful fountain. Some women were talking until they arrived. All those women were dressed the same as Roti and Praan.

Aryan turned to look left, and he saw girls similar to Sundar's age playing with a huge tiger, treating it like a dog. His eyes fell on the huge bull they had entered the building to hide from. But that wasn't all; there were many animals, some of the same species, others different. From the corner of his eye, he saw a lioness. The day looked the same as when he got knocked out.

"Are we in the jungle?" asked Daksh, turning right to look at Aryan.

Aryan was still a little uncomfortable with how his hands were tied behind his back, and Praan was pushing them forward like a relationship of rich and peasants.

"Wait a minute," said Daksh, looking down at his chest. "Where is my *denim* jacket?"

"Oh, that thing you were wearing," said Praan. "It is over there."

Daksh looked to his left, and Aryan also turned to look. Two girls and a cub had each end of the jacket in their merci until it tore into two rough pieces. Praan gave a nasty, merciless laugh.

Daksh looked over his shoulders, "You will pay for this, you Giant."

Praan looked down at Daksh, shook him by pulling him towards her, and then pushed him forward constantly.

"Stop—stop—please," begged Daksh when he started to feel uneasy.

Praan stopped shaking him, laughing. Daksh groaned and looked forward. Aryan wanted to speak but thought against it, deciding it was better to keep his mouth shut.

It was normal that every woman and those little girls were giving them angry looks. Aryan's eyes met with some of those women; they had their killer looks on their beautiful faces. Aryan looked forward, and he saw Roti leading them towards the fountain.

There was a change in the environment as the sky turned orange. The sunlight flashed its way between those sky-touching buildings and then landed on the ground. The fountain looked magnificent, and the milieu matched perfectly.

Daksh was sure, as he saw those women coming close and starting to gather behind them, that Roti and Praan were leading them to their sacrificial ceremony.

They arrived at the fountain. Water was flowing slowly and steadily from the top of the statue. Roti put Sundra down. Then she hopped on the periphery of the fountain, facing them and others who were now gathered behind them.

"SISTERS," said Roti, in a gallant voice, "THESE MEN ARE NOT FROM THOSE SLUGGISH, EVIL, MEN TRIBE. THESE MEN ARE NOT THOSE CITY PEOPLE WHO ARE IN DEEP SLUMBER. THESE MEN ARE HERE BECAUSE THEY TRIED TO STEAL FROM CORBEAU—"

There was a loud murmur; Aryan and Daksh kept their heads down.

"BUT...CORBEAU IS A NICE—"

"Yeah! Right!"

Even though Daksh spoke in a low voice, every head turned to him. Daksh's anxiety piled up seeing this; he looked at Aryan. Aryan shook his head constantly. Daksh got what Aryan was trying to express; he gave him a slight nod.

"You have something to say, Slugger?" said Roti, looking down from the periphery.

Daksh's throat constricted; he regretted saying those words. Daksh straightened himself, the back part of the t-shirt still in the merci of Praan, and looked directly at the tall, beautiful figure standing on the periphery of the fountain.

"What I mean is," Daksh started fabricating, "that that blue eye—I mean *Corbeau* is even lovelier. Look at us...he is allowing us a chance to give him back those gold coins we stole. Even though those gold coins are in your possession, and he can take them with just one swing of his dark wings."

"Why do I sense sarcasm in your tone?" said Roti, in slight rage.

Roti jumped down and started to walk towards Daksh. Daksh trembled seeing her approach. He struggled, but Praan looked at him, and he looked at her. Roti came close; Daksh's head was barely reaching her shoulders.

"I apologize for him," said Aryan boldly. "It is not entirely his fault…this is what happens—er—when you live in a city for too long."

Roti looked at Aryan and then at Daksh.

"You *Men* are from the city?" asked Roti.

"Yes, Roti," said Aryan, with a bow.

He was anxious about saying her name directly. He thought Roti might stab him for that. But she didn't react.

"I knew it," said Praan. "Look at their clothes…odd and disgusting."

Aryan quickly looked at Daksh and gave him a cold look.

"Free them," commanded Roti, looking at Praan.

Praan cut the tied ropes and released them from her grasp, too. Daksh rubbed his wrist. Aryan checked on his wounds. The blood was now dry. Although he was able to see tight marks of those ropes on both his wrists.

Roti walked towards Sundra, who was right in front of them. Aryan looked at her and then at her ears. Aryan knew that Roti was not going to give them those gold coins that easily; they certainly had to fight for them. But there is no way he would do anything to hurt this little girl. Aryan sighed in relief when he saw Sundra taking off those earrings and placing them in Roti's palm.

Roti turned, and she was now face to face with Aryan. She untangled her hair. Seeing her hair flowing like the almighty Ganga from the top of the Himalayas, her hair went below her waist. Her dark hair matched with her bold personality. The orange sun put a glow on her visage as she looked up at the sky. Aryan was oblivious to her beauty;

he muttered "beautiful" under his breath. Aryan turned his gaze instantly as Roti looked directly at him.

Aryan looked at her again, but not in the same way as before. He saw Roti placing her fingers behind her red lips and then blowing some air out in the form of a high-pitched whistle. At that same time, the land beneath them shuddered, and there were heavy rumbling noises. The bull they were hiding from earlier came between Aryan and Roti. Aryan's body started shaking as he saw that bull closely again. The bull was so massive Aryan thought he could fit comfortably inside its stomach.

Aryan blinked as Daksh came in front of him, facing Roti.

"C-c-can I say something?" asked Daksh, raising his hand up.

Roti looked at him coolly while stroking the bull. The bull was acting like a rejoiced dog in front of her.

"OK...I know it is going to be hopeless to say this," said Daksh, standing two steps away from the bull, "but why go through all this trouble? J-just give us the gold coins, and we will never show our filthy faces to you, noblewoman. I give my word I will not speak of this with Corbeau, I swear."

The whole Mumbai roared with the laughter of those women; even Praan laughed heartfully, patting herself on the lap. Most of the laughs were like evildoers.

"I like the idea—but NO," said Roti, stroking the bull.

"S-S-So—so what...we—we have to fight this bull?"

"Yes," said Roti, looking at Daksh, smiling.

Daksh placed his hand on Aryan's shoulder. Aryan knew what was about to happen now. And like before, he proved himself right, unwillingly.

Roti plucked out some of her hair strands and tied those earrings on the bull's horns each.

Aryan and Daksh started to walk backwards, away from the bull, while keeping their eyes on him. They kept moving backward suddenly, their back hit something. Aryan thought it might be a wall or something. They turned together and saw Praan looking at them with her notorious smile. Aryan and Daksh shared a look of terror.

"MOOO!"

Aryan and Daksh turned and saw the bull was now facing them. Praan patted hard on their back, saying, "Hope you die!" and jumped towards the right. All those women who were gathered behind them were now moving to the corner.

"Why—why in the name of me we had that need to enter that forsaken — tomb..." said Daksh, regrettably.

Aryan had his eyes fixed on the bull. He thought of a plan so quickly that even he was impressed with himself.

"Shut up!" snarled Aryan, looking at Daksh. He looked back to the front. "I have a plan. At first, we will run right towards that fountain...I am sure the gate is somewhere nearby. Once we find the gate, we will find the car and hit the bull with it."

"What if we fail?"

"Then we will surely get eaten."

"Hai Shiv!"

"Do not run until I tell you to."

"WHAT?"

They had no time as Roti tapped on the bull's back. The bull charged right at them, the land trembled with his heavy footsteps.

"ARYAN, HE IS COMING CLOSE!"

Aryan didn't answer. He was busy looking at the bull. The bull came closer, and his horns were a couple of inches away. Just then, Aryan pushed Daksh away, and the bull passed between them. Aryan fell towards the right, Daksh towards the left. Just behind them, women lined up, they took a step back as they fell.

Aryan and Daksh instantly got up on their feet. The fountain was now at their back.

"The gate is a couple of distances away from the fountain," said Daksh.

Aryan nodded, inhaling some air, and got himself ready to run. They saw the bull shaking his head, blowing out some air facing them. Together, with no other thoughts, they showed their backs to the bull and ran like athletes running for their lives. Aryan knew that the bull had begun to chase them as his heavy footsteps echoed in the area. He saw those women laughing, enjoying themselves. Aryan brought back his focus and looked straight at the fountain. He looked to the left. Daksh was matching his pace with him, his eyes fixed on the fountain. Daksh was just a hand's distance away from Aryan.

They ran towards Roti as she was still in front of the fountain. Aryan thought she would take out her sword or knife, but she stayed still. They passed behind her. Aryan went to the right, while Daksh passed from her left. Both of them jumped on the periphery of the fountain, Daksh on the left, Aryan on the right, and walked on it to the other side. They jumped down as the circle met.

The rumbling got close; Aryan turned his head backwards without slowing down. He saw Roti bending down, and in a whoosh, she jumped so high that the bull passed from below her and banged himself straight on the fountain. The bull broke the fountain right from where it was pouring water down. The bull jumped out of the fountain, and with an angry "Moo," he ran after them. Aryan turned his gaze front.

"CURSE YOU BASTARDS!"

Aryan recognized it was Praan, and she might have fallen in love with that fountain.

"There! There is the gate."

Daksh was right, and the gate was right in front of them, a couple of meters away. They reached the gate it was wide, and tall. Daksh kicked it, it swung forwards, and both of them passed behind it and shut it back.

They were now back on the quiet roads of Mumbai.

"Where did we park the car?" asked Daksh.

The area was completely foreign to them. It was winding left and right. They walked and stood in the middle of the road, which was sandwiched between rows of buildings, just like before.

BANG

There was a loud sound of metal falling hard on the road. They looked to their right and saw that it was the bull's doing.

"RUN!"

Aryan paced forwards, and so did Daksh. They had no idea where they were running towards. They just kept running straight, with buildings and shops pacing behind. Aryan was in a lot of pain, as the air stung the wounds on his face like someone rubbing salt on them. Aryan looked back and saw the bull closing in on them. He looked forward and focused all his power on his legs.

He looked to his left, Daksh was running like a focused man, his hands moving front and back, his hair flowing back.

The road in front was turning in four directions. Aryan quickly looked at Daksh, who was already looking at him. They nodded, hearing each other's thoughts. When the four-way came close, Daksh turned left, while Aryan turned right. As Aryan was the one wearing the bright red colour, the bull went after him. Just then, Aryan turned in a circular motion and veered left. He ran towards Daksh. Keeping their pace, they looked back. The bull trembled, and the quick turn by Aryan made its legs cross, but the bull didn't fall. It shook its head and continued to chase them.

And here comes the tricky part! The road was now turning in four directions after every building they passed behind. Aryan's hands were shaking as he didn't know what to do. His mind was already focused on running as fast as possible. His ears could hear those heavy footsteps, getting closer with each step they took.

Aryan didn't know how much longer he could run he was panting badly, and slowing down with each footstep. He turned his head to check on Daksh, and his heart stopped beating as he saw nothing. He turned right, and Daksh was gone. A part of him was worried, another was not. Aryan thought that Daksh might have found the road towards the car or the car itself.

Each side of the road was covered by tall buildings. Aryan kept running straight. He looked left and right, those turning roads were passing behind him. As he ran forward, the sun showed its divine body, the almighty was right in front of him in the middle of the sky. The rays of sunlight were directly falling on him. Aryan's left side of his face was burning with pain. The part above his left eye, at the end of his left eyebrow, was stinging badly.

It happened in an instant as a drop of blood flowed down and entered his eye; he was blinded in one eye. His left foot was on the ground, right in the air. The right foot came down but hit his left foot instead of the ground, as the blood distracted him. As the right foot gave a focused hit at the heel of the left foot, the left foot went in the air, and Aryan fell down on his bottom. He wiped the blood away from his eye with his hands, trying to get up, but his legs refused as they got twisted. He turned without getting up in the middle of the four-way road, and right in front of him was the bull. The bull was three to four meters away, also steady, but then he moved as he saw his prey motionless on the road.

This it is—here comes my death.

The bull was now only a meter and a half away, his head getting wider. Aryan closed his eyes. Aryan opened them again after a second, realizing he was still alive. There was the roar of an engine; the bull had already turned himself, facing right. From the road, which was turning left (right for Aryan), came Daksh with his car. The bull was not ready for it.

The car hit the bull hard, and the bull fell on the road and gave a roll. The car was right there, but the bull got up. The bull tried to get back on his feet.

CRASH

Daksh hit the bull again, but this time, the blow was targeted right at his stomach, left side. The bull left the ground and fell at some distance. He gave a pitiful *Moo*, but it was time for Daksh to be merciless. He hit the bull again with his car—and again—until it went unconscious. The bull was still breathing; an opening was created right at the left side of his massive stomach, and blood was flowing out from it.

"Take that you—killer—bull."

Aryan sighed and smiled, turning his leg with his hand gently. He managed to get up on his feet and walked towards the bull. He saw that the front of the car was totally damaged, and smoke was coming out of it.

"I love this car," said Daksh, kissing the steering wheel.

Aryan walked close towards the bull, feeling sorry for him, lying on the floor, bleeding in the middle of the road. Bending down, Aryan pulled off those earrings from his horns and got up. Daksh was standing up on his seat, looking at him, and then he started clapping.

"You just had to wear red!" said Daksh.

"Well, I had no clue that there would be this huge *bull* chasing me."

They both laughed, Aryan went inside the car, Daksh started the engine, and they drove away.

Chapter 20

Helping Hand

"Yash—Yash!"

Yash felt gentle taps on his face and warmth. Opening his eyes, he saw the blue sky in front of them, surrounded by grass. For a moment, Yash thought he was back home on his soft bed, relaxing.

"Hey, talk to me, Yash…are you alright?"

Yash sat up and found Mahir to his right, also seated on the grass.

"Yes—yes—I am fine."

Observing the far side beside Mahir, he noticed the field they were in was ending, and just beyond it, a road began. Turning back twisting his spine, Yash saw the road leading towards a massive mountain. Mahir faced the mountain to the east, while Yash's body faced west. The sun was glowing above the mountain.

"How—how—did we end up here?" asked Yash curiously.

"Beats me, I jumped out of that window...next thing I know, I opened my eyes here."

Yash sighed; he had no thoughts about getting up and starting to move. He gazed and saw they were surrounded by farmlands. A breeze was touching them momentarily.

"It might sound farfetched, but I really have some serious thoughts about moving towards that mountain," said Mahir, looking at Yash, then at the mountain.

"I was thinking the same," said Yash, nodding.

Yash noticed that Mahir's flannel jacket was missing. Then his eyes eventually directed towards Mahir's wounded leg. The jacket was tied tightly over the wound.

"Is it still—"

"Paining? Oh, hell yeah!" said Mahir. "But I can walk."

Yash smiled and patted on his back. Yash got up on his feet, he helped Mahir to stand up. Mahir put his arm around Yash, and they started walking towards the road.

As they were walking, Yash didn't stop observing. Just beside the road, left or right, farmlands had conquered the place. To the left side, he saw wheat farms and some flowers that were unknown to him. The view was bucolic.

Those rays of the sun, which were gentle and smooth, now were harsh. Yash and Mahir were panting, walking towards the mountain. Their T-shirts clung to their bodies because of sweat. The mountain was still a distance away, shining green and brown in some parts.

Yash scanned the area repeatedly, searching for a tree where they could find shade and rest. Unfortunately, there were none—only vast fields, wheat farms, and scattered flowers. Trees appeared in the distance, where the mountain began.

"Oh, God, I think I am going to die here," panted Mahir.

Yash lifted Mahir, supporting him with his arm as he limped.

"No time for gloom, or else we are doomed," said Yash bluntly.

Mahir gave Yash a bemused look. Yash rubbed his eyes with his free hand, trying to alleviate the discomfort caused by the sweat.

"Just put me down, Yash. I cannot walk anymore," said Mahir, his eyes closed.

"Yes, let us rest," agreed Yash.

They both sat down on the road. Yash briefly considered moving to the grassy area, but dismissed the thought. Mahir's leg didn't look good; the jacket displayed a dark, roughly circular stain. Yash felt a deep sense of sympathy for Mahir.

"Is it hurting badly?" asked Yash.

"No," breathed Mahir, "I lost sense of my leg since we started walking... I think it must be—"

"No negative speaking!"

There was no one around them. Yash's throat was so dry that even breathing was a challenge. Adding to their troubles, the merciless sun showed them no mercy.

Yash didn't know why he did what he did; he looked up at the sky, closed his eyes, and muttered—

Help us.

He then observed some strange colors when his eyes were closed.

"I—I think I heard something," said Mahir, in an alert voice.

Yash opened his eyes and looked at Mahir. He was about to say that it was his mind, but then he, too, heard something. The voice was soft and coming from a distance. It was like the *ting-ting* of bells, pleasant.

Then came the sound of a cart being pulled. They alerted themselves because the sound was coming from behind.

Yash and Mahir turned to look back. They saw two domestic bulls—one brown and the other white. Their horns were big and pointy. Strangely, neither Yash nor Mahir felt any fear.

Yash helped Mahir to get up. As the cart got closer, they were able to see a man seated behind those bulls in front of the cart. A few seconds passed, and the cart was now at arm's length from them. Yash and Mahir looked at the man who was seated in the driver's seat. The man, too, looked at them. He was wearing a yellow kurta, his head was covered with a purple turban and a white dhoti. His face was calm. He appeared to be older than Yash and Mahir, although his face had no wrinkles except for one scar on his left cheek.

"What are you two boys looking at me for?" asked the man, his voice a combination of rough and calm. "Go on, hop on the cart... you are heading towards the mountain, right?"

Yash and Mahir gave no answer. Their eyes sparkled with tears. After all this running, getting hurt, and being shocked, they did not expect that someone would come and offer them help.

"Thank you," said Mahir, sniffing.

"My dear boy! You are bleeding!" said the man, looking at Mahir's leg. Suddenly, his expression changed. "Don't worry—Pandit will fix this."

Mahir looked at Yash, Yash was already looking at him. They turned to the man.

"Thank you..."

"Krishna—my name is Krishna."

"Thank you so much, Krishna," said Yash, expressing his gratitude.

Both of them walked to the back of the cart. With great difficulty, Mahir finally climbed onto the cart. Yash sat on the right side, Mahir sat on the left in front of him. The cart was empty, with some dry grass here and there, but that didn't bother either of them.

Krishna clucked his tongue, and the cart began to be pulled by those bulls.

"My name is Yash."

"I am Mahir."

"Namaste, Yash and Mahir," said Krishna, turning his head back to face them.

Yash and Mahir joined their hands in a formal Namaste. That is when those two bulls *mooed*.

"Hai-Hari! How did I forget them?" said Krishna, shaking his head. "Meet my sarthis, Atul," the brown one lifted his head up, "and Tul." The white one lifted his head up.

Mahir and Yash chuckled—

"Namaste, Atul and Tul," said Mahir and Yash together.

Both bulls *mooed* happily and continued pulling the cart.

"There is a pot of water if you want to do—"

Yash picked up the pot and had already started drinking from it. Then, he passed the pot to Mahir, who emptied it in one gulp. Huge relief passed from their throats to their hearts. Their bodies were now relaxed. Yash looked at Krishna, realizing he hadn't listened to what he said. He saw Krishna smiling, facing him, his right hand holding a metal glass. Yash gave him an embarrassed smile, to which Krishna responded with loud laughter.

At last, the area with trees arrived. As those trees covered the area, a silence fell upon them. All they could hear was their own cart moving forward. It was at this time Yash realized that there are types of silence. The silence right now was calm, and languor fell upon him.

Mahir was relaxed, his eyes were closed. Yash sighed seeing him like this. He too was tired but chose against going to sleep. Yash observed that most of the trees were wild. The lord of light was showing his presence through the gaps in the branches and bushy leaves. Suddenly Yash's nose twitched as it smelled something like a sour mango. And soon, they were surrounded by many mango trees. Even Mahir opened his eyes when he sensed the smell.

There were also some unknown trees that had white flowers blooming on them. Yash and Mahir so wished that those mango trees had some mangoes.

The journey was silent and wonderful. Yash turned his head as he heard some birds twittering. Soon, the whole mountain echoed with the singing of those birds. Yash searched and searched but failed to locate those birds. Right then, he saw a bird resting on a branch of a mango tree. Her body was covered with yellow feathers, except for her neck, which was blue like she put on a necklace. Yash thought it was this species that made those ear-soothing sounds—just then, he saw another bird sitting on a branch of a wild tree. She was completely blue. Yash chuckled.

The land has now got a slope. They were now surrounded by trees which had thin branches but were tall about ten meters. Those birds kept singing, and Yash was enjoying it fully. He turned his head back as he heard the sounds of water flowing down. Krishna clucked his tongue and with one crafty movement, they turned right, from where the water flowing sound was coming from.

Atul and Tul stopped, and Mahir opened his eyes. They arrived at a narrow rivulet. The place was bucolic, with many butterflies moving here and there as there were many flower plants near the rivulet. The cart stopped about a three-tree distance away from the rivulet. Yash observed that the other side of the rivulet had open ground and that trees covered the rest.

"Er, Yash—if you don't mind—can you fill back the pot?" asked Krishna politely. "I know you are tired, but it would mean a lot for my journey back down."

"No, Krishna, there is no problem at all," said Yash.

Yash picked up the pot and looked at Mahir.

"Oh, look at that!" said Krishna, looking at his own hands, which were slightly muddy, then he looked down at his feet. "Well, I guess I have to join you anyway, Yash. Can't go in front of Pandit looking like this."

Yash smiled, seeing how amusing Krishna is. Thoughts of Daksh and his other friends passed through his mind, and he frowned.

"I am not that bad of a company," said Krishna, observing the sudden change in Yash's expression.

"No—no—I just remembered..." Yash started to say.

Krishna smiled and hopped down from the cart. Yash did the same, then he turned to Mahir.

"You better stay here," said Yash, looking at him.

"Don't worry, Mahir," said Krishna confidently. "Pandit will fix your leg in no time, I give you my word for that. Plus, someone has to stay here...these two will not think a minute to wander around for tasty grass."

"Not to worry, I will keep my eyes on them, it is the least I can do for you. I'll be a burden if I tag along," said Mahir cheerfully.

Yash and Krishna walked their way towards the rivulet. It was a heavenly view, even though the sun was right above them; its rays did not displease them. From the other side of the rivulet, there were sounds of birds singing.

"Yash, come here."

Yash turned back and saw Krishna had already entered the rivulet. Standing against the flow, his dhoti folded up, he washed his hands, and his legs were already inside the water. Yash walked towards him. Right in front of Krishna, there was a layer of stone, water was flowing down from there.

"Give me the pot," demanded Krishna.

Yash passed the pot. Krishna placed the mouth of the pot right below those layers of stones, and it began to fill. Yash was just standing there, hands inside his pockets, gazing, turning his head here and there. He really adored the place and the beauty of it.

"Here!" said Krishna, stretching out his hand, which was holding the pot.

Yash took his hands out of his pockets and took the pot from Krishna. Krishna stepped out of the rivulet, wore his chappal, and walked towards Yash. He gave a wave to his dhoti while walking.

"How unlucky!" sighed Krishna. "The trees you see here are filled with fruits…but now, because of the weather, they are not."

Yash knew that Krishna might have sensed his hunger; he smiled in response. Suddenly, Yash saw, for the first time, a grave look on Krishna. He bent down and came back up, holding a gold coin in his fingers.

****

"Nuh-uh."

"You have to."

"I am not going over there!"

"You have to—"

"Why?"

"Daksh, those are domestic bulls over there. Not that giant beast we saved our lives from."

"I know that, you idiot. Look in the cart."

Aryan peeked his head out from behind the tree. He was covert. He saw, in the cart, there was a man, his shoulders were wide and well-built. Aryan was only able to see the back of the man. The way his head was tilted towards his right shoulder gave a piece of information that the man was asleep.

"I think he is napping," said Aryan in a hushed voice, looking at Daksh.

Daksh was hidden behind a tree left from Aryan, but a little bit further.

"Oh, so you think it is a good idea," said Daksh, "to walk up to him and say, "Hello, kind sir, can you drop us somewhere we don't know? Oh, and yes, it must be the place where there are no women—or bulls"."

"Do we have any other option then?" hissed Aryan, like an angry serpent. He raised his eyebrows to show his anger, but the pain kissed him. "Look, I am tired, Daksh. My face is throbbing as if somebody has burned it. My legs are done walking. You have no idea how I pulled myself all the way up here on this sudden mountain that came in front of us."

Daksh did not want to agree with Aryan, but seeing Aryan, especially his face, Daksh exhaled, then nodded and shook his head at the same time.

"Alright, but we will approach together."

Aryan and Daksh started to approach the cart on their tiptoes. Aryan was able to hear the singing of birds that were close by. Then he heard the sound of water flowing down, he sighed.

I beg you, O lord, please let this man be a kind one. And for once prove my thoughts wrong, for pity's sake.

Aryan's anxiety levels were increasing as they passed from one tree to another on their tiptoes towards the cart.

They were in the open area now, with no trees to hide behind, just in case. Right in front of them was the cart, horizontal. Aryan saw those bulls they had their noses pointed to the ground sniffing, and then plucking a bunch of grass with their teeth. They were walking on their tiptoes skillfully. They must have years and years of experience to come all the way towards the cart without making any sound. They were now about to reach the back of the cart. Aryan slowed down his speed as the figure inside the cart looked strangely familiar to him. They took the turn and were now at the back from where you can enter the cart.

"OH MY GOD! IT—IT'S MAHIR!"

Mahir opened his eyes at once. His face was instantly directed towards these two familiar faces. Mahir's expression was identical to theirs, as if looking in some expression mirror.

"Hey...Atul—Tul—am I dreaming? Because I can see Aryan and Daksh over here."

Atul and Tul *mooed*; Mahir didn't comprehend what they said.

Daksh looked up at the sky and sighed; then he looked straight at Mahir.

"Look, you thoughtless creature," Said Daksh, showing his right palm to him. "I am real."

Saying that Daksh patted hard on Mahir's leg. The birds flew away, and the whole mountain echoed with the ear-piercing screech of Mahir.

"YOU MANIAC!"

"OH MY GOD—YOU ARE BLEEDING!"

"STOP SCREAMING!"

"You are screaming."

"MAHIR!"

The voice came from behind. Aryan and Daksh turned and saw two men running towards them. One was tall, and the other was about Aryan's height.

"Yash…" breathed Daksh.

Aryan paced towards Yash and wrapped him in his arms. Yash also welcomed him. They both laughed, and some drops of happy tears flowed down from their eyes.

"Thank God that you are safe," said Aryan, coming back the amount of happiness was too much for his heart.

"Yes…you too are safe," said Yash, his eyes sparkling with tears, his expression changed suddenly. "What happened to your face?"

"Oh—it is—let's say: never fight with a woman."

Aryan and Yash walked towards the cart. Yash looked at Daksh, Daksh came forwards and hugged him.

"I missed you, freak—it is so good to see you," said Daksh, his eyes closed.

"It is good to see you too, Daksh." Pulling himself back.

Krishna was watching all this from behind. Yash took notice of it.

"Oh—yes—this is Krishna, he helped Mahir and me to come all the way on this mountain," said Yash, he looked at Krishna. "Krishna, these are my friends, this is Aryan, and this is Daksh."

"Namaste Aryan, Namaste Daksh," said Krishna, joining his hands in formal Namaste.

"Namaste," said Aryan and Daksh together.

Krishna walked forwards towards Aryan. He came close, his height was exactly the same as Aryan's. He scanned his face, which made Aryan very uncomfortable.

"Wow, you are badly bruised," said Krishna, nodding.

Aryan frowned in worriedness as he was only able to feel the pain. He was utterly unaware of how he looked.

"Come with me, Aryan and Daksh," said Krishna.

Aryan and Daksh looked at Yash. Yash smiled and then nodded.

"Don't worry, I am not going to eat you. I am vegetarian," said Krishna, amusingly. "And I have no purpose to steal your gold either."

Aryan and Daksh looked at each other, while Mahir sat up straight. How Krishna knows about gold, they had no idea.

"Hang on—how do you—" said Daksh, puzzled.

"How do I know about gold coins?" said Krishna. "Let me tell you this—and keep this in mind as the journey ahead will not be easy—you are not the only ones who tried to steal from that tomb."

They were surely taken by surprise, although Yash remained calm, observing others" baffled faces.

"So—*you* tried to steal?" asked Mahir, leaning forward.

"Yes," Answered Krishna, smiling.

"When?" asked Daksh.

"Oh, it was way long ago," said Krishna, still smiling his smile was calm, not mischievous, "I think years have passed by…maybe decades."

"What are you still doing here then?" asked Aryan. "I mean, didn't you find back your gold and return it?"

Krishna opened his mouth to answer but then he chose otherwise, he smiled, looking up at the sky and then at them.

"I think I am not the right person to explain what is actually going on in the Hoax," said Krishna, smiling. "Don't worry, though...Pandit will have answers for every question *you* have, Aryan."

"Krishna—this Pandit you keep referring to—where is he?" asked Yash, politely.

"In the *mandir*, of course," said Krishna. "The mandir is located on the other side of this mountain."

Yash nodded, and Krishna looked at Aryan, then turned to Daksh.

"You both come with me," said Krishna, appealingly. "You will feel better when you sprinkle some water on your body."

"I will stay here with Mahir," said Yash.

Aryan and Daksh returned after a few minutes, and Krishna was walking in front. They looked energetic, having enjoyed the refreshing water. Krishna jumped on the cart and took his driver's seat. Yash sat beside Mahir, and in front of them, Aryan and Daksh settled. Atul and Tul started pulling the cart when Krishna gave them the signal.

"What happened with you guys?" asked Mahir, curiously.

Daksh revealed everything about their time in Mumbai, the eerie quietness, the powerful women, and the bull chase. He also described how he saved Aryan with that beautiful car. Mahir and Yash listened attentively, their hearts rising and falling with excitement.

"Oh, so you met Roti, huh," said Krishna, turning his head towards them, then he looked ahead again. "A very nice and beautiful woman she is."

"Seriously?" said Daksh, disbelievingly. "I don't know about the *beautiful* part—but nice, my as—"

Daksh's whole upper body came forward as Aryan pushed his fist hard on his spine. Daksh screamed in agony.

"At least have decency about how to speak about a woman," said Aryan furiously.

"Classic Daksh," said Yash, laughing.

Daksh looked at Yash coolly, rubbing his back.

"What the hell happened to your feet, Mahir?" said Aryan, concerned about Mahir's well-being.

Mahir told them everything that happened in that lunatic place. About that furry, big, brown dog and how he attacked him, he also spoke admiringly about how Yash took control of the situation and how they managed to escape.

"Crazy!" said Daksh, after Mahir was done. "You were in the dodgy house—that is messed up."

"I know, right," said Yash. "So, these are our gold coins."

Yash showed them two thick gold coins. Aryan buried his hands in his pocket and took out two gold coins identical to those Yash was holding.

"A piece of advice, boys," said Krishna earnestly, "these gold coins are serious havoc creators."

They put away those gold coins instantly. The area they were passing by was like God's own garden. Here, they were indeed able to smell nature, like wood, and some strange nose-tingling fragrances. The mountain was really like the royal garden and smelled like an *apsara* had just passed by them.

"How gorgeous it looks!" sighed Krishna.

They matched their gaze with Krishna, and then they saw the temple. Aryan was amazed that they came to the other side of the mountain so quickly. Although their will died instantly to meet the Pandit. The thorn was that the temple was almost at the top of the mountain. Their eyes came down and finally reached the ground. There were certainly more than two hundred stairs. The outer, white, marble walls of the temple were shining with the sun.

The cart came to a halt right in front of where those endless stairs started. Both sides of the stairs were covered by trees.

They all jumped down from the cart, now came the time to think about how Mahir would manage to climb up. Krishna came to the rescue. He told everyone to stand aside, then he calmly instructed Mahir to "calm down." Placing his right hand below Mahir's legs and his left arm below Mahir's upper body, Krishna effortlessly lifted Mahir, who was twice his size in width and placed him in a standing position. Daksh and Yash quickly approached, offering their support as they put Mahir's arms around their shoulders.

"Woah," exclaimed the three of them simultaneously.

"You are strong, Krishna," Said Mahir, still not able to comprehend the fact that Krishna picked him up.

Krishna chuckled. "Well, these two bulls made sure during their teenage years that I got some weightlifting practice."

Everyone laughed, and they began walking towards the stairs. Aryan, Yash, Mahir, and even Daksh patted Atul and Tul on the head, and the helpful bulls *mooed* happily.

"Hey, I'm sorry, but I don't think I'll be able to climb even one stair properly," expressed Mahir with concern.

"Oh no, your leg is bleeding again," exclaimed Yash, horrified.

"No worries, I'll pick you up," offered Krishna.

"No, Krishna, we already owe you a lot," said Yash, patting Krishna's back.

"I'll do it," volunteered Daksh.

Daksh bent down, and Mahir walked to his back. Daksh grabbed his leg and passed his hand from behind them, and Mahir put his arms around Daksh's neck. With some effort, Daksh stood up with Mahir on his back.

"My—God—you are heavy."

Chapter 21

Creator-Nurturer-Destroyer

"Looks like I am the first to arrive," said Daksh, hands on his hips.

Daksh turned and glanced towards the countless steps he had climbed to reach the top. Aryan was ahead, Yash carrying Mahir on his back behind him and Krishna bringing up the rear with a pitiful look at Yash.

Aryan reached the last step and stood beside Daksh. Krishna arrived shortly after. They both wiped their sweat-soaked faces with their elbows. Then came Yash, almost crawling up the last step, with Mahir on his back looking guilt-ridden. Yash collapsed on the marble floor, and Aryan and Daksh helped Mahir to stand up, relieving Yash of the weight on his back.

"You okay?" Mahir asked Yash.

Yash looked up and, with Krishna's assistance, stood up. He gave Daksh the coldest look.

"You...you...bastard," panted Yash. "You son of a—" Yash coughed. "You knew, didn't you? That if you pick Mahir at the beginning, you don't have to at the top, as your turn was over."

Yash took a break for breath's sake.

"I could say—No—but then I would be lying to you," said Daksh with a cunning smile.

Yash grunted in anger, and Daksh smiled, making his eyebrows dance. Krishna grabbed Yash tight as Yash tried to make a move on Daksh. Daksh hid himself behind Aryan.

"We are in God's place!" said Daksh.

"Both of you, *shut it*," barked Mahir.

They both calmed down, and Daksh came forward. Yash exhaled and looked away. Aryan was enjoying the view from the top. The temple entrance was behind them. Aryan sighed when a cool zephyr touched his cheek.

"Look—look—we came from there," said Aryan urgently.

Yash, Mahir, Krishna, and Daksh matched his gaze. They saw, to the north, a wall of fog that extended up to the clouds.

"Wait...that is north...you said you guys came from *south* Mumbai," said Mahir, with a perplexed look.

Everyone's head turned to Mahir with a *matter-of-fact* look.

"This is a cryptic place, Mahir," said Krishna.

Mahir opened his mouth and nodded in response.

"It is indeed," said Daksh. "You remember when I told you that we had a beautiful car, but then you asked us where it is. Yeah, the answer is—when we passed from that fog, our car coughed out smoke and stopped working right there on the road. We had no choice but to leave that beauty behind."

Daksh sniffed as if suppressing himself from crying.

"If you stand here longer, your head will start to melt."

The heavy, but soothing, voice came from behind. They all turned together. Right in front of them was a tall man, taller than Yash, almost touching the target of seven feet. He was wearing a white dhoti, and his upper body was covered with a single thin, long cloth. His shining white hair flowed back with the wind; his hair was brighter than the marble floor. His face was hairless, apart from eyelashes and eyebrows. His eyes were so dark they didn't even reflect the rays of the sun. His diamond-cut face gave him a strong look.

"Panditji!" said Krishna, joyfully.

He is the Pandit?

Aryan was not able to comprehend that the tall Godlike man was indeed the Pandit Krishna was talking about.

Krishna walked ahead and touched Pandit's feet. Pandit smiled and placed his hand on Krishna's head. Krishna came back up with a rejuvenating smile.

Pandit then looked at Yash, then at Daksh, Aryan and Mahir. Yash and Daksh went ahead and touched Pandit's feet. Aryan, who was helping Mahir to remain stand, looked at Mahir, and he nodded. They took one step—

"We can do this all day, Aryan," said Pandit in a pleasing tone.

Aryan smiled as he was about to ask Pandit how he knew his name.

"First task first! Your friend Mahir needs medical help, and that includes you too, Aryan. Now follow me, children."

By not even moving their tongues, they followed Pandit inside the temple. At the entrance, beside the door, there were huge pillars made of marble. The entrance door opened inside, it was made entirely of bronze. The entrance was obviously tall so that Pandit could go in and out at ease. Aryan saw many carvings on those two-parted doors, he was about to observe them, but his feet touched the calmingly cold floors of the temple. They had already taken their shoes off when they were on the very first stair.

The view inside the temple was enchanting, as if darkness had no place, even in the concealed corners. The room was expansive and circular, adorned with pillars at every turn. Aryan looked up to notice a chandelier lit with candles, casting a warm orange hue throughout the room. The pillars seemed to glow, reminiscent of gold. Numerous windows allowed the air to flow freely, creating a serene ambience.

Aryan looked ahead, right in front of the entrance. There, a little to the left, was the divine sculptor of Lord Brahma, standing about five feet tall. Lord Brahma was seated inside the lotus. In the middle was Lord Vishnu, his eyes open and looking straight at them. Lord Vishnu's smile was always the mysterious one, leaning comfortably on the *Adi-Anantha-Sesha*. A little to the right, seated on a white stone, was the God of destruction, who has the heart of a loving mother, the almighty Mahadev.

Aryan couldn't take his eyes off those divine, colorful *murtis*. He simply wished to sit there and stare at them for no reason.

"Aryan, Mahir," said Pandit, bringing Aryan back from his reverie, "come with me, please. Daksh and Yash, stay here with Krishna."

Aryan noticed Daksh nodding silently, and Yash and Daksh instantly turned their gaze toward the Creator-Nurturer-Destroyer. No, they weren't looking at them. Aryan observed that right in front of the Gods was a rectangular table covered in yellow cloth, with bowls filled with fruits on it.

Pandit's laughter roared through the whole temple.

"Oh, my dear boys, I am so sorry," said Pandit. "Go ahead, eat some if you want to. I can assure you that the Gods will not mind at all."

Daksh and Yash, waiting for approval, attacked immediately. They picked an apple each and started eating. Krishna smiled embarrassingly, observing the way they devoured the fruits.

"I know that you two are also famished," said Pandit, looking at Aryan and Mahir, "however you both have to wait. Now, follow me."

Pandit turned right, and Aryan, supporting Mahir, followed him. Aryan could hear the sound of Daksh and Yash jamming their jaws on those fruits.

"Take it easy boys—no one is running away."

Krishna's voice reassured them. The ceiling was adorned with hanging candle chandeliers supported by long chains. A wave of pure saffron aroma wafted through their noses, calming their minds from racing thoughts.

There was now a door in front of them, a two-door-in-one-frame pattern. Pandit pushed them aside, and as he did, his cloth—covering his upper body—lifted, revealing to Aryan a deep scar just below his wide shoulder, on the long head of the triceps.

They entered a passageway illuminated by lamps in the corners. It extended forward, leading to yet another door identical to the one they had just entered. The passage walls were not bare but adorned with pictures. On the right wall, Aryan saw *Asuras* pulling a thick rope, later realizing it was the snake he often came across in stories. On the left wall, *Devas* were pulling the snake. Every detail was magnificently painted. Before Aryan could notice more, Pandit pushed open the other door.

The room was rectangular, stretching forward. At the end of the room, facing Aryan, were two wooden cupboards, about shoulder height for them and way smaller for Pandit. The room had six gothic-shaped windows in total, three on the left and three on the right. On the right side, just below the middle window, lay a *khat*, also known as a rope bed.

Pandit walked towards the cupboards immediately. Aryan went to the *khat* and settled Mahir on it. Aryan sat down on the floor in Sukh asana. He observed Pandit opening the left cupboard and taking out something, which he placed in his palms. From the second cupboard, Pandit retrieved a small mortar and pestle and started crushing and mixing herbs. He added some more herbs and mixed them firmly before turning and walking straight toward Aryan.

"There is a mirror over there," said Pandit, his voice resembling a poet singing verses. He offered the bowl to Aryan, saying, "Apply this paste on your face. Mahir, lay down flat and relax; no one will mind."

Mahir nodded, giving Pandit a warm smile. Aryan got up on his feet and turned, noticing a circle-top-shaped mirror hanging on the wall just beside the door. To Aryan's left, it was on his right. Indeed, the left side of his face was badly beaten by Praan. Thanks to Krishna, when Aryan sprinkled some water on his face, he noticed how pacified his wounds became. He looked at his reflection and then at the paste in the bowl, which was greenish in color. Using his first two fingers, he started to apply the paste. The scent was initially saffron, followed by rose, and then another herb Aryan was certain of but had forgotten the name. Aryan felt completely relaxed as the cooling substance embraced his face. His visage was now entirely green.

Aryan turned and was stunned to see Mahir in deep sleep. His leg had already been taken care of, with a thick layer of green bandages applied to the wound by Pandit.

Seated in the middle of the room on a small mat on the floor, in Sukh asana, Pandit was already looking at Aryan. He gestured with his hand for Aryan to sit in front of him. Aryan instantly went and, by setting a mat, sat down in Sukh asana too.

"Thank you—thank you so much for helping us, Panditji," said Aryan, expressing his gratitude gracefully.

Pandit nodded, simultaneously closing his eyes. He opened them and looked at Aryan.

"I heard from Aigile that you understand situations instantly," said Pandit, smiling.

"You know him?"

"Yes, my dear boy, I know Aigile."

"Can I ask you a question?"

"You certainly can."

"We stole those gold coins from the tomb—I know you know that very well—but then why help us?"

"My dear boy, just like you know that I know about the attempted stealing, I think you also know why I am helping you."

Aryan was puzzled for a second, but then he found the answer himself.

"You chose to do this."

Pandit smiled and nodded.

"It seems like your mind asked you to ask a question, yet your lips conjured a totally novel question," said Pandit, looking straight into Aryan's eyes.

"I—er—of course," Laughed Aryan. "You can read minds, too."

Pandit and Aryan laughed together.

"You had your fair experience with Aigile, I presume."

Aryan nodded in response.

"The question is worthless, Panditji," said Aryan, looking down.

"Aryan," Pandit's Panditas soothing voice touched his ears, "no question is worthless, because of these questions we have that spark, the spark to move ahead in the journey to find the answer."

I am tired of asking the same question again and again.

"Tiredness is the first step towards demolishing dreams," said Pandit. "Do you know I have my own definition of a *coward*; want to hear what it is?"

Aryan nodded.

"It is that the person knows he or she is on the right path, however, when the person notices that ahead there are difficulties and sacrifices, so the person chooses to bail, away from the darkness to his own made-up bliss."

When Aryan looked into those dark eyes of Pandit, he knew that the Pandit had that discerning quality. Aryan closed his eyes to get ready to ask the question he was meaning to ask. He allowed those perplexed thoughts, he let go of those feelings that told him asking this question would be fatuous. His eyes opened right at Pandit.

"How is this happening with us?" Aryan let out his feelings. "Yes, I know all this is happening because we tried to steal those cursed objects, and now we are paying for it. But how is it possible that we are in a *different* world? I certainly don't remember going through some…portal…or some ancient magic door. How can this be happening, and in reality, am I dead?"

Aryan inhaled some air, and he gazed towards Mahir. Seeing him still asleep, he calmed down.

"Hmm, do you know what *Somras* is, Aryan?" inquired Pandit.

"The drink of Gods, the nectar of immortality."

"Exactly," beamed Pandit, "now answer me this: who created the *Somras*?"

"Lord Brahma, the creator."

"Yes, yes, correct indeed." Said Pandit, nodding. "Are you aware that while creating the *Somras*, Lord Brahma accidentally created a terrible poison…Do you know which poison I am talking about?"

Aryan started working on an answer; his brain didn't ask any further questions. Suddenly, the passageway he came past to arrive at this room came to his mind. Then he remembered some stories people who were close to him had told him when he was a kid and for what reason Mahadev is called—

"*Halahal*, the poison that stays in the throat of Mahadev."

"Exactly." Pandit beamed again. "You surprise me a lot, Aryan…I now see what Aigile was trying to express. Now listen carefully, everyone knows about the first side of the story, not the second. *Asuras* were indeed down-spirited by the discrimination of Lord Vishnu—"

"I am very sorry for interrupting, Panditji, but why does Lord Vishnu discriminate? Almost in every legend, he favors *Devas* and not *Asuras*; he is the nurturer, right?"

Pandit laughed out loud.

"Believe me, Aryan, this exact question was asked of me way long ago." Said Pandit, smiling. "Lord Vishnu is indeed the nurturer of this world; let me explain in a different way. Mahadev, there is one of the reasons why Mahadev is known as the destroyer, and the answer, to be put into an understandable way, is that Mahadev does not know how to discriminate."

"Is that a bad thing?"

"Not entirely, see the whole world, if you have observed it enough, you will notice that the world moves ahead because of discrimination. If everyone, everything, to be called the same, the world will stop and come to an end."

"Oh, I understand now," said Aryan, he was not letting his mind divert for even a second.

"Lord Brahma, well, he cannot take sides, can he?"

"Why?"

"Lord Brahma is the creator; his children are the *Asuras* and *Devas*, parents don't discriminate either, Aryan. So, the whole burden of doing what is needed is left to Lord Vishnu. As he is a God, he gets future visions just like you are observing me and knows very well of the outcome."

"I see...please continue with the second side of the story," Aryan insisted.

"As I was saying, *Asuras* were not pleased by the discrimination. The guru of the *Asuras* clan, the great Shukracharaya, thought that if he couldn't have the *Somras*, he would demand the poison. With all focus on *Tapasya*, he demanded the poison from Mahadev; Mahadev gave some drops of *Halahal* to guru Shukracharaya. The poison was so pernicious that guru Shukracharaya had to put it in a different vessel, which he had already demanded from Lord Brahma—

Aryan commanded his brain to take every piece of information and note it down mentally without any further questions.

—Guru Shukracharaya did many experiments on *Halahal* and made it egregious. Now, what *Halahal* can do is unimaginable even for Gods. The poison now can blend with any liquid material without notice, even for the people who possess sharp vision. Whomsoever is the host is possessed by a mantra, the power in which the host himself will die, although his memories will still be in present. And now comes the horrific part, if some other person even touches that liquid, in which the poison is mixed, it will instantly alert the host. If the host commands the victim's body will flow away like ash, all it remains is his memories, which the host can transfer into his, for all those reasons, now the host will be the master of the victim—mortal or immortal."

Aryan was staring at Pandit, his eyes wide open.

"T-the Water!" said Aryan, his voice shaking with fear. "When we went deep in that—*tomb*, we did come to a point when there was water, and our foot was in it."

"So now you understand the whole answer."

"When we took out those gold coins and diamonds, we touched the water...that alerted Corbeau and...and we got transferred in his memory."

"That is correct. You may have heard it somewhere, supporting that theory is what I do, *life is nothing but a memory which we only realize it fully when it is deemed to be.*"

"There is still one question I cannot find the answer for."

"And what that question is Aryan?" asked Pandit, curiously.

"How did Corbeau get his hands on the other version of *Halahal*? I know that Corbeau is like thousands of years old, still all about guru Shukracharaya and the battle of *Asuras* and *Devas* was way back than that, wasn't it?"

"Again, you are right, Aryan," said Pandit, smiling. "The poison was passed to every single *Asura* who lived on earth and not underground. Corbeau's master was an *Asura*, well half, so he had the poison."

"So, his master agreed to give such an evil poison—so he can possess others memories?"

"He was not the person you think he is right now," said Pandit, defensively. "Roots of *Karmas* are way deep. He was a nice, good-souled man. All he wanted to do was to see the look of pride in his king's eyes for him, that is all he ever wanted."

"That didn't answer my question," snapped Aryan. He realized and changed his tone. "I am sorry, Panditji, this is way too much for me."

"I understand," said Pandit, calmly. "The answer is quite straightforward: his master was on his deathbed, and as Kan—

Corbeau was the only one close to call as a son, he passed the poison to him. Believe me, Aryan, he was not the same person he is today—he still isn't…"

"Who was his master?"

"His name: Avyay."

"He died?"

Pandit didn't answer. He looked up at the ceiling, then gazed at Aryan.

"Avyay is presently reflecting in your eyes and answering your questions…" said Avyay.

…to be continued…

www.ingramcontent.com/pod-product-compliance
Lightning Source LLC
LaVergne TN
LVHW041910070526
838199LV00051BA/2563